James Craig [...]
more than thirty [...]
His previous Inspe[...]
Apologise, Never [...]
Circus; *Then We Die* [...] *[...]y*
the Fathers; *Nobody's Hero*, [...]s of [...] [...]nd *All Kinds of*
Dead are also available from Constable.

Also by James Craig

Novels
London Calling
Never Apologise, Never Explain
Buckingham Palace Blues
The Circus
Then We Die
A Man of Sorrows
Shoot to Kill
Sins of the Fathers
Nobody's Hero
Acts of Violence
All Kinds of Dead

Short Stories
The Enemy Within
What Dies Inside
The Hand of God

JAMES CRAIG

THIS IS
WHERE I SAY
GOODBYE

Constable • London

CONSTABLE

First published in Great Britain in 2018 by Constable

A CIP catalogue record for this book is available from the British Library.

ISBN: 978-1-47212-220-9

Typeset in Times by TW Type, Cornwall
Printed and bound in Great Britain by CPI Group (UK) Ltd, Croydon CR0 4YY

Papers used by Constable are from well-managed forests and other responsible sources.

Constable
An imprint of
Little, Brown Book Group
Carmelite House
50 Victoria Embankment
London EC4Y 0DZ

An Hachette UK Company
www.hachette.co.uk

www.littlebrown.co.uk

For Catherine and Cate

This is the twelfth Carlyle novel.
Thanks for getting it completed go to
Krystyna Green, Rebecca Sheppard,
Hazel Orme and Michael Doggart.

'There comes a time when you look into the mirror and you realize that what you see is all that you will ever be.'

Tennessee Williams

ONE

Feeling seriously unwell, Josh Sandberry stumbled away from the phosphate glare of the streetlight by the bus stop and ducked into the alley that ran away from Tottenham Court Road, towards Whitfield Street. His head was spinning and the chorus to 'Get Lucky' was playing on a loop in his head. It was almost three in the morning and six hours of steady drinking was taking its inevitable toll. 'Eight vodka and Cokes on a school night!' He giggled. 'Not good, old boy. Not good at all.'

Reaching the entrance, he toe-poked an empty wine bottle, sending it clattering down the alley.

'Mwargh.' As Josh blundered forward it was clear that he was not the first person tonight who had sought out an al-fresco bathroom. Grimacing at the smell of ammonia, he felt his knees buckle slightly.

I'm going to puke.

Placing a hand on the brick wall to his left, he lowered his head and took a couple of shallow breaths, preparing to retch.

'Come on, you'll feel better.' He knew that it was best to decant the contents of his stomach before making the journey home. In the middle of the night, it would take an hour or so to get back to Wood Green. He didn't want to have to jump off the bus halfway home to spill his guts on the pavement.

Through the swirling fog of alcohol, he reflected on how he hadn't intended to get pissed at all. Tonight was supposed to be one quiet drink, maybe two. But he had fallen in with a group of boisterous LSE students and one drink had become three, four, five. By midnight, it had turned into quite a session and there didn't seem much point in calling a premature halt to proceedings. Apart from anything else, Josh had got his eye on one of the students, name of Debby or Sally or something, all pink hair and massive cleavage, just his type. For her part, Debby – he was fairly sure that was her name – had seemed quite interested in him, too. Josh remembered a hand on the knee at one point. As it had begun creeping surreptitiously towards his crotch, he'd thought his luck might be in. Then the next thing he remembered it was almost one thirty and the girl had disappeared. He hadn't even got a phone number.

Ah, well, these things happened. Even if she had taken him home, Josh reflected philosophically, the chances of him getting it up would have been small to none. All he wanted to do now was go home and sleep. If he was going to wake up with a monster hangover, much better that he was in his own bed. With his mouth feeling like a small animal had expired in it, he coughed violently, trying to raise some spittle. One thing was for sure: tomorrow would have to be a duvet day. Cautiously rolling his head on his shoulders, the senior customer engagement manager tried to remember if a day off might nix his chance of receiving an end-of-month performance bonus. Highly unlikely that he was up for one, was his immediate conclusion, given that he had already missed his performance targets both last week and the week before.

Without any money at stake, he turned his fragmented thoughts to the politics of the situation. When was the last time he'd thrown a sickie? Not in the last month or so. He hoped not, anyway. His supervisor, a sullen cow called Andrea, hated him. It was your basic personality clash: Josh had a personality; Andrea didn't. Josh was the life and soul of the party; Andrea didn't like the idea of people enjoying themselves, even out of office hours. He had already had two warnings this year about

2

absenteeism. And it had been made clear to him that another day off could be fatal.

Finally raising some moisture on his tongue, Josh spat into the gutter. The prospect of getting the sack from his shitty little sales position didn't really bother him. Getting another job in London would be a piece of piss, even if he didn't have a reference. What did rankle was the pleasure Andrea would get from sacking him. He knew she would happily deliver his P45 personally if he gave her the chance. It would probably be the most exciting thing that happened in her miserable little life all year.

Pushing the offensive Andrea from his mind, he began fumbling with his flies. Whether or not he managed to puke, he definitely needed to relieve his aching bladder. Steadying himself, he heard a disgusted cluck from the mouth of the alley. Half turning, he saw a girl in a red coat staring at his crotch, mild disgust on her face. Nobody's forcing you to look, Josh thought. Even in his befuddled state, though, it was clear that getting arrested for indecent exposure – or worse – would not be a good idea. Cock in hand, he turned his back on the gawper and waddled deeper into the alley, his shoes squelching across a sticky mess of alcohol and bodily fluids on the cracked tarmac.

Standing in the shadows, Josh glanced over his shoulder, checking that his audience was gone, before unleashing an arc of piss towards the pile of black bin bags that awaited the arrival of the refuse collectors in a few hours' time.

Aaaaaah.

Impressed by the distance he was getting, Josh began hosing the bags, slowly moving left and right. Suddenly the sound of water on plastic was replaced by something altogether less distinct. Frowning, he peered into the darkness.

'Holy shit!' Stumbling backwards into a pile of cardboard boxes, he finally managed to throw up.

This time tomorrow she would be fishing. Well, maybe not this time tomorrow, but in thirty-six hours, for sure. WPC Wendy

Granger closed her eyes and tried to imagine the bucolic scene in all its soft-focus beauty. Before she could compose the image in her head, a siren brought her back to her current reality. Tottenham Court Road at chucking-out time, the street decorated with vomit, piss and blood, a motley collection of teenagers reluctant to go home.

Granger looked down at the girl in the red coat standing in front of her. Petite, maybe five foot two, with long dark hair and the kind of pale skin that shimmered under the street lighting, she was claiming that she was eighteen. Granger very much doubted it. Fifteen seemed a better guess, sixteen at a push. There was a clear smell of alcohol on her breath but her eyes were bright and she didn't seem intoxicated. Even at this late hour, the girl retained a fresh-faced look that suggested a stamina Granger had lost years ago.

There's no point in hating her, the cop admonished herself, just because she's young. Granger had a vague sense of being young herself, once, nights up the West End, too much to drink, followed by embarrassing behaviour of one sort or another. It was a rite of passage.

On the other hand, it was impossible not to feel a lingering sense of resentment at being confronted by the next generation, kids getting ready to push her off the stage before Granger had achieved anything. The handful of gawkers standing behind the police tape, next to the bus stop, couldn't have contained anyone older than twenty, all of them happily chatting and filming the scene on their mobile phones, as if this was simply an extension of the night's entertainment, put on for their benefit. Granger had to fight an irrational urge to have them all arrested and shipped back to the station. Whoever said that youth was wasted on the young had probably been thinking about the stupid little sods stumbling around Westminster at closing time. So much energy, so little imagination. A properly enforced curfew on the under-twenty-fives would cut the workload of the nightshift by about 75 per cent. At least. Granger herself would be thirty this year.

4

I'm turning into Mum, she thought morosely, overlooking the fact that her mother, by the time she had reached that particular milestone, had already popped out three kids and was well on the way towards the unsuccessful conclusion of her second marriage.

'Is this gonna take long?' The girl pointed towards a bus approaching the stop. 'I want to get that.'

'I just need to take some details.' Granger pulled out the battered Moleskine notebook that had been a present from her dad three Christmases ago. The pages were covered with densely packed notes, mostly relating to long-forgotten cases. Granger deliberately kept her handwriting small and neat to make the notebook last as long as possible. She flipped towards the back for a blank page. 'You can get the next one.'

'But they take ages at this time of night,' the girl complained.

'Sorry,' Granger lied. 'Won't take long. The alternative would be to go down the station.'

'I didn't do anything,' the girl whined, every word making her sound even younger than she looked. As the bus came to a halt, she looked like she was considering making a run for it. The doors opened and, after a moment's debate, a couple of gawkers jumped on board. The doors closed behind them and the driver glanced at the goings-on in the alley before pulling away, heading towards Camden. The girl watched it depart with a mixture of annoyance and resignation in her face. 'Okay,' she turned back to face Granger, 'so I've missed my bus. Thanks a lot. What do you need to know?'

It took a moment, but Granger recalled the name the girl had given her. 'Hayley Cooper?' she asked, as she scribbled it down.

'That's right.'

'Where do you live?'

Cooper gave an address in upmarket Highgate. 'My mum's a lawyer,' she added, as if to explain the posh address, 'a partner at a Magic Circle firm.'

'And she lets you stay out at this time of night?'

The girl shrugged. 'She's in Singapore.'

Granger didn't bother to ask about the father. 'So,' she asked, 'you were the one who called it in?'

'More fool me,' the girl muttered.

'What happened?'

'How would I know?'

Gritting her teeth, Granger reframed her question: 'What did you see that caused you to call nine-nine-nine?'

'Not a lot.' Cooper gestured towards a young man sitting on the back step of an ambulance parked on the pavement. There was a green blanket wrapped around his shoulders and he stared vacantly into the middle distance as he took occasional sips from a small plastic water bottle. Even at a distance of five yards, they could smell the mixture of vomit and urine emanating from under the blanket. Cooper wrinkled her nose. 'He was in the alley having a wee. Men are such dirty little sods, aren't they?'

'Mm.'

'They'll go anywhere.'

'Yes, I suppose so.'

'Anyway, I saw him doing his business and I turned away. I mean, you don't want to watch that, do you? A few seconds later he started screaming, like he was being murdered. I couldn't really see what was going on but he just kept shouting, so I called nine-nine-nine. The cops were here in, like, thirty seconds.'

Hardly surprising, Granger thought. The West End, throwing-out time. Lots of cops on the street. Everyone on high alert for trouble.

Cooper pointed down the alley. 'They found him in there.'

'You didn't go in?'

'No fear.'

'And you didn't see anyone else?'

'No.' Cooper shook her head. 'He just went in for a pee. There was no one else.'

'Someone could have come from the other end,' Granger hypothesized.

'If they did, I didn't see them.'

'And you didn't see the girl?'

'No.'

'You didn't hear any arguments, any screaming?'

Cooper gave the question some thought. 'I was just arriving at the bus stop. I didn't even know she was there.'

'Okay.' Granger began doodling in her notebook.

'One of the other officers said she was dead.' Cooper gestured at the guy perched on the back of the ambulance. 'I don't think he killed her – otherwise why would he have started screaming? I think he just went in there for a pee.'

'She's not dead.' Granger immediately regretted saying it. You were not supposed to share crime-scene information with the public.

'No? That's good, isn't it?'

'Yes.'

Cooper peered into the alley. 'Is she still in there, then?'

'Dunno,' the WPC admitted. 'I think they took her out through the other end.' From further down Tottenham Court Road, another bus was heading towards them. Handing over one of her business cards, Granger tried to think of a final question. She pointed her biro at the guy in the blanket. 'Did he have any mates with him?'

'No.' Cooper brought out her Oyster card for a second time. Giving Granger a look that said, *You promised*, she edged towards the bus stop. 'I think he was on his own. He was just a bloke who'd had too much to drink.' The bus pulled up at the stop and the driver opened the doors. 'I've gotta get to bed.' Cooper turned away from Granger and broke into a jog. 'I've got double Spanish in the morning and Mr Bueno-Rodriguez doesn't let you into class if you're late. I'll call you if I think of anything else.'

WPC Granger watched the girl take a seat as the bus pulled away, heading towards north London. 'Double Spanish,' she muttered ruefully. 'Those were the days.'

7

TWO

Standing under the harsh corridor lighting, Granger stifled a yawn. Bleary-eyed, the policewoman stared through the large window that gave the hospital staff an easy view of their latest patient, without having to go in and out of the room every five minutes. The girl from the alley had been cleaned up but the injuries on her face still looked fresh and raw.

Someone really did want to kill you, Granger thought, didn't they?

They still didn't know the victim's name. For the moment, she had been given the imaginative moniker of 'Miss X'.

After finishing her interview with Hayley Cooper, Granger had spoken to half a dozen other bystanders. None had provided her with any information of any relevance. The injured girl, meanwhile, had been taken the short distance – no more than a few hundred yards – to University College Hospital. There, she had been given a preliminary examination by an exhausted-looking junior doctor before being hooked up to a range of machines and placed in an induced coma.

Granger had informed the duty sergeant at the station that Miss X was not going to be giving any interviews for the foreseeable future. The wife was shamelessly angling to be stood down. Instead, she was told unceremoniously, 'Stay put and await further instructions. And while you're at it,' said the sergeant, 'see if you can come up with an ID for the victim.'

'How I am I supposed to do that?' Granger shot back, her frustration levels rising as her sugar levels dropped.

'Sit tight,' was the sergeant's final word, 'in case she wakes up.'

'But—'

'And keep your wits about you, in case her attacker turns up to finish the job.'

Yeah, right, Granger thought glumly. This isn't the bloody movies, you know.

'I'll send someone to relieve you later on.'

'I—' Before she had been able to point out that her shift had technically ended four hours ago, the line had gone dead.

'Bollocks.' Granger cursed herself for not being more assertive. Not for the first time, she wondered if she was really cut out to be a cop. After more than eight years on the force, she should have moved up the ranks, at least a little. Instead her job was pretty much the same mix of social work, form-filling and endless hanging around that it had always been. Mindlessly doing what she was told – regardless of how stupid or pointless – was beginning to grate.

Moving away from the window, the WPC looked around for somewhere to sit down, groaning as she realized that there wasn't a chair in sight anywhere along the entire length of the hospital corridor. Moving from foot to foot, she tried to ease the dull ache in her calves.

'Hey.'

Granger looked up to see her sometime partner, PC Paul Dombey, appear from round the corner. Dombey was carrying a cup in each hand, with a paper bag hanging from his mouth. Granger stifled a giggle.

Coming to a halt, Dombey let Granger retrieve the bag. It was warm to the touch. She felt herself start to salivate, like Pavlov's dog.

'What are you up to?' he asked, gesturing at her feet. 'Practising your dancing?'

'Cramp.' Returning her elevated foot to the floor, Granger peered inside the bag and groaned. Two large iced doughnuts. She knew that even one bite of the additive-stuffed sugar bomb would blow her latest health regime completely out of the water. Resistance, however, was futile. She sucked in her stomach. 'Didn't they have anything else?'

Dombey looked mortally offended by her lack of enthusiasm. 'Fresh from the shop,' he pointed out. 'It was either that or a KitKat. The bacon rolls won't be ready for another twenty minutes or so.'

Thank God for small mercies. Granger wondered how much cholesterol there was in a doughnut.

'I couldn't wait that long,' Dombey admitted. About six foot three, he looked like a giant seven-year-old. Three years in London had done little to take the edge off his comedy Yorkshire accent. Granger considered the amiable giant uniquely ill-suited to big-city life. She imagined that his natural habitat was more like a two-man police station deep in the Dales where he could hunt sheep rustlers and rescue missing ramblers. The kind of place that had disappeared in the 1960s.

Paul Dombey, man out of time. Granger tittered.

'What's so funny?'

'Nothing.' Granger took a piece of icing from the bag and nibbled it daintily. 'Why is the food in hospitals always so crap?'

'It's comfort eating.' Handing her a cup, Dombey stuck a hand into the bag, pulled out one of the doughnuts and took a large bite.

'Mm.' Granger removed the lid from her cup and took a sip of tea. 'Thanks.'

'No problem.' Dombey grinned. 'This is the kind of grub I'd want if I was in hospital.' To emphasize the point, he demolished the rest of his doughnut in a succession of rapid mouthfuls.

Grub? Who used a word like that any more? Granger smiled. It was the kind of thing she'd expect her dad to say. 'You'd think a hospital would be a bit more focused on promoting a healthy diet, wouldn't you?'

'Not really,' Dombey said. 'If you're in here, you've got more important things to worry about than your five-a-day.'

'Maybe.'

'No maybe about it, Wend.' Taking a slurp of his tea, he made a grab for the remaining doughnut with his free hand. 'Don't you want that?'

Granger instinctively jerked the bag away from him. 'Maybe half.'

'Deal.'

Taking the doughnut from the bag, Granger carefully pulled it apart, offering her partner the larger piece.

'What are you doing?'

Granger turned to see a middle-aged woman in a white coat striding towards them. She had an iPad in one hand and a mobile phone in the other. The expression on her face was at the extremely pissed-off end of the annoyed spectrum. She pointed to a noticeboard on the far wall. 'What does that say?'

'Check your balls?' Dombey pointed his doughnut at a poster about testicular cancer.

Glaring at the young constable, the woman indicated an adjoining notice that bore the stark message: 'No food or drink in the corridor'. 'This is supposed to be a clean environment,' she snapped, coming to a halt in front of Granger. The name badge on her coat said 'Dr Hendricks'. She was tall, maybe five foot nine, with angry brown eyes. Her brows were knotted together, with deep furrows lining her forehead. Her long black hair was streaked with grey. Attractive but more than a little worn at the edges.

Burnout victim, Granger thought. It'll take more than a week at a health spa to get you back on your game, she decided.

'You can't eat here.'

Grinning like the idiot he was, Dombey shoved the remains of his doughnut into his gob, swallowing quickly.

Granger dropped her half back into the bag and placed the lid on her tea. 'Sorry,' she said meekly.

'We have enough problems with vermin already.' The doctor gestured towards a series of small boxes that had been placed along the wall at floor level. The mouse traps were branded with the logo of a famous pest-control company. Granger was so tired that she hadn't noticed them until they were pointed out to her. Hendricks eyed the two police officers suspiciously. 'How did you get in here anyway?'

How do you think? We walked straight past the front desk. Granger gestured towards the girl in the bed. 'We're here about the girl who was assaulted.'

'Well,' the doctor observed, 'you're not going to be able to talk to her for a while . . . days, maybe weeks.'

'We need to make an ID,' Dombey pointed out. 'There was nothing on her where she was found, no driving licence, credit card, anything like that.'

'So what are you expecting?' Even accounting for the fact that she was frazzled, the doctor's sneering tone was rather over the top. 'A tattoo on her inner lip? Her name sewn into her clothes? Dog tags?' She pointed to a small pile of clothes lying on a chair next to the bed. 'When she came in, as you probably know, she was wearing a flimsy dress, knickers and a pair of shoes. There's nothing with her name and address on it.'

'We don't know who she is.' Dombey provocatively sipped his tea.

'Then you'll have to come back later,' the doctor looked like she wanted to give him a smack with the iPad, 'when she wakes up.'

The three of them stood there, no one apparently sure of what to do next. Granger watched as a second doctor, a youngish guy with blond hair, approached Hendricks, smiling sheepishly.

'Any developments?' he asked. His English was so precise and clear that he had to be a foreigner.

Hendricks looked as irritated by her colleague as she did by the police. 'Only bloody cops, wasting our time,' she snapped.

The man shot an apologetic glance at Granger and Dombey. 'Markus Siebeck.'

'I'm Dombey and this is Granger.' Dombey gestured towards the girl's room. 'We were the ones who brought her in.'

'What are her injuries?' Granger asked.

With a theatrical sigh, Hendricks began tapping on the screen of the tablet. 'Two broken ribs, a collapsed lung, multiple bruises,' she intoned mechanically, 'TBI—'

Dombey frowned. 'Eh?'

'Traumatic brain injury,' Granger explained quickly, not wanting the good doctor to think they were totally thick.

'That's why we've put her in the coma,' Hendricks explained, 'while we assess her condition.'

'Was she sexually assaulted?' Dombey asked, a bit too eagerly for Granger's taste.

Hendricks shook her head. 'There was no evidence of that. She was just beaten half to death. Isn't that enough?'

Granger stared at the floor.

'I've got to get on with some work.' Turning to her colleague, Hendricks pointed towards the exit. 'Markus, will you see the officers out of here, please?'

Granger started to protest, then thought better of it. Being a cop, you learned to pick your battles. This one wasn't worth fighting.

THREE

From the flat next door came the sound of mid-morning television. Raised voices followed by applause. The modern form of confessional. He had seen the show once – at least, he had looked at maybe two minutes of one episode. That was as long as he could bear watching stupid people arguing about stupid things, egged on by a smug presenter and the representative cross-section of the underclass that made up the audience – people with nothing to do, no purpose but to broadcast their stupidity and pointlessness across the airwaves. The kind of people who, in earlier times, would have been at the front of whatever lynch mob had been up and running at the time.

His neighbour, Mrs Fox, watched the show every morning while she waited to see if her home help would show up to rifle her purse and pretend to clean the flat. Mrs Fox was pushing ninety now. Not right in the head. Not able to get out and about. Ignored by her family, the poor woman was being relentlessly exploited by a succession of 'carers', each of whom would appear for a couple of weeks at a time before moving on in search of richer pickings. It was so shameless that he had written to the council about it – both by letter and email – without getting any response. When he had tried calling them, it had taken almost twenty minutes for someone to pick up the phone, then immediately – and deliberately – cut him off.

The TV's screeching was replaced by music, the jingle for a ubiquitous mobile-phone game. Richard Furlong smiled grimly.

Everything in life was a distraction. Everyone had to deal with it in their own way.

He had tried to intervene, to no avail. The unfortunate Mrs Fox would have to fend for herself. His mind was a mix of thoughts, ideas and regrets. Holding tightly to the side of the sink, he took a succession of deep breaths as he tried to switch off his brain as he waited for his heart rate to return to something approaching normal.

You always knew that this day would come, he told himself. There's no point in acting surprised now.

Staring out of the window at the orange building on the opposite side of the road, Furlong waited until he was sure that his tremors were under control before relaxing his grip and reaching for the tap. Turning on the cold water, he splashed his face. Wiping his eyes on his sleeve, he stifled a sob. Next door, the arguments had resumed. Tuning out the noise, he began carefully washing the blood from his hands.

Picking up a tea-towel emblazoned with a drawing of a Routemaster, Furlong dried his hands as his stomach started to rumble. Despite everything, his hunger demanded to be satisfied. Bemused by what his body was telling him, he folded the cloth into quarters and placed it carefully on the windowsill, next to the small trophy that was now just a vague memory of happier times.

From the landing came the sound of Mrs Fox's front-door bell. Two short rings followed by a brief pause, then the key going into the lock. The usual drill. A woman calling her name. Probably the girl Furlong had passed on the stairs the week before. All peroxide hair and dark rings under the eyes. Translucent skin. Purple lipstick. Like a vampire.

The vampires were taking over. The idea crossed his mind that he should go next door and put Mrs Fox out of her misery. Place a pillow over her face and hold it down. Switch off her television set. Save her from the undead. One last simple act of mercy.

His stomach rumbled again. 'All right,' he muttered. 'Food.' He would have a last supper. Filling the kettle, he set the water to boil and stepped over to the tiny table that almost filled the kitchen's available floor space. On it was a letter. Picking up the sheet of paper, Furlong ran a finger along the embossed heading. He had received many such letters. The usual frisson of excitement that he received from holding the heavy paper in his hand was today absent, but he still felt compelled to read the carefully typed instructions with exaggerated care.

Once he had memorized its contents, he lifted the sheet to his face and breathed in its scent. Furlong knew it intimately: Oud Silk Mood by Maison Francis Kurkdjian. He had bought enough of it over the years, a necessary luxury, even at almost three hundred pounds for a small bottle.

Furlong let the sheet flutter to the table. A step to his left was enough to allow him to reach out and pull open the fridge door. Inside it was empty, apart from six cans of lager, a pizza two weeks past its sell-by date and a small Tupperware box, which sat alone on the top shelf. Taking the box from the fridge, he wiped his palms on his shirt before loosening the lid. As instructed in the letter, he carefully placed the box in the microwave, set the reheat programme for ninety seconds, slammed the door shut and hit the start button.

As the machine hummed into action, Furlong thought about the events of the last few days. Things had moved so quickly, spiralled so far out of control, so fast, that the whole thing seemed unreal. And yet he felt strangely resigned to what was happening. Deep down, he had always known that this – or something very much like it – was how things were destined to pan out.

The ping of the microwave brought him out of his reverie. Wiping his nose on the sleeve of his shirt, Furlong took out the box and placed it on the table, then removed the lid to let the steaming contents cool. Moving mechanically, he placed a couple of slices of white bread in the toaster and switched it on.

Dropping a teabag into his RPRA mug, he added a splash of milk and some boiled water from the kettle, resting his backside against the sink as he let the mixture brew.

After twenty seconds or so, he took a teaspoon from the drawer next to the sink, stirred the contents of the mug for several seconds, then lifted out the teabag and dropped it into the sink. A tentative sip suggested that the tea was a bit on the weak side but, after some equivocation, Furlong decided it would do. He placed the cup on the table as the toast obligingly popped out of the toaster. On inspection, the bread was slightly browner than he would have liked, but not quite what you would call burned. Burned toast could give you cancer – he had read that somewhere not so long ago. His stomach rumbled again, as if to remind him that this was not the time to be too pernickety. He put the toast onto a plate, took a knife from the cutlery drawer and moved to the table.

Sitting down, he reached forward and removed some of the contents from the box, spreading it evenly across the first slice of toast. Once he was satisfied with the result, he took a deep bite, chewed determinedly – four, five, six times – then swallowed. Although the smell was quite arresting, the taste was disappointingly bland. He drank some tea, ate the rest of the toast in his hand, then started on the second slice.

From the street below came the rise and fall of a car stereo pumping from a vehicle as it made its way slowly through the traffic. Furlong shook his head in dismay. People had so little respect for their environment. Not for the first time, he reflected on how he had been incredibly lucky to get a flat so high up. How anyone living close to ground level could put up with the incessant noise he would never know.

Popping the final piece of toast into his mouth, he ran his tongue across his lips and drained the last of his tea from the mug. After placing the lid back on the box and returning it to the top shelf of the fridge, he put the cup and the plate in the sink. Licking the knife clean, he ran the hot-water tap, added a squirt of washing-up liquid and washed each item in turn, placing them on the draining-board to dry. Stifling a modestly satisfied burp, he stepped around the table to a large single-pane window. A shaft of sunlight was pouring through the glass, highlighting the grime that had collected on its outer surface. The sun's warmth made him feel thick-headed. Shaking the torpor from his skull, he fumbled with the lock, pushing the window as far open as it would go.

Sticking his head outside, he felt a blast of warm air on his face.

Nice day for it.

Looking down, he could see a steady stream of vehicles and pedestrians moving in each direction on the street below.

'No point in hanging around any longer.' A frisson of excitement tickled his chest. Pulling his head inside, he took a chair from the table and placed it under the window, listening to his knees crack as he stepped onto the seat. From there, he tentatively lifted one foot over the ledge and sat down, grimacing as the metal frame cut into the flesh of his left buttock. Manoeuvring his second foot out was trickier but, after a few moments of grunting effort, he managed it. Sitting on the windowsill, he found himself looking straight into the office opposite. At a desk by the window, a woman drank from an outsized paper coffee cup while she tapped away at a computer keyboard. For several seconds, Furlong waited to see if she would turn away from her screen and see him sitting there, about to let go.

When she didn't oblige, he jumped.

FOUR

Dr Markus Siebeck glanced glumly at his watch. It had stopped at three minutes past nine. He would have to get a replacement battery. Or maybe he would just throw the damn thing away. It was too chunky for his taste, like something a teenage boy would wear.

Back in the 1980s, maybe.

No one even needed a watch these days, did they? In the digital world it was impossible not to be aware of the time unless you went and sat on top of a mountain. And even then it would take some effort.

The young doctor started to undo the strap, then thought better of it. The watch had been a present from his girlfriend. Markus remembered waiting impatiently in the Galeria Kaufhof, watching the passers-by on the Neumarkt, while Helma hummed and hawed over which one to buy, as if her budget was five thousand euros, rather than seventy-five. After the best part of half an hour, she had come up with the Casio model that now adorned his wrist. Markus had offered no input whatsoever into the final decision; nor had he cared.

That had been, what, eighteen months ago? Something like that. Markus knew that if he were to stop wearing the damn thing, Helma would read far too much into it.

As usual.

The truth was he didn't much like the watch, even when it was working.

Despite the non-functioning timepiece, Dr Siebeck was acutely aware that he was barely two hours into a twelve-hour shift. This was the fourth day in a row the young German had been on duty. After this, he had another two days to go before the reward of a couple of days off. He was in a permanent daze. The English were supposed to be lazy and, by and large, they were, but for some reason they liked to work their doctors like dogs.

Standing outside Lampard Ward, he watched impassively as a gaunt, shaven-headed woman of indeterminate age, wearing a tracksuit, shuffled down the corridor, carefully wheeling the pole holding the drip bag attached to her arm. In her free hand, she clutched a packet of cigarettes and a lighter. Reaching the end of the corridor, she manoeuvred her way out of the door and immediately began the ritual of lighting up.

Siebeck tried to remember the last time he had felt so tired. Yesterday, probably. Breathing in deeply, he almost gagged. The cleaners had been round minutes before and the smell of cleaning products made his stomach somersault.

I need to get out of here, he thought. This place is making me ill. He was a doctor who hated hospitals. How had that happened? He had studied for more than a decade to get here. Then again, UCH was a long way from the kind of small practice in Nordsachsen he had envisaged while making his way through medical school.

The day's round of consultations had barely started but Siebeck was already more than twenty minutes late for his next patient. The delays would get longer as the day progressed. The poor souls originally scheduled for late afternoon would probably be sent home without being seen. The English health system had been something miraculous, once. Now it was just an unsustainable black hole falling in on itself.

Outside, he watched the woman with the drip start on a second cigarette. She was one of a small knot of sallow souls gathered round a bin specially designed for butts, each greedily sucking down their nicotine fix. None gave the impression of enjoying the experience. It was like a race to the grave. When Kurt Vonnegut described smoking as 'a classy way to commit suicide' he clearly didn't have the good patients of University College Hospital in mind.

An often-recalled image of his grandfather slipped into Siebeck's mind: the old man sitting at the kitchen table, unshaven, an unfiltered Pall Mall in one hand, a half-empty packet in the other, his fingers permanently stained yellow. Joachim Croy had easily smoked more cigarettes in a day than his grandson did in a week. Siebeck had once estimated that his grandfather had burned through something in the region of 350,000 in his lifetime. A lifetime that had been, not surprisingly, cut short by throat cancer. Croy was dead at sixty-two. More than thirty years later, his grandmother, a devout non-smoker, was still going strong. Siebeck smiled. Sometimes it seemed there was some justice in the world, after all.

Just sometimes.

Casting a guilty look back in the direction of the consulting rooms, the doctor wondered if he could, in all conscience, step outside for some fresh air and a quick smoke with his fellow untouchables. Staff were not supposed to light up on the hospital steps like ordinary folk. Indeed, according to the hospital trust rule book, such behaviour constituted misconduct; it was a disciplinary offence that could lead to suspension, or even dismissal in the case of repeat offenders.

Siebeck reluctantly pushed the idea from his head. The front entrance to the hospital wasn't his preferred location for a smoking break anyway: the chances of getting any fresh air while standing fewer than two metres from Euston Road were slightly less than nil. The six-lane highway that rolled past the eponymous railway station to the north was one of the most polluted in the city, and therefore in the whole of the country and, indeed, Europe. For somewhere that liked to style itself as a twenty-first century 'world capital', London had a curiously nineteenth-century attitude towards air pollution. The relentless traffic, Siebeck thought sadly, was probably doing more to shorten his own life expectancy than his unfortunate taste for Mayfair king size.

All thoughts of a 'crafty fag', as the English put it, vanished as he watched his next patient approach from the direction of the hospital lobby. Looks like I'm not the only one who's behind schedule, Siebeck thought. Running through the details from the case file in his head, he watched the man approach. Alexander Carlyle. Seventy-five years old. One metre seventy-three tall. Sixty-two kilograms the last time they weighed him but probably well south of sixty now.

All in all, Alexander Carlyle didn't look like much. Then again, he was well on the way to being dead. Alexander – never 'Alex' – had been one of Siebeck's first patients when he had arrived at UCH. As Siebeck was a new arrival, and a foreigner to boot, the hospital administrators had had no compunction about dumping the terminal cases on his desk. At the time, Siebeck would have given this guy maybe nine months. A year at the most. For him still to be standing three years later was a minor miracle.

A fluke of nature.

A triumph of the human spirit.

Or something.

From the road outside came the shrill sound of an emergency siren. Siebeck tensed until he realized the ambulance was on its way out. Whatever they brought back was not likely to be his problem anyway. The doctor gave silent thanks that he didn't work in Accident and Emergency, which was all drunks and timewasters.

'Mr Carlyle.'

The old man came to a halt in front of him. He looked as if he was already dressed for his coffin. His suit was crumpled and his shirt, originally white, had turned a rather murky shade of grey. Siebeck realised belatedly that the man's son was hovering behind him. 'How are you, today?' he asked the patient.

'Fine, Doctor, fine.' 'Fine' was just about the only word Alexander Carlyle ever used. Stoicism was the man's saving grace.

'Good.' Siebeck probably knew more about this man than he did about almost any other person in the entire city. A Scotsman who had come to London to find work more than fifty years ago. Widowed. Just the one son – a mid-ranking policeman who worked somewhere not far from the hospital.

'Sorry we're late,' the son muttered, shooting his father a dirty look. 'We had to wait ages for a bus on account of the tube strike.'

'I thought that was last week?' Siebeck instantly regretted querying such a convenient lie.

'Last week's strike was three days,' the old man explained. 'This week only two.'

'Ah, yes, of course.' The doctor tried to recall what the dispute was about, but his mind was a blank. 'It's seems like it's almost all the time at the moment, doesn't it?'

The son muttered something to the effect that heads needed to be knocked together.

'I know we're not supposed to be late under any circumstances,' Alexander Carlyle sounded genuinely apologetic, 'but the first couple of buses that went past were so full we couldn't get on them.'

'That's okay,' Siebeck said, relieved not to be on the end of yet another complaint about the NHS's grotesquely over-optimistic timetabling. 'These things happen.' Lifting an arm, he gestured towards the consultation room. 'Shall we go inside?'

Taking up his standard defensive position, sitting up straight, shoulders back, hands resting on the desk, Siebeck felt the gaze of the son fall upon him. The fact that the man was a cop changed the dynamic in the room somewhat, making the doctor feel a little less sure of himself than usual. It was irrational but no less real for that. Like most doctors, Siebeck was not used to being scrutinized and he didn't much like it. He felt guilty of something.

Sitting next to his son, Alexander Carlyle stared straight ahead, focusing on a point on the wall somewhere above Siebeck's head. On first inspection, there wasn't much of a resemblance between the two men. On occasion, Siebeck had found himself idly wondering if his patient might not have been the biological father. Look more closely, however, around the eyes, the corners of the mouth and the line of the jaw and you could see the makings of a likeness.

The old man began to cough.

'Would you like some water?' the doctor asked.

Holding up a hand, Alexander Carlyle shook his head.

The son fumbled in his pocket for a paper handkerchief and handed it to his father. 'He'll be fine in a minute.'

That word again.

Ubiquitous and meaningless at the same time.

At least he was present this morning. The son had a decidedly mixed track record when it came to accompanying his father on his hospital visits. The two men, it seemed to Siebeck, were distant, almost wary of each other. He remembered reading somewhere about the Scots being emotionally retarded. It was down to a mixture of their Protestant heritage, a terrible diet and the appalling weather, apparently. Siebeck had been there once, a weekend in Edinburgh with Helma. All he could remember was that their northbound train had been three hours late and he had been cold the whole time. They had argued a lot. She accused him of running away. He didn't deny it. He accused her of fucking her boss. She didn't deny it. They had travelled back on different trains. It was the only time he had ever felt happy coming back to London.

From the way he spoke, the father seemed considerably fonder of the daughter-in-law than he was of the son. There was a grandson as well – or maybe a granddaughter. Siebeck had heard the potted family history several times. It was the usual unremarkable stuff; the kind of thing you heard from all your patients, if not normally at such length. Now that it was all over, Siebeck was confident that the information would decay and be flushed from his brain in the next few months.

With a bit of luck.

Finally, the old man's coughing subsided.

'Now, then.' Siebeck tapped at his keyboard and stared intently at the information that popped up on his computer screen, even though he knew well enough what it said. 'Where we are on this, right now . . .'

FIVE

Ten minutes later, the three men were back out in the corridor, shaking hands.

'So,' Siebeck grinned uncomfortably, 'thank you again for coming.' He stared at his shoes, seemingly unable to close off the conversation and be on his way.

Poor lad, Alexander thought. He doesn't know what else to say. The German was tall and gangling, far too big for his white coat, which didn't come close to encasing his frame. He had a high forehead and a mop of golden hair that was already receding markedly at the temples. Although he must have been well into his thirties, he looked little more than eighteen. His nervousness was surprising but, then again, maybe some doctors never got used to waving their patients off to die.

'You have everything you should need,' Siebeck stammered.

'Yes.'

'If there's a problem—'

'We'll ring,' Alexander said quickly.

'Yes, good.' Siebeck took a half-step backwards but still couldn't bring himself to turn and flee.

Alexander watched a woman wander past, pushing her drip bag on its pole. In her free hand was a packet of cigarettes. Some people never learn. He watched Siebeck track the woman's progress back to the ward with what he took to be dismay. It really is quite a shite job, being a doctor, he mused. I've never really understood the attraction. Apart from the nurses, maybe.

His gaze alighted on a guide to colonoscopy services that had been pinned to a nearby noticeboard, next to an advert for the current junk food offers available in the hospital shop. At least his days of being poked and prodded were now over. There would be no more investigations, no more humiliating procedures with bored-looking girls sticking things up his backside while he tried not to pass wind in their face.

It was all over.

The thought cheered Alexander considerably. Not for the first time, he reflected on how all of his worries were falling away. No one mentioned it, of course, but there was a good side to dying. There was some pain, obviously, but that was manageable. He had finally started taking the illegal extra-strong tablets that his son had managed to rustle up from one of his criminal pals and, much to his surprise, they were working a treat. As long as the boy could keep them coming, Alexander could look forward to his remaining days being spent increasingly in a drug-induced haze, keeping a smile on his face before he headed off for the big sleep.

Why is he smiling? Siebeck wondered what was going on inside his patient's head. The psychological side of things was someone else's problem, but Mr Carlyle's reaction to being told to go home to die was far removed from the usual wailing and bluster. The doctor noticed how the stubble on his chin glinted under the strip-lighting. The old man's eyes, shrinking into their sockets, were focused on a poster on the noticeboard. It was obvious that he was in considerable discomfort, even with the drugs he was taking.

Doesn't he realize what's happening?

Maybe he's in denial.

Maybe he's just too doped up to understand.

Initially, the additional pain relief was something of a surprise. Tests that the hospital had run the week before had shown an extremely high level of opiates in the old man's bloodstream.

The levels were much higher than you would get from his prescription. Clearly he was using illegal drugs to supplement the medication Siebeck had arranged for him. Some form of heroin, most likely. Given that the man's son was a cop, the doctor had a fair idea of where the drugs were coming from. However, after giving the matter some thought, he had decided not to report it. When his time came, Siebeck knew that he too would want to be doped up to the eyeballs. All in all, it was an easy decision to let it lie; knowing when to look the other way was a key skill when you worked for the NHS.

The cancer was firmly in control now, even if it seemed to be in no particular hurry to finish Mr Carlyle off. Siebeck shifted his weight from one foot to the other, wondering why he had come all the way from Saxony for this. Pain and suffering seemed worse somehow in a foreign country. A familiar stab of self-pity shot through him as he contemplated being a thousand kilometres from home. After a month in Kentish Town, Helma had packed her bags and gone back to Leipzig. Siebeck knew he would have to follow her or their relationship would be dead more quickly than his patient. He had tried to weigh up the pros and cons of that but had failed to reach any conclusion.

A cough brought him back to the here and now. The son. A look of irritation passed across the cop's face. Standing next to his father in a pair of tatty jeans and a T-shirt bearing the legend 'Lonsdale', he resembled a dishevelled teenager.

'The focus now will be on making you as comfortable as possible.' Siebeck focused on the father. 'This is where I say goodbye.'

The old man nodded. 'Thank you for all your help.'

The doctor bit his lower lip. 'Good luck.'

From Euston Road came the sound of screeching brakes, followed by a series of car horns. Taking a deep breath, Siebeck finally turned on his heel and began marching down the corridor towards A and E. The ambulance bay just outside would be the best place to go for a discreet smoke. His next patient would just have to wait.

The cigarette was in his mouth, dangling, he liked to think, from his lower lip in a rather louche fashion, when he realized that his lighter was still in the office.

'Damn.'

As Siebeck looked around in vain for a fellow smoker who could help him out, he saw the familiar figure of Sonia Gavril heading towards him. In her early twenties, Sonia was a porter who had come to London from a small town in Romania. Her nickname around the hospital was Tank Girl, because of her resemblance to the cartoon character, both in appearance and attitude.

'Hi, Doc.'

'Hi,' Siebeck replied nervously. Ever since she had arrived at UCH, almost a year ago now, Sonia had made no attempt to hide her interest in the German doctor. Given half a chance, Siebeck feared, she would eat him alive.

'Don't worry,' Sonia said cheerily. 'I'm not gonna try and jump your bones.' She gestured around the dreary car park. 'Not here, anyway.'

Siebeck was only partially reassured. 'How did you know where to find me?'

'Doc, c'mon.' Sonia planted her feet apart and her hands on her hips. 'If you're not in your cubicle—'

'Office.'

'Whatever. If you're not there, where else are you gonna be? Everybody knows you've got a terrible nicotine habit.'

'They do?'

'People worry about you, Doc.'

Siebeck felt slightly disoriented by the idea. 'Well,' he huffed, 'they shouldn't.'

'Don't be so grumpy.' She aimed a lazy punch at his arm; he was relieved when it missed. 'I've got something for you.'

29

'A light?' Siebeck asked hopefully.

'No.' She made a grab for his smoke, but he ducked out of the way. 'Those things are bad for you. I thought you medical professional people knew that?'

'My choice,' Siebeck mumbled, removing the cigarette from his mouth, just in case she made another grab for it.

'You should show your body more respect.'

The last thing he wanted to talk about was his body. 'What have you got for me?' he croaked, not sure that he wanted to know.

'This.' Sonia held up a small piece of plastic in a latex-gloved hand.

'What is it?'

'Looks like a data stick. I got it from Anne.'

'Anne?'

Sonia pointed towards the heavens or, at least, towards the upper floors of the hospital. 'Miss X, upstairs. I thought she deserves a name, don't you?'

'You mean she's awake?' Siebeck asked, feeling totally confused.

'No, not yet.' Sonia looked over her shoulder, checking that no one was eavesdropping on their conversation. 'I pulled it out of her diaper.'

Nappy, Siebeck thought. Sonia's English was peppered with Americanisms that he found irritating.

'I pulled it out of her shit.' Sonia tossed him the flash drive.

'Urgh.' Siebeck jumped backwards, letting it bounce at his feet.

'Don't be so squeamish,' Sonia admonished him.

'Why didn't you give it to Nadine – I mean Dr Hendricks? The girl is her patient.'

Sonia's face darkened. 'That stupid cow has gone off shift. Anyway, she wouldn't want to know.'

'I don't want to know,' Siebeck wailed.

'Course you do.' Sonia's expression instantly returned to its usual breezy self. 'You want the bastard who put her in a hospital bed nailed, don't you?'

Nailed? Siebeck glanced towards the gutter. 'What's that got to do with the contents of her, er, bowel movement?'

'Come on, Doc. How many people swallow computer sticks? It's evidence, isn't it?' Grinning, she headed back in the direction she had come. 'Check it out. I need to get back to work.'

'What shall I do with it?' Siebeck shouted after her.

'How should I know? Give it to the cops. You never know, if it breaks the case open, it might even help you get to second base with Hendricks.'

Second base? What the hell was second base? As Sonia disappeared through the doors, Siebeck had an idea. Picking up the data stick, he hurried back inside.

SIX

Thank God that's over. Inspector John Carlyle watched the doctor disappear down the corridor. The German seemed a bit strange, but that was not so surprising. What a terrible job, telling people that they were dying. With a vague sense of guilt, he checked his phone. No missed calls. That was something, at least. Theoretically, he was on duty but things were quiet at the moment. As far as he could tell, most of Central London's criminal fraternity were on their holidays.

Long may it continue.

Pushing thoughts of Charing Cross police station from his mind, he placed a hand on his father's shoulder. 'Fancy getting something to eat?'

Alexander Carlyle winced.

'Are you okay?'

'Ach.' His father's face crumpled. 'I need another of your fancy pills.'

'I'm glad to hear they're working.' Carlyle had gone through a lot of aggravation to come up with a supply of opiates to boost the old fella's pain relief. Alexander had initially been reluctant to take them, which had irritated his son immensely. Now that the pain was getting worse, though, he was gobbling them up like sweeties.

'Aye, they're no bad.' Alexander pulled a lozenge from his pocket and popped it into his mouth. 'My special cough sweets.'

'How many have you got left?'

'A few.' He sucked the tablet. 'I'm getting through them at quite a rate at the moment, though.'

Carlyle stuck his hands into his pockets. 'I'll speak to Dom.' Dominic Silver, ex-copper turned art dealer – with a long and successful spell as a drug-dealer in between – was one of the inspector's longest and closest associates. Dom was a handy man to know when your father was in need of a reliable supply of drugs above and beyond the feeble pharmaceuticals provided by the NHS.

'Thank him for me. I'm very grateful.'

'I will.'

Alexander bit down on the pill. 'About the money.'

'Don't worry about that, Dad. Dom's taking care of it.'

The old man's face relaxed as the opiates began to kick in. 'This stuff must be expensive.'

'No idea,' Carlyle said airily. It was true enough. This was the first time he had ever taken a backhander of any sort from his criminal mate and he didn't want to dwell on the details.

'They're certainly better than anything the doctor gave me.'

'That's why we got them.' Carlyle tried to edge his father towards the door. 'Anyway, food. You should get something to eat.'

Alexander muttered something inaudible, then said: 'Maybe just a cup of tea. Not in here, though. It's depressing as hell. And the café is rubbish.'

'Agreed,' Carlyle smiled. He was pleased that the old man was finally talking in something approximating the Queen's English. In the last few months, as the end drew nearer, he had been speaking in a kind of cod-Scots accent, like something out of the Broons. The inspector assumed it was some subconscious attempt to return to his youth. Whatever the reason, a visit to the doctor seemed to have knocked it out of him.

'There used to be a place just round the corner,' Alexander reminisced, scratching his chin. 'Delph's, I think it was called. That would be okay.'

Carlyle vaguely remembered the place. It had been owned by a large woman from Leytonstone with a useless husband and a bad drink problem. It was not such an uncommon story, when you came to think about it. The place had closed down in the early 1990s and had lain empty for years. Now, the site was occupied by a bookmaker.

'It does a decent cuppa,' Alexander offered.

'I'm not sure Delph's is still around.'

'Bound to be.'

Carlyle backed off, not wanting a row. 'We can have a look.' In his head, he took a quick trip down Tottenham Court Road, alighting at another old-school café near Goodge Street tube; one of the few remaining places that wasn't part of some chain or other. 'If Delph's isn't there, I know somewhere else we can go.'

His father turned and gave him a weak smile. 'Grand. Let's get out of here.'

'Sure.' Carlyle slipped his hand through Alexander's arm and they began moving slowly towards the exit.

'I'm sorry.'

The inspector felt a tap on his shoulder. He looked round to see Dr Siebeck standing in front of him, a sheepish look on his face. What is it now? he wondered grumpily. Surely we've had enough bad news for one day.

'I was wondering if I could take a few minutes of your time.'

Carlyle glanced at Alexander. What else could possibly be wrong with the old bugger?

'It's not about your father,' Siebeck said quickly.

Carlyle frowned.

'I wondered if I could ask you to meet another patient,' the doctor explained. Suddenly it seemed as if he was struggling to express himself in English. Pushing a strand of hair away from his face, he lowered his voice. 'In your capacity as a police officer.'

A police *officer*. He made it sound like something from the

1950s. Carlyle looked at the unsmoked cigarette in the doctor's hand. Siebeck stuffed it into the pocket of his coat. The inspector was about to protest when Alexander gave his arm a squeeze.

'Go and look, son,' he said quietly, pointing. 'I'll just have a wee seat here and then we can head off to Delph's when you're done.'

'But Delph's . . .' Carlyle stopped himself. If the old man wanted to go to Delph's, they would go to Delph's. He signalled to Siebeck. 'Okay. Lead on.'

He let the German usher him back down the corridor. Round the corner, they walked into an empty lift and hit the button for the third floor.

'So,' said Carlyle, as he watched the doors close, 'how did you know I was a cop?'

'Your father mentioned it on one of his earlier visits.'

'Oh?' Carlyle raised an eyebrow. Ever since he had gone home one night – decades since – and announced that he was joining the Metropolitan Police, his parents had done little to hide their disappointment.

'Yes. He seemed quite proud of the fact.'

'Mm.' The lift shuddered and began its upward journey.

'He says that when you get the bit between your teeth you don't give up.' Siebeck smiled. That bit was true enough, although Alexander had expressed it rather differently: 'He's an awful difficult bugger to throw off the scent,' had been his verdict.

Carlyle stared at his feet. He could do with a new pair of shoes. Whether he could afford the expense, however, was another matter entirely.

'Which is why I wanted you to see Anne.'

'Does Anne have a surname?'

'We don't know. Anne's not her real name. I—' Siebeck corrected himself: '*We* just thought she should have something. Better than calling her Miss X.'

Oh, I dunno, Carlyle thought. Miss X sounds quite good to me.

The lift made it to the third floor and the doors slowly opened. Siebeck jumped out and gestured left. 'This way, please.' He led Carlyle down the corridor, stopping outside the first of a series of private rooms. Standing aside, he gestured for the inspector to take a look through the porthole window in the door.

'Female, mid-twenties. She was found in an alleyway in the early hours of this morning. No identification papers.'

Looking at the woman lying in the bed, hooked up to an array of tubes and monitors, Carlyle winced. 'She looks like she's been in a car crash.'

'There are cuts and bruises all over her body. Someone gave her a terrible beating.'

You don't say, Carlyle thought glumly.

'Bruised ribs, multiple—'

'I get the picture.' Squeamish at the best of times, Carlyle didn't want to wallow in a checklist of despair. Dealing with his father's diagnosis was more than enough medical misery for one day. 'Is she going to make it?'

'The next few days are critical. She'll stay in an induced coma for the moment. But I think there's a reasonable chance that she can make a decent recovery.'

'Let's hope.' Carlyle let out an extended breath, not wanting to interrogate the doctor on the possible meanings of the word 'decent'.

'It could have been a lot worse. Whoever did this left the poor woman for dead. She was very lucky that someone found her when they did. A few hours later it would have been all over for her.'

Carlyle adopted an expression of concerned officialdom. 'You spoke to the police when she first came in, right?'

'Not me.' Siebeck gave an apologetic shrug. 'She's not really my patient. My colleague, Dr Hendricks, has been looking after her. She met with a couple of your colleagues. They didn't seem that interested.'

'Police officers are always very busy.' Carlyle took another look at the girl in the bed and felt a fleeting sense of outrage. Some bastard had given her a right going over. Not that there was anything he could do about it. 'I'm sure they're doing all they can,' he added.

'They didn't seem that interested,' Siebeck repeated, refusing to be fobbed off so easily.

'What's it to you?' the inspector asked brusquely.

'Nadine – Dr Hendricks – is really quite exercised about it.' He paused. 'She's very angry. She says that the police aren't doing enough.'

Nadine, eh? A vision in a white coat flitted through Carlyle's brain. Did he imagine it or was Dr Siebeck blushing slightly? It seemed that the good doctor fancied his co-worker and wanted to get some Brownie points by championing Miss X.

'We see a lot of injured women in the hospital,' Siebeck continued. 'The police sometimes come but they never do much. Nadine says that violence against women just isn't a priority. They – you – are more concerned about people who have their mobile phones stolen.' Evidently the doctor had realized this line of argument was hardly going to endear him to Carlyle because he added, 'So she says, anyway.' He stared at the floor. 'I don't know.'

The inspector contemplated being used to help Siebeck get into his colleague's knickers. He should be outraged but somehow he wasn't. After all, Siebeck had spent the last three years looking after Carlyle's father. The least that the boy deserved was a little help in the romance department. It was a strange way to play Cupid, but what the hell? He rubbed his chin thoughtfully. 'Maybe I should speak to Dr Hendricks. Is she around?'

'She comes back on duty at eight,' Siebeck said, a bit too quickly.

'Okay.' Carlyle frowned. 'What about the other cops? The

ones who were here earlier with, er,' he had already forgotten the name, 'Miss X.'

'Anne,' Siebeck corrected him.

'Yes, Anne.'

'There were two constables in uniform. A man and a woman.' The doctor paused to recall their names. 'Dombey and Granger.'

'I know them. WPC Granger is a good officer. Let me speak to her when I get back to the station.'

'And you'll come back to talk to Nadine – Dr Hendricks?'

No. 'Let me see what I can find out in terms of how the investigation is progressing.' Carlyle gestured towards the room. 'Presumably the officers checked through all of Anne's effects.'

'There was nothing on her when she came in. No handbag or anything.'

'Where was she found?'

'I don't know exactly.' Siebeck waved an arm in the direction of Warren Street. 'Somewhere near here.'

'Dombey and Granger will have checked it out.' Hopefully.

'There was this, however.' Siebeck pulled a small transparent plastic bag from his pocket and offered it to Carlyle. Inside was a piece of green plastic, slightly bigger than the size of a thumbnail.

Lifting his glasses onto his head, Carlyle bent forward for a better look.

'It's a mini-USB stick,' Siebeck explained.

'Anne's?'

'Yes.'

Carlyle took the bag. 'Why didn't you give it to Dombey and Granger?'

'We only found it an hour ago. It was in her stool.' Siebeck had tentatively cleaned the stick before placing it in the bag but evidence of the journey it had taken was still visible.

The inspector took a moment to process that particular piece of information.

'Almost got thrown away.'

Carlyle grimaced. 'She ate it?'

'That's right.'

'Why would you do that?' Carlyle answered his own question. 'Because you wanted to hide it from someone.' He glanced again at the comatose Anne. Maybe there was more to her story than random violence and depressingly routine misogyny. Feeling a twitch of interest somewhere deep in his brain, he shoved the bag into his pocket. 'I need to get back to my dad. Let me see what I can find out.'

He returned to the ground floor to find his father sitting where he had left him, staring vacantly into space.

'What was all that about?' the old man asked, finally registering Carlyle's presence.

'Tell you later.' Carlyle helped his father slowly to his feet. 'Let's go and get that cup of tea.'

SEVEN

As the inspector had suspected, Delph's café was long gone. The entire block where it had stood had been flattened at some point in the preceding decades, and a generic office tower thrown up. The newish building was already looking more than a little shabby. In another twenty years or so, it too would be gone.

Alexander accepted this latest evidence of the mutability of London life with a dismayed shrug. Trudging down Tottenham Court Road, they ended up in a small place serving health food, round the corner from the Heal's furniture store. After twenty-five minutes of weak tea and even weaker conversation, Carlyle saw his father onto a number fourteen bus. While the old man headed home, the inspector reluctantly headed off in the direction of work.

By the time he had climbed the stairs to Charing Cross police station, Carlyle was technically more than three hours late. The world, it seemed, had not stopped spinning on its axis as a result. In the lobby, the usual random selection of people waited patiently to be seen. Avoiding making eye contact with any of them, the inspector wandered over to the front desk where the duty sergeant, a square-jawed Geordie by the name of Callum Lee, was engrossed in the latest Police Federation newsletter.

'Looks like more cuts are coming,' was Lee's greeting.

'There are always more cuts coming,' Carlyle responded. It was true enough: he couldn't remember a time in his working life where the force hadn't been under pressure to reduce its spending.

Dropping the newsletter into the desk, Lee yawned. 'You're late in this morning.'

'Chasing up some loose ends on the . . . er, Bamford case,' Carlyle replied, trying not to sound too defensive.

'Mm.' The Bamford case – a bike-theft ring in Bloomsbury – had been wrapped up months ago. They both knew it was due to come to trial in the next few weeks and the idea that the police investigation was in any way ongoing was fanciful.

'I'm looking for Granger,' Carlyle said, moving the conversation on. 'Is she in today?'

''Fraid you're out of luck there, sir.' Lee tapped daintily at his keyboard and stared at the screen. 'She's on leave, back in . . . three weeks.'

'Three weeks?' Carlyle scowled. 'What the hell's she doing? A round-the-world trip?'

'Gone to Ireland,' Lee explained. 'Wendy has a timeshare on the River Sheen. She likes her fishing. Takes it very seriously.'

'Good for her,' Carlyle muttered. 'What about Dombey? Is he around? Or has he fucked off for a month to paddle up the Amazon?'

Lee gave him a weak smile. 'He's on an early. But he's out on a call. A disturbance in Walton Court.' The sergeant mentioned an address within walking distance. 'Some bloke threw a fridge out of a fourth-floor window.'

'Must have been a fairly small fridge,' Carlyle mused.

'Nearly killed a woman walking her dog.'

'What the hell did he do that for?'

'How should I know?' Lee groaned. 'That's what young Dombey's endeavouring to get to the bottom of. He should be back soon.'

'Okay. You don't remember a call that Dombey and Granger responded to, a woman assaulted in an alleyway? She's up in UCH.'

Lee shook his head. 'I'm only just back from leave myself.'

Stands to reason, Carlyle thought sourly. At any given time, more than half the people on this bloody police force are either on holiday or off sick.

'Took the kids to Center Parcs,' Lee ventured. 'It was great. Not cheap, mind.'

'I can imagine,' Carlyle replied, struggling to have any sympathy. 'Anyway, when Dombey gets back in, tell him I want to see him. I'll be upstairs.'

'Sure thing.' Looking over the inspector's shoulder, Lee contemplated the dribble of humanity that had washed up in his domain that morning. 'All right,' he shouted. 'Who's next?'

On the third floor, Carlyle was still waiting for Dombey to show up when the phone started ringing on his desk. With some reluctance, the inspector tore his attention away from the Fulham FC website and picked it up.

'Yeah?' He was slightly embarrassed to realize that he sounded like a petulant teenager.

'Your presence is required.' For his part, Sergeant Lee's impersonation of an exasperated parent was more than passable.

'What've you got?'

'Man jumped out a window on Bucknall Street.'

'Bucknall Street.' For once, the *A–Z* in Carlyle's head failed to come up with a location.

'It's just behind that new development on St Giles High Street,' said Lee, giving him a helping hand, 'the one with all those horrible-coloured offices – green, orange and so on.'

'Yes, yes,' Carlyle snapped, unhappy at being given a lesson in local geography by a refugee from Newcastle.

'Looks like today's the day for things flying out of windows,' Lee observed, his tone suggesting that this kind of thing never happened on Tyneside. 'Made quite a mess, apparently.'

'That's gravity for you.' For no obvious reason, Carlyle's mind defaulted to Michael Caine in *Get Carter*. Didn't a man get thrown off a multi-storey car park or something in that movie? 'Who's there at the moment?'

'Palin.'

Carlyle groaned. Sergeant Adam Palin was – in the inspector's opinion – a useless little scrote who had arrived from the Rosslyn Hill station earlier in the year. For reasons he couldn't quite remember, Carlyle had immediately taken against him.

To makes matters worse, his regular sidekick, Sergeant Alison Roche, was on maternity leave, meaning that Carlyle had to work with whoever was around. Over recent weeks, however, he had found himself having to resist the attempts of the powers that be to pair him with Palin on an increasingly regular basis.

'He's waiting for you,' Lee advised.

'Surely he can manage that on his own, can't he?'

'Apparently not.'

'For fuck's sake,' Carlyle hissed. 'Is there any evidence that an actual crime has been committed?'

'How should I know?' Lee shot back, the inspector's grumpiness starting to rub him up the wrong way. 'All I've been told is that you need to get over there. Palin won't do anything till you've had a look.'

'Okay.' Carlyle knew when he was beaten. 'Okay, okay, okay.' He forced himself to his feet, grabbing his jacket from the back of the chair. 'I'll go and find out for myself. Tell them I'm on my way.'

Turning into the narrow Bucknall Street, he was surprised to see a scene that looked like something out of a Hollywood movie. Traffic was backed up in both directions. In the middle of the jam, a car had jumped the pavement and ploughed into a plate-glass window at the back of a restaurant whose alarm was relentlessly blaring. Lying in the middle of a pool of shattered glass was a crumpled racing bicycle. Further along the street, a temporary medical station had been set up between two ambulances. Carlyle watched as a group of paramedics attended to the most serious casualties while the walking wounded waited patiently to be seen.

Adam Palin appeared from behind a pillar and gave him a toothy grin. Palin was a small bloke, shorter than Carlyle, with a pudding-bowl haircut and a confused expression on his face. He had been in London for the best part of fifteen years but still looked and sounded like he'd just arrived in the capital from darkest Snowdonia.

'What's all this?' Carlyle shouted over the noise of the alarm. 'I thought it was just some bloke who jumped out of a window.' The alarm fell silent and he felt himself relax a little. A couple of seconds later it started up again. 'And can't you get that fucking noise turned off?'

'Dombey's in there now,' Palin shouted back, 'trying to switch it off.'

'Well, he's not doing a very good job,' Carlyle grumbled. At least he had managed to locate the young constable: he could speak to him about the unknown woman in UCH. First things first, however. 'What happened?' he repeated.

'He bounced.' Palin pointed to the car.

'Bounced?' Looking around, Carlyle belatedly realized that there was no sign of a body on the pavement.

'He bounced off the bonnet of the Lexus,' Palin's tone was one of almost child-like glee, 'which promptly hit a bloke on a bike, took out a couple of pedestrians and ended up in the back of Il Grillo's.'

The inspector looked at him blankly.

'It's a new chain,' the sergeant explained. 'Mediterranean fusion.'

'Expensive pizza,' Carlyle translated. The alarm stopped again. This time, the inspector waited ten seconds before assuming it would not restart. After taking a couple more seconds to savour the silence, he pointed towards the ambulances. 'So, if the jumper's in Il Grillo's, who are all the other folk?'

'Three other cars had slow-motion collisions. Four other

pedestrians were knocked down and another four were hit by flying glass. Oh, and a cat was run over.'

'Fatally?' Like most Londoners, Carlyle's instinctive concern was for the animal, rather than his fellow human beings.

Palin shook his head. 'Just a broken leg. But brings the grand total to one dead – the jumper – two seriously hurt, more with minor injuries and the cat.'

'Jesus Christ,' Carlyle harrumphed, 'if this was America, it would take a teenager with an assault rifle to wreak so much carnage. How could one man cause such destruction to both people and property just by jumping out of a window? It looks like a bloody terrorist attack.'

'It certainly was a suicide attack.' Palin giggled.

Carlyle was distracted by a small square screen, slightly smaller than a mobile phone, hanging from the front of the sergeant's jacket. 'Is that what I think it is?'

'The body-camera trial started this week.' Palin tapped it with his finger. 'This is the first time I've had the chance to use it at a crime scene.'

Carlyle stiffened.

'Only five hundred officers are getting them.'

Just my bloody luck, Carlyle groused. More than thirty thousand coppers to choose from and they have to give one to bloody Palin. 'It's not switched on, is it?'

'Nah. The guidelines about when cameras are to be used are quite strict.'

The inspector let out a breath. 'Glad to hear it.'

'They can't be permanently switched on. When they are switched on people have to be informed if they're being filmed. I can store images for a month only, unless they're required for evidential purposes.'

'Whatever you do,' the inspector muttered, 'don't bloody film me.' Since the advent of smartphones, Carlyle, like a lot of officers, had lived in a permanent state of mild dread of being caught on camera doing something improper. Now, as well as members of the general public, he would have to keep a wary eye on his colleagues. Big bloody Brother was getting ever more in his face, and Carlyle had more than enough self-awareness to grasp that this presented a real threat to someone like him, someone who was prone to bending the rules now and again. Well, probably rather more than 'now and again'. In the past, he had pushed his luck to the limit. And beyond. That would have to stop. No more intimidation, no more violence, no more manipulating evidence or 'engineering' convictions. The inspector preferred not to think about many of the things he had done in the past. He had to focus on his future behaviour. That meant acknowledging he had reached the stage of his career where he was a man out of time. Colleagues like Palin were barely half his age. They owed him no loyalty. And they were running around with cameras, able to record his every misstep for a waiting disciplinary hearing.

Under no circumstances could Carlyle ever get caught on film doing anything that wasn't kosher. He couldn't get caught doing anything that didn't *look* like it was kosher. Cameras didn't do context and they certainly didn't do extenuating circumstances. If he allowed himself to be caught out, the inspector had no doubt that the Met would happily hang him out to dry.

'Don't worry,' Palin remarked sheepishly. 'I haven't quite worked out how to use it yet.'

'Good.' Carlyle looked past the Lexus into the restaurant. The car had not reached any of the tables, which stood undamaged, ready for service. Even so, there was no way the place would be able to open for the next few days. Mediterranean fusion was off the menu tonight. The inspector made a mental note to avoid being the one who had to give the manager the good news. 'The jumper,' he asked, 'where is he?'

'Still inside. The body's trapped under the front of the car.'

'Can we go and have a look?'

Palin pointed back in the direction from which Carlyle had first arrived. 'Better go round the front.'

EIGHT

Burdened by a squeamishness that was not entirely helpful in his line of work, the inspector did not normally like to get too close to dead bodies. In this case, however, the scene looked so staged, the victim's pose so frankly comic, that the whole thing seemed slightly less than real. Snapping on a pair of rubber gloves, Carlyle listened to his knees creak as he squatted on his haunches in front of the corpse. The jumper had ended up stuck under the front bumper of the Lexus, which had demolished a serving station and wedged itself in a kitchen doorway. His arms were outstretched and there was a bemused expression on his face that reminded Carlyle of Wile E. Coyote immediately before he was flattened by a rock.

'How am I ever going to process that?'

Shuffling through ninety degrees, the inspector looked up to see Susan Phillips standing behind him with a large metallic case containing the various tools of the pathologist's trade. Phillips, a well-preserved blonde with a perpetually complicated private life, was one of the Met's most experienced scientists. She was among the few colleagues who had been on the force about as long as Carlyle and they had known each other for decades.

'You took your time getting here,' Carlyle observed drily.

'Don't pretend you haven't just got here yourself,' she replied, dropping the case at her feet. 'Palin told me you arrived a few minutes ago.'

'Welsh twerp,' Carlyle muttered. He looked around. The sergeant was nowhere to be seen.

'Is that the guy?'

'No,' Carlyle grunted. 'It's his stunt double.' With his thighs burning, he returned his attention to the stiff, thrusting a hand forward and reaching into the back pocket of the dead man's jeans. 'At least he had the good grace to jump with something on him.' Levering himself with the help of the crumpled bonnet of the car, he got to his feet, shaking out his legs, then turning the cheap black leather wallet in his hand. Opening it, he recovered a ten-pound note, a couple of receipts and a membership card from something called the RPRA.

'Richard Furlong.' Squinting, Carlyle pushed his glasses back up his nose with the knuckle of his index finger. 'Have you ever heard of something called the RPRA?'

'Eh?'

Carlyle held up the card for Phillips to inspect. 'The RPRA,' he repeated slowly.

'What's that? Some kind of club?'

'No idea.' Carlyle gestured towards the pathologist's case. 'Hand me an evidence bag, will you?'

'God.' Placing her hands on her hips, Phillips rolled her eyes to the ceiling. 'You never come prepared, do you?'

'You should know me by now.' Carlyle grinned. Muttering to herself, the pathologist bent down and opened her case. After rooting around inside for a couple of seconds, she handed him a bag. 'Thanks.' He dropped the wallet and its contents inside.

Phillips pointed at the body. 'Can I have a look at him now?'

'Sure.' Carlyle stood aside and watched as she got down to business. 'There's not a lot of blood, is there?'

'Well, he didn't land here, did he?' Phillips ran a hand underneath the car's bumper. 'Looks like he broke his neck, among other things.'

'Mm.' Carlyle poked at a piece of glass with his shoe.

48

'Haven't you got something else to be getting on with? I don't really need an audience.'

'I'll go and have a look at his flat.'

'Good idea.'

'See if there's any evidence that someone pushed him.' The inspector gazed out of the shattered window, towards the block of flats opposite. Above the front door was the legend: Hugh Childers House. 'Hugh Childers . . . Who was he?'

Phillips glanced up. 'Never heard of him.'

'Me neither.' Carlyle returned his attention to the corpse. 'I don't suppose he's got a set of keys on him by any chance?'

'John,' Phillips tutted, 'I'm not here to be your skivvy.' She made a half-hearted search of the guy's pockets. 'Doesn't look like it.'

Carlyle was distracted by a uniform wandering towards him, hands in pocket. 'Don't worry, I'll just get Dombey to kick the door down.'

Hearing his name mentioned, the giant young constable grinned.

'Our very own Fred Trueman.'

'Eh?'

Carlyle shook his head. The boy was an imbecile. At least he didn't have a camera strapped to his jacket. 'Took you a while to get that alarm switched off,' he observed.

'The damn thing was indestructible,' the constable moaned. 'And it was impossible to switch it off.'

'Bloody alarms.' Carlyle tried not to sound too sympathetic. 'Total waste of time. Total waste of *our* time. Most of the time it's a false alarm. People only have them because the insurance companies insist on it.' The more he thought about it, the more it appeared like a monster conspiracy to make his working life more difficult. 'I must have been called out to hundreds of false alarms in my time . . . thousands.'

'In the end,' Dombey admitted, nonplussed by the inspector's ramblings, 'I had to hit it with a big wine bottle.'

Carlyle gave an approving nod. 'Improvisation.'

'I just smacked it and it kind of whined and died.'

'Jolly good.' Maybe Dombey wasn't totally useless after all.

'The manager's not very happy, though.'

Then again, maybe he was.

'She muttered something about compensation.'

'She's not around now, is she?' Carlyle cast a nervous glance towards the restaurant entrance.

'Nah. She went round the corner for a coffee and a fag. She said something about needing to call head office, who would call their lawyers.'

That would be something for Palin to deal with. 'Don't worry about it.' Keeping a wary eye out for the unhappy manageress, the inspector made his way back to the door. 'C'mon,' he said, signalling for the PC to join him. 'Let's see what else we can find for you to hit.'

Leaving Palin to direct operations at ground level, Carlyle found a resident willing to buzz him into the block of flats. A quick inspection of the mailboxes in the lobby told him that Furlong had resided on the top floor. Eschewing the lift, he set a steady pace as he led Dombey up the stairs. Reaching the top, he paused for breath. From the outside, Furlong's flat looked well looked after. The front door had received a recent coat of green paint and the small brass nameplate was polished to a high sheen. On either side of a newish doormat was a small potted plant.

As his heart rate returned to a more normal level, Carlyle gestured at the door. 'Reckon you can kick that in?'

Dombey's expression was doubtful. He contemplated the three different types of lock, lined up on the door. 'Not if all those are locked.'

'Give it a go,' the inspector instructed.

'If you say so.' Scratching his chin, Dombey walked up to the door and dropped to one knee, lifting up the plant pot to his right. Finding nothing underneath, he put it back and lifted the one on the other side of the door.

'Bingo.' A wide grin spread across his face as he held up a set of keys on a yellow plastic key ring.

'Smartarse.' Carlyle scowled.

'My mum was always losing her keys,' the constable explained, 'so she kept a spare set in a plant pot by the back door.'

'This is London, though,' Carlyle reminded him.

'People are the same everywhere.' Dombey unlocked the door and pushed it open, inviting the inspector to step across the threshold.

Inside, the flat was as neat and tidy as the landing. After a quick search of the other rooms, they congregated in the kitchen.

'Looks like he jumped from here.' Dombey pointed at the open window and the chair beneath it.

'Don't touch anything,' Carlyle grunted, 'until you put some bloody gloves on.'

Taking the admonishment in his stride, Dombey stuck a hand into his pocket. 'No sign of any struggle.'

'No.' Carlyle clocked the crockery on the draining-board. 'It's all very neat and tidy.'

Dombey shrugged. 'You wouldn't want to leave a mess, would you?'

'I don't think I'd care very much,' Carlyle said. 'Who does the washing-up before topping themselves?'

'Force of habit?' Dombey ventured.

'Maybe.' The table was clear, apart from a single sheet of paper. Bending forward, Carlyle sniffed the letter.

'Smell nice?'

'Heavily perfumed.'

'What is it?'

'No idea.' He knew that it wasn't Chanel No. 19 – his wife Helen's perfume – but, other than that, he didn't have a clue. At the top of the page was an embossed letterhead in Gothic script. 'Madam Monica, House of Pain'.

'House of Pain?' Dombey almost pushed him out of the way in his eagerness to see what the letter said.

For a few moments, they stood, side by side, reading in silence.

'What's that got to do with anything?' Dombey asked, once they had finished. The disappointment in his voice was clear. There was nothing titillating in the letter at all. 'What does it mean?'

'It's a set of instructions,' said Carlyle, stating the obvious.

'Instructions about toast?'

'Looks like it.' Carlyle looked around the kitchen. Sitting between an expensive-looking red toaster and the fridge was a breadbin. On top of the bin were the last few slices of a white loaf, still in their wrapper. A scattering of crumbs lay on the work surface. 'Looks like the condemned man had toast for his last meal.'

Dombey had another squint at the letter. '*Soooo* Madam Monica wrote to tell him to eat some toast and then top himself?'

'There's nothing in the letter about throwing himself out of the window.' Carlyle stepped over to the fridge and opened the door. Inside was empty, apart from some lager, a pizza and a small Tupperware box, which sat on the top shelf. Reaching up, he took out the box, inspected the contents and carefully removed the lid.

'What is that?' Dombey asked. 'Curry?'

Carlyle took a tentative sniff and winced. 'Not quite.' He was spared the need for any further explanation by Palin's appearance in the doorway.

I thought I told you to stay downstairs, Carlyle thought angrily. Why can't you ever just do what you're told?

Palin ignored his boss's scowl. 'Inspector,' he said urgently, 'you've got to see this. We've got more bodies upstairs.'

NINE

'What kind of sick so-and-so would do something like this?' Palin carefully picked his way between the body parts that had been strewn across the flat roof. Scratching his head, he looked like he was about to burst into tears. 'I mean,' he opined, sounding more Welsh than ever, 'it's a massacre. A bloody *massacre*.'

Dombey appeared at the top of the stairs and stuck his head through the door. 'Bloody hell.' He grinned. 'What happened here?'

'Get back downstairs,' Carlyle commanded. 'No one comes up here until the flat has been fully processed.'

'The forensics team have only just started in the restaurant.' The constable's grin ebbed away. 'It's gonna take ages.'

The inspector waved him away. 'You'll be in line for some decent overtime then, won't you?'

'But I've already pulled a double shift,' the boy whined, 'been on all night.'

'Just as well you have youth on your side.' Carlyle aimed a kick at the door. 'No one comes up here,' he repeated, 'until I say so.'

As Dombey beat a reluctant retreat, Carlyle considered the vista. How many cameras must overlook this roof? How many offices? Hugh Childers House was hemmed in by taller buildings on all sides. Somebody must have seen something. Canvassing potential witnesses, however, would be a nightmare. And the idea that they might have the manpower to sift through hours of video was laughable. To the east, between the high-rises, a glimpse of the British Museum and St Pancras lifted his spirits slightly. All around them, London was going about its business, undisturbed by the carnage laid out in front of them.

Palin accidentally kicked a decapitated head across the asphalt. Fortunately, it came to a halt before disappearing over the edge of the roof and falling into the street below. 'Do you think the jumper did this?' The jumper. It took Carlyle a moment to recall the guy's name. Richard Furlong. 'He could have lost the plot, killed them and then ended it all.'

'Perhaps.' Carlyle had yet to form any view on what might have happened. At this moment, he wasn't even sure that he wanted to have a view. His only real interest was in finding a way to walk away from this mess as quickly as possible. He watched Palin trying to remove some blood from the toe of his shoe.

'So what do we do now?' the sergeant asked, pawing the ground with disgust.

'Dunno,' Carlyle admitted. 'Call the RSPCA?'

Inspector Fiona Cope tapped the side of the mug. 'I don't suppose I could get a cup of tea, could I? I've been on the go since six.' She shot Carlyle a rueful smile. 'Getting the kids up, doing the school run, it's like you've done a day's work before you even make it into the office.'

'Tell me about it.' His days of taking his daughter, Alice, to school were long gone but Carlyle could still sympathize. Once a parent, always a parent.

'All I had for breakfast this morning was a couple of Digestive biscuits. If I don't get something soon, I think I'm going to faint.'

'This is a crime scene,' Carlyle replied, rather too curtly.

'Yes, of course.' She shot him a naughty-schoolgirl look that was, frankly, rather disconcerting.

'We can go out and grab something in a minute,' he offered,

breaking eye contact, 'leave the techies to it.' There didn't seem much point in going through Richard Furlong's pristine flat, but process was process.

'Okay.' The RSPCA officer placed the mug back on the draining-board with an excess of care. 'I shouldn't have picked that up, sorry.'

'Don't worry about it.' Carlyle shrugged. He had never been that big on the CSI side of things. In his experience, crimes were normally solved by a mixture of confession, betrayal and luck. Science didn't really come into it. Anyway, it was a moot point as to whether the kitchen should even be classified as a crime scene.

'But what if that mug's got the killer's fingerprints on it?'

Was she taking the piss? The inspector decided to give Cope the benefit of the doubt. 'It looks like he jumped. Suicide.'

'Poor guy. He must have been in a right state to do something like that.'

'Yeah.' Carlyle's thoughts turned to local cafés. In the face of his wife's relentless long-term campaign to wean him off coffee and pastries, he didn't want to pass up the opportunity to ingest the maximum amount of caffeine and sugar.

'Doesn't it affect you,' Cope asked earnestly, 'things like this?'

'They're not that common,' Carlyle told her. 'Most of the things we see are more mundane.'

'I know what you mean. Sometimes, though . . .' Cope let the thought trail away as the sound of raised voices came from next door.

'Bloody Dombey,' Carlyle muttered. He had sent the young constable to speak to the neighbour but the Yorkshire giant was making heavy weather of the interview. From what Carlyle could tell, it seemed that the resident was a gaga old woman with a carer who professed not to speak any English. Instead of making his excuses and moving on, Dombey had already spent the best part of twenty minutes trying to interrogate the pair about their recently deceased neighbour. It was a total waste of time. Carlyle needed to get going. It was imperative that he didn't get caught up in canvassing the rest of the building: there were distractions around every corner and his day had been badly enough disrupted already. He still wanted to speak to Dombey about the battered woman at UCH but that could wait until they were both back at the station.

A scene-of-crime officer appeared in the hallway, awaiting permission to come into the kitchen. He was a fat guy with a beard that would have been fashionable in Kabul, or maybe a ZZ Top tribute band. Around the man's mouth, the crumbs from a recent snack were clearly visible.

Making a show of removing his latex gloves, Carlyle focused on the SOCO. 'We're just leaving.' He shoved the gloves into his jacket pocket, next to Furlong's letter. Madam Monica was one loose end that he would check out himself. 'We haven't touched much.'

'You're not supposed to have touched anything,' the SOCO snapped.

The feeble smile on Carlyle's face made the point that he couldn't care less about the admonishment. 'Sorry.' He turned to Cope. 'Time for us to get out of here.' He pointed at the mug as he shuffled towards the door. 'By the way, what is the RPRA, would you know?'

'The RPRA?' For a moment, Cope looked nonplussed. Then she unleashed the most wholesome smile Carlyle could remember seeing in a long time. 'Don't tell me you haven't heard of the Royal Pigeon Racing Association?'

Using the fire escape, he crept away from Bucknall Street, leading his new acquaintance into deepest, darkest Soho. Carlyle's intended destination was a bit of a schlep – almost all the way to Regent Street – but it took him halfway to his next appointment. Enjoying the sunshine, Cope didn't seem to mind the walk. As they made their way through the traffic and the oncoming pedestrians, they chatted amiably about nothing in particular, an unspoken agreement between them that the unpleasantness of Bucknall Street could wait until some sustenance had been taken.

Ten minutes later, they were sitting in the clean and calm surroundings of the Nordic Bakery in Golden Square. Contemplating coffee and a cinnamon bun, Carlyle was suddenly transported back to his schooldays. Afternoons in Albiston's café on the Fulham Road, bunking off 'Mad' Melvin McEwen's A-level maths class. Reading the *NME* from cover to cover while lingering over the dregs of his cold cappuccino.

Too cool for school, even at that age. He still enjoyed the sense of being AWOL. Where once he'd hidden out in Albiston's, now he wandered around Central London, studiously ignoring the occasional attempts of the management to track him down. On the other hand, he had collected only a C for A-level maths. At the time McEwen had been very disappointed. Decades on, Carlyle remained irked by the result.

Taking a mouthful of his coffee, he sat back in his chair and gave Cope a belated once-over. A fresh-faced blonde, her blue eyes sparkled from under an erratic fringe, giving the lie to the idea that she was some poor drudge being stomped into the ground by the impossible demands of family and work. The chipmunk cheeks and narrow chin added to the healthy girl-next-door look, as did the pink polo shirt underneath a navy fleece with a discreet RSPCA logo emblazoned above the left breast.

From a speaker above his head, Carlyle tuned into the sound of Dexy's Midnight Runners. As the saxophone on 'Let's Make This Precious' kicked in, the sense of nostalgia was complete. Sailing back to the 1980s, he decided that Cope reminded him of an old geography teacher from his sixth-form years – the saintly Ellen Smith.

Miss Smith – always in a tracksuit, always smiling. All the boys had fancied her something rotten. He recalled with some embarrassment how they had been driven half mad by the news that she was going out with Melvin McEwen: he had dumped his wife and three kids to set up home with Smith in a flat in White City.

Maybe he hadn't been so crazy after all.

Like many teachers, Smith and McEwen had lived for the holidays. They were serious climbers, who would take off to distant parts whenever the opportunity presented itself. Carlyle seemed to recall that Smith had fallen off some mountain in Scotland, not long after he'd joined the police. She'd had to be airlifted to hospital. He couldn't remember if she had made a full recovery.

Ellen and Melvin. Where are you now?

'Is that a police technique,' Cope took a modest nibble from a slice of Tosca cake, 'or are you just checking me out?'

'Er, no.' Carlyle struggled back into the here and now. 'Neither really.'

She shot him a deeply doubtful look. 'Uh-huh.'

'You just reminded me of someone.' He blushed. 'One of my teachers when I was at school. It was a long time ago, obviously.'

Enjoying his discomfort, Cope continued to probe: 'And you had a thing for her?'

'No, no,' he lied. 'She was a teacher. I was just wondering what happened to her.'

'I see.' Cope licked the crumbs from her fingers and reached for a napkin.

Feeling his embarrassment increase exponentially, Carlyle glanced nervously out of the window, half expecting to see his wife walk past to find him gossiping with this attractive woman. Cope dabbed at the corners of her mouth with the napkin and he was relieved to see that she was wearing a wedding ring.

Once again, she caught him out. 'Don't be fooled by that. Mr C is long gone. When the going got tough, he decided he'd rather work in Dubai.'

'Ah.'

'He likes to spend his holidays in Thailand, rather than visiting his kids.'

Realizing he had hit a nerve, Carlyle returned his attention to his bun.

It had started to rain, a sharp, intense shower that sent people on the street scurrying for cover. Cope watched a woman struggle to raise an umbrella. A passing van raced through a puddle, giving the unfortunate pedestrian a soaking. 'I try not to think about what he gets up to over there.'

'Erm . . .' Carlyle had no idea how to respond to that. Thailand had never been on his must-see list. As the soaked pedestrian disappeared from view, he contemplated his own ring finger, bereft of any band. 'Funnily enough,' he stammered, 'I *am* married. I just don't like wearing jewellery.'

Cope laughed. 'I was only teasing about you checking me out.'

'Oh.' He tried to disguise the disappointment in his voice.

Cope took a sip of her tea. 'What does your wife make of you not wearing a ring?'

'Nothing, as far as I know. She doesn't wear one either. We have them, of course,' he tried to remember where in the flat they were currently located, 'we just don't wear them.'

Cope pursed her lips in contemplation. 'That seems a bit sad.'

'Not as sad as being divorced,' Carlyle blurted out, immediately regretting the crassness of the remark.

Her eyes opened wide as she sat back in her chair.

'Sorry.'

'I'm not divorced,' Cope shrugged, 'just separated.'

Very separated, Carlyle thought.

'But it's a fair point,' she conceded. 'The kids haven't seen the useless sod in more than eighteen months.'

It was getting to the point where he wished Helen could miraculously appear and spare him from any more of this conversation. Reflexively, he glanced at his watch.

'Need to be somewhere?'

'Yes. Busy day.'

'Tell me about it. I was supposed to be on a job out by Heathrow this morning – checking on a couple of horses that seem to have been abandoned in a field. Neighbours rang our hotline last week but we don't have the resources to deal with everything straight away.'

'Sounds familiar.' As talk turned to work matters, Carlyle felt himself relax a bit.

'Police calls get prioritized. That's why I came straight to you.'

'I don't suppose you get many calls about pigeons.' Carlyle grinned.

'We get all sorts, you'd be amazed.'

I doubt it, Carlyle thought. An idea popped into his head. 'Maybe I should have called the RSPB instead.'

'It's a bit late for that. We don't want a turf war.'

'No, I suppose not.'

'People do get confused, though,' Cope admitted. 'There is a lot of overlap, obviously. And we work together quite a lot. But they tend to be a bit more genteel than us. We're more at what I would call the social-worker end of things.'

'I know what you mean,' said Carlyle, with feeling.

'People can do such horrible things.'

'Very true.'

A look of disgust passed across Cope's face. 'Whoever did that was a right bastard. Those birds weren't just killed, they were torn apart.'

'Richard Furlong was clearly in a very distressed state,' Carlyle ventured.

'Furlong?' Cope shook her head. 'It wasn't him. At least, I'd be very surprised.'

Carlyle raised an eyebrow. 'Why is that?'

'From everything we saw in the flat, the gentleman had been a devoted bird owner for many years. There was no evidence that his life had been falling apart over a period of time. The flat was clean and tidy. The birds were healthy and well looked after – their coops were clean and in good condition.'

Carlyle suppressed a grin. Bloody hell, he thought, who's the cop here?

'There was food and water. Everything was in order. I don't know if you saw it, but there was a list of upcoming races pinned to the side of one of the coops.'

'Races?'

'You've heard of pigeon races, haven't you?'

'Yes,' Carlyle stuck out his lower lip, 'but I thought that was stuff people did in, I dunno, the 1950s or something.'

'It's not as big as it was,' Cope explained, 'but it's still popular. I suspect that if you check with the RPRA, you'll find that Mr Furlong was quite an active member.'

'I'll do that.'

'Most people who keep pets over a long period of time look after them very well. I wouldn't be surprised if Mr Furlong spent far more on his birds than he did on himself. Neglect and abuse might happen if the owner has suffered a major dislocation in their lives – perhaps they've lost their job or gone through a divorce – something that has negatively impacted on their mental health and their finances. There was no evidence of that here.'

'We haven't started digging into his private life yet,' Carlyle reminded her.

'Yes, but what did you see in that flat? A single man living a quiet life. A man who had no obvious passions beyond his birds. A guy who didn't make much of an impression on the outside world.'

'Now you're speculating.'

'I would be very surprised if he killed his own birds,' Cope said firmly.

'Okay. So someone killed the birds and threw him out of the window?'

61

'Not necessarily. Someone could have killed them and that caused him to take his own life.'

'Have you ever thought of joining the police?' Carlyle laughed.

'Nah.' Cope smiled. 'That's definitely not my kind of thing. It's bad enough seeing the kind of thing people do to animals. Having to deal with what they do to each other would be too much. Anyway, the hours wouldn't work for a single mum.'

'Oh, I dunno about that. My sergeant's on maternity leave at the moment. God knows when she'll come back.'

'Spoken like a man.' Cope sighed. Pushing her plate away from her, she got to her feet. 'I need to get going myself. Thanks for the tea.'

'My pleasure.' Standing up, Carlyle offered a hand and they shook.

'I'll send you a copy of my report.'

'Thanks.'

'In the meantime, you'll need to get the council to clean up the mess as soon as possible. Otherwise you'll have a health hazard on your hands.'

'Understood.' Carlyle let her pass the buck with good grace. It was something else he could give Dombey to do to keep him busy.

'Off to Heathrow?'

She shook her head. 'No time now. I wouldn't be able to get there and back before school pick-up. Maybe tomorrow.'

'There's always tomorrow,' Carlyle agreed. Watching her make for the exit, he reached for the largely untouched Tosca cake as he sat back down. Waste not, want not.

TEN

Having cleaned every last crumb from the plate, the inspector wiped his hands on a napkin, feeling rather guilty. Two cakes in one day was not unknown, but two cakes in one sitting was fairly unforgivable. As Helen was never slow to point out, middle age meant a slowing metabolism and – should he fail to keep his sweet tooth under some measure of control – an expanding waistline. Leaving the bakery, he made a vow not to touch another pastry, at least until tomorrow.

Stomach sucked in, he headed towards Regent Street. Arriving at a pedestrian crossing, he waited patiently behind a small group of elderly Chinese tourists and their guide. On their way to the Royal Academy, no doubt, Carlyle mused, as he endured an interminable wait for the lights to change.

When finally given permission to cross, the inspector was irritated beyond belief that the green man disappeared before he was barely halfway over the road. In front of him, one of the tourists, a woman, struggled past a row of impatient drivers, aided by a walking stick. Off to his right, a motorbike revved loudly, unceremoniously suggesting that the old dear get a move on.

The inspector felt a spasm of anger as he glared at the offending road-user. The impassive rider looked through him as if he wasn't there. Only with considerable force of will did Carlyle not step up to the biker and demand to see his papers in the hope of fabricating some motoring offence.

Ignoring the traffic, the woman slowly reached the sanctuary of the opposite pavement. Swerving past her, Carlyle jumped across the gutter and ducked into a space between two of her companions. Lengthening his stride as he moved on to the relative calm of Vigo Street, his annoyance at the motorcyclist was already forgotten, marking just another fleeting interaction in the big city.

Passing the Ozwald Boateng store, he cast an envious look at the selection of finery in the window. A boy could dream.

Trying not to dwell on his sartorial shortcomings, the inspector moved on, reaching into the breast pocket of his jacket for his mobile as he did so.

'Fuck.'

Patting down each of his remaining pockets in turn served to confirm what he already knew: he had left the damn thing at the station. In his mind's eye, he could see it sitting charging on top of an old copy of the *Metro*.

'Idiot.'

A passing gentleman in a tweed jacket gave him a quizzical look. Ignoring him, the inspector stomped onwards, head bowed, still muttering to himself.

Turning into Cork Street, he crossed the road and stopped outside the rather shabby façade of Molby-Nicol. Not only was the art gallery closed, it was empty. Carlyle peered at a small poster in the window advertising an exhibition of Irish landscapes. Squinting at the small print, he saw that the opening date was almost three weeks away.

Carlyle felt himself sinking into an ooze of self-pity. 'Christ,' he groaned, 'this really isn't your day, is it?'

For a moment, he stood in the doorway, wondering how best to proceed. Reluctant to return to the station, he considered the practicalities of tracking down the mysterious Madam Monica. If she was based in London, it was a job that could be knocked off this afternoon. If not, he would rather send Palin to speak to her than have to put up with a trip to the provinces.

Still undecided as to his next step, Carlyle turned and started towards Piccadilly, walking straight into an oncoming pedestrian. Eyes on the pavement, he mumbled something that could barely be construed as an apology.

'Well, well, look who's here.'

The inspector belatedly looked up to see Dominic Silver grinning at him. He held a large paper cup in one hand, a bunch of keys in the other.

'Careful where you're going,' Dom chided him. 'I nearly got coffee all over me.'

Carlyle took a step backwards. 'Sorry, I didn't see you.'

'No worries.' Dom's grin grew so wide that it looked like his skin was about to tear along the lines of the cheekbones. 'No harm done.'

What's happened to his face? Carlyle wondered, trying not to stare.

Dom stepped past him and walked up to the door. 'You okay?'

'Yeah. Sure. Fine. You?'

'All good. You're lucky you caught me. We're closed at the moment.'

'I noticed.'

'Felt like a break.'

'Yeah,' Carlyle replied enviously. For Dom, the gallery was essentially a hobby. It was supposed to wash its face but the inspector doubted it managed to do so. The cost of running a business on Cork Street was eye-watering: you didn't see any of the other gallery owners closing on a whim for weeks at a time.

Choosing a key, Dom began releasing a succession of locks. 'I've only popped in to do a bit of admin and pay some bills. Eva and I are off to Lanzarote in a couple of days. A week in the sun by the pool – just what the doctor ordered.'

'Nice.' Carlyle thought back to a family holiday he'd had with Helen and Alice in Playa Blanca, six or seven years ago. That was the only time in relatively recent memory that they'd been able to afford to go further than Brighton. To the best of his memory, the trip had been okay, not brilliant, not crap.

'The kids do their own thing, these days,' Dom ventured, 'so we might as well too, eh?'

'Absolutely,' Carlyle agreed, stealing another glance at his friend's distorted visage.

Pushing open the door, Dom keyed off the alarm and bent down to pick up a selection of mail that was splayed across the floor. Switching on the lights, he gestured for Carlyle to follow him inside. 'Come on in.'

'Thanks.'

The gallery was one large room, with a small office at the back. By the far wall there was a desk with a phone and a computer from which a receptionist would admit visitors. Dom clumped across the wooden floor in his brogues and dropped the mail onto the desk. Turning to Carlyle, he gestured at the empty walls. 'We're between shows at the moment.' He tossed his keys on top of the mail and took a sip of his coffee. 'Gonna take advantage of the break to get the place redecorated.'

'Uh-huh.' Carlyle imagined that he could make out the suggestion of a scar behind Dom's left ear. The skin had been pulled back across his face, leaving him with a slightly reptilian look. It wasn't the worst facelift the inspector had ever seen. On the other hand, it wasn't exactly invisible – at least, not to someone who had known Dominic Silver for more than thirty-five years.

Vanity, thy name is man.

A giggle rose in his throat and he had to stifle it with a cough. Dom looked at him, expressionless. 'You okay?'

'Yeah, sure.' Carlyle kept up with the coughing until he was sure he had the giggles under control. 'Just a frog in the throat.'

'Want some water?'

Carlyle held up a hand. 'I'm fine.' Once he was sure he could control himself, he met Dom's gaze. 'What's next?'

Dom looked at him blankly.

'What's the next exhibition?'

'An up-and-coming Irish painter.' Dom slipped effortlessly into salesman mode. 'Very nice guy. Ridiculously talented. His stuff is all stormy seas and murky skies. Very atmospheric. Appeals to a certain type of buyer. Guaranteed to do okay.' He perched on the edge of the desk. 'Eva likes it. I think it speaks to her Celtic side.'

'Oh?' Carlyle wasn't aware that Dom's wife was in possession of a Celtic side.

'Her great-great-grandparents came from Cork originally. Like a lot of people, they got off their arses and headed to the United States. Boston. At some point, however, the family made the reverse trip. Ended up in London sometime before the Second World War. It's quite a story.' Dom scratched his ear. 'Speaking of family, how's your dad?'

'That's why I'm here.'

'I thought it might be.' Dom nodded. 'How's he getting on with the tablets?'

'Good. It took him a while to get round to trying them but now he's popping them like sweeties.'

'Running low on supplies, is he?'

'Yeah. I don't know precisely how many he's got left but a couple of bad days and I think he'll be out.'

'Fair enough. Leave it to me.'

'Thanks.' Carlyle didn't ask Dom where the tablets were coming from. The less he knew the better.

'Give Alexander my best.'

'I will.'

'We should all go for a drink sometime.'

Carlyle shuffled uncomfortably on the spot. 'He's not really up for a pint, these days.'

'No, I suppose not.'

'We're reaching the end game,' Carlyle admitted. 'I was with him at the hospital and the doctor said as much. He was a nice enough bloke, but he was basically waving the old fella off to die.'

'When you get down to it,' Dom observed, 'dying is really quite a mundane thing. At least Alexander has been able to keep his dignity.'

'So far.'

'Don't worry.' Pushing himself away from the desk, Dom headed towards his office. 'We'll keep a smile on his face for as long as possible. Let me make a couple of calls. I should have something for you before we go away.' He headed towards his office. 'Oh, and by the way, I need to get a new receptionist before we reopen. If Mrs C could suggest anyone we'd be very grateful. Finding someone reliable who'll stick around for more than five minutes is a total nightmare.'

'I'll mention it to Helen.'

'Thanks.'

'No problem.' Carlyle nodded at the gleaming machine sitting on the receptionist's desk. 'Would it be okay if I used your computer for five minutes?'

'Sure.' Turning in the doorway, Dom pointed to a power socket under the desk. 'Just fire it up. Password is Procktorzero3.'

'How do you spell that?' Carlyle grabbed a pencil that was lying on the desk.

Dom slowly repeated each letter in turn while he scribbled them down on a yellow Post-it note. 'Patrick Procktor was an artist who worked with one of the other galleries along the street. I really liked his stuff – we have one of his paintings at home. He died in 2003.'

'Interesting. Thanks.'

'No problem.' Dom disappeared into his office, shutting the door behind him.

Settling into the chair behind the desk, Carlyle switched on the computer. Waiting for it to boot up, he picked up a copy of the catalogue for a previous Molby-Nicol show – an exhibition of photographs from China – and began flicking through the pages. As he did so, a small press cutting fell out. Picking it up, Carlyle looked at it and frowned. 'Bus engine bursts into flames?' He turned the clipping over. On the other side was a story headlined *Property developer jailed for two years*. Next to the headline was a picture of an elderly man in a suit throwing a punch at a photographer on the steps of Southwark Crown Court. Even in the grainy black-and-white image, Lucio Spargo's eyes blazed with an intense fury that hinted at a profound sense of frustration and injustice. Given that he had just been sentenced for the possession of drugs that had been planted on him by Carlyle, these were not totally unjustified emotions.

Carlyle carefully put back the cutting and returned the catalogue to its place on the desk. Would Spargo be out yet? Quite possibly. On a two-year sentence, he could end up doing nine months, or even less. The inspector made a mental note to check when he got back to the office. Once he was out, Spargo would be one more enemy walking the streets he would need to keep half an eye on.

Carlyle had no qualms about framing the developer. Spargo was a thug who had escaped incarceration during a long and nasty career through a mixture of coercion, bribery and good fortune (conveniently timed car accidents and the like). Looking to redevelop a stretch of Cork Street, he had tried to force Dom out of his gallery, threatening Eva in the process. That was when Carlyle had stepped in. With Spargo behind bars, his development project had collapsed and Molby-Nicol was saved.

The Spargo episode was an example of how Carlyle and Dom's relationship had worked over the years. It was also an example of the inspector's willingness to bend the rules or, to be precise, break the law. For the second time that day, he admonished himself that such activities had to be consigned to the past or he would be toast. 'You've gotta change,' he told himself, 'or you'll find yourself sharing a cell with someone like Spargo before too long.'

ELEVEN

Dom wandered out of his office and over to where Carlyle was still sitting at the desk. Hovering at the inspector's shoulder, he squinted at the small video playing in the middle of the computer screen. 'What the hell's that?'

Pointing at a leather-clad figure, Carlyle adopted an air of insouciance. 'That's Madam Monica.' The dominatrix was standing in front of a saltire cross, whip in hand. Lashed to the cross, the frankly unappealing torso of a white male of indeterminate age quivered in anticipation of a taste of her whip. 'She runs one of west London's leading BDSM dungeons, apparently.'

'Good for her.' Dom rubbed a hand across his forehead. 'I thought we had firewalls to stop that kind of thing. Why are you watching porn on my computer?' He pointed towards the street. 'You know that people walking past can see you?'

'They can't see the screen.'

Dom glanced towards his lap. 'It's not the screen I'm worried about.'

'Don't be disgusting. This is work.'

'Yeah, right.'

'No, seriously.' Sitting back in the chair, Carlyle placed his hands behind his head and quickly ran through the events of the morning. He was explaining how Richard Furlong had ended up as pavement pizza when Dom started waving his arms around.

'Rewind, rewind. He had *what* in his fridge? That can't be right.'

On the video, Madam Monica had set about thrashing her client with gusto. Impressed by her energy, Carlyle kept one eye on the screen while addressing his host. 'I can assure you that it was.'

'And he was eating it? I don't believe it. *Nooooo.*'

'Believe it.' Monica began working over a particular part of the punter's anatomy with the heel of her boot. Wincing, Carlyle looked away. 'She sent him the stuff, along with a set of precise instructions on how to use it. He had to heat it up in the microwave and spread it on his toast. I've got the letter in my pocket.'

'Bloody hell.' Dom laughed. 'Not exactly Delia Smith, is it?'

'Not quite.'

'Why would someone do that?'

'That's what I'm going to find out.'

Dom's eyes grew wide. He glanced back at the screen before scrutinizing the inspector. 'You're gonna see Madam Monica?'

'Yeah. She's based in Ealing.'

'I hope you're taking backup.'

'Don't be daft.'

Dom pointed at the screen. 'She'll have you for breakfast – pun intended.'

'Hardly.' He had seen more than enough. Reaching across the desk, Carlyle closed down the video. 'There's no reason to assume she won't want to assist the police in our enquiries.'

'Let's hope she doesn't come after you with her whip.'

'You can always come along,' Carlyle suggested, 'if you're that curious.'

Dom gave it a moment's thought. 'Nah. Not my thing. I had a client who ran a place like that. Adults playing those games always seemed a little silly to me.'

'Back in your drug-dealing days?'

'No, no. A Molby-Nicol client. She collected ceramics.'

'A dominatrix who collected pots?' Somehow, it just didn't seem quite right.

'Well, you can't spend your whole life in the basement, whipping fat bankers,' Dom reasoned. 'She liked to have nice things to look at when she was off the clock. Seems reasonable enough to me.'

'I suppose so.' Clicking on the mouse, Carlyle pulled up a calendar under Dom's beady eye. 'I need to book an appointment to get the full address.' He shot Dom a hopeful look. 'And I need a credit card to confirm the booking.'

Dom took a quick step backwards. 'Don't look at me.'

'C'mon,' Carlyle pleaded. 'I can't use my own card for this. Helen will have a complete fit.' In reality, he was less worried about the potential for embarrassment than the potential for the £225 'introductory offer' to push him beyond his agreed overdraft limit.

'I'm sure you can find her on the PND.'

'When was the last time you tried to access the Police National Database?'

'Want me to do it for you?' Dom still had plenty of contacts in the Job and was not slow in using them. Without the need to follow standard data-protection protocols, he could probably extract information from the PND considerably faster than Carlyle could.

'Thanks, but making an online booking is the quickest way to get to the woman *and* ensure she'll be there to see me when I arrive.'

'Whip in hand.' Dom smirked, his semi-synthetic face sliding awkwardly across his cheekbones.

'Don't you have a company credit card?'

'Yeah, but Eva does the books. How would I explain a visit to Madam Monica? You're not the only one who's kept on a short leash, you know.'

With penury staring him in the face, Carlyle made one final

plea. 'They probably put it down on the bill as something innoc-uous, like Acme Services or something.'

Dom was unmoved. 'No chance. Use your own card. Claim it back on expenses.'

'Okay.' Carlyle groaned, reluctantly reaching inside his jacket for his wallet.

'Helen will understand.'

'Let's hope so.' Carlyle was unconvinced. Over his long police career, he had never taken a formal posting in any of the Met's various vice units – largely at the insistence of his wife. When it came to the demands of the job, Helen was unstinting in her support and forbearance. Equally, she was clear-eyed when it came to human nature and, in particular, human weakness. As such, she saw no need to have her hus-band exposed to the inevitable temptations that came with that particular territory.

'Just don't go home with a selection of scars across your bum.' Dom chuckled. Discussion concluded, he gave Carlyle a consoling pat on the shoulder. 'Good luck, old chap. I'll be interested to hear how you get on.'

Dropping his MasterCard on the desk, Carlyle began slowly typing in the details. 'I bet you will.'

Still smiling, Dom retreated to his office. 'I'm sure you'll have fun.'

'Where were you? I thought you were going to come round the other night. You owe me some money. Ella needs new shoes and you still haven't given me the money for her school trip. There's also—'

Deleting the voicemail, Umar Sligo tossed his iPhone onto the coffee-table and yawned. Lying back on the sofa, he closed his eyes, trying to remember how he had ended up in this posi-tion. Technically, he and Christina were still married. More importantly, they had a joint mortgage and, last but not least, a kid, Ella.

Voices in the hallway were followed by the sound of the door opening.

'Hey, hey. What's this?'

Umar reluctantly opened his eyes.

'What are you doing?' Harry Cummins aimed a desultory kick at Umar's feet. 'Get your shoes off my table.' He grinned. 'This is a place of work, not a doss house.'

Blinking, Umar struggled into a more upright position. 'I was just thinking about things.'

'Bollocks.' Harry laughed. 'You were asleep.'

'Leave him alone, Harry.' Slipping through the doorway, Zoë Connors carefully placed a couple of takeaway paper bags on the table as she directed an apologetic look at Umar.

'It's just a bit of banter.' Slipping off his jacket, Harry hung it on the coat stand behind the door and took up his usual position behind his desk under a large framed oil painting of a brooding Donegal landscape.

The sharp, citrus fragrance of Zoë's perfume brought Umar back to full consciousness. Pushing a lock of blonde hair behind her ear, she shot him a smile. 'I got you some coffee and a bacon roll.'

'Thanks.'

Harry grabbed a roll from one of the bags. Unwrapping the greaseproof paper, he took a large bite.

Umar watched in dismay as a drop of grease trickled down Harry's chin. 'Aren't you having anything?' he asked Zoë.

'Are you kidding?' Harry scoffed, through a mouthful of dough and bacon. 'Zoë's body is a temple.' Popping the last of the roll into his mouth, he picked up a selection of paper napkins, wiping his fingers and then his mouth.

Reaching into her bag, Zoë retrieved her mobile and began tapping on the screen. 'Jocelyn's Juice Factory opens in twenty minutes, I'll think I'll go and get a Wellness Smoothie.'

'Six quid fifty for some chopped-up apples and a bit of spinach,' Harry moaned. 'Now that's what I call a business.'

'It's seven pounds now,' Zoë corrected him. 'They put their prices up last week.'

'Even better.' Harry shook his head. 'It's good to know that I'm doing my bit to keep the London juice-bar industry afloat.'

Zoë placed a hand on her hip and wiggled her backside. 'Surely I'm worth it.'

Harry grunted something noncommittal.

Umar tried not to stare at the curve of her jeans.

'You would be the first person to complain,' Zoë pouted, 'if I started to let myself go.'

'There's no chance of that,' Umar blurted out. 'You're in great shape.'

Zoë beamed at the compliment.

Harry sent him a look that, while friendly enough, carried a clear message: *Watch it*. 'How are you progressing with my list?' he asked.

'I'm getting there,' Umar took the roll and the coffee from the second bag and placed them on the table, 'but it's gonna take a while. It's a hell of a mess. And you know that paperwork isn't my thing. Mike would be better suited to this.' Michael Difford, Harry's accountant, was the only person other than Harry himself who was allowed to scrutinize the books under normal circumstances.

'He would be, if he were here.' Harry threw his arms into the air in exasperation. 'Last heard of, he was trekking across the desert in Peru or Chile or somewhere. What a great time to have a mid-life crisis.'

'There are other accountants . . .'

'No, no, no.' Harry waggled an admonishing index finger at his associate. 'We have to keep this strictly in-house. And I need something today. At least an idea of where we're at.'

I need a smoke. Umar struggled to his feet. 'That's going to be pushing it.'

'Pull your finger out,' Harry snapped. 'If you hadn't lost the data, we wouldn't have this problem in the first place.'

I didn't lose the data, Umar reflected. One of your girls stole it and then erased the original files. Harry's rewriting of history needled him but he limited his observation to 'We should have had it backed up.'

'Thank you, Mr IT,' Harry scoffed. 'Ten out of ten for hindsight.'

'Well, we should.' Umar shuffled towards the door.

'Today,' Harry repeated.

'Yes, boss.'

'Oh, and, Umar?'

'Yes, boss?'

Harry's face brightened slightly as he pointed towards Umar's untouched bacon roll. 'Don't you want that?'

TWELVE

Spitting into the gutter, Umar placed a Benson & Hedges between his lips, sparked up and took a deep drag. Feeling the smoke percolating into his lungs, he held his breath for the maximum time possible before exhaling into the grey sky.

One of the cleaners, Angela, appeared with a mop and a bucket of boiling water. Short, maybe an even five feet, she was a woman of indeterminate age, indeterminate origin, indeterminate everything. One of the invisible army of people who cleaned the place and kept the show on the road. Acknowledging Umar's presence with a nod, she set about washing the pavement.

'Smoke?' Umar already had the packet open.

Quickly finishing the job, Angela muttered her thanks in some indecipherable language as she grabbed a cigarette. Taking a cheap green lighter from the pocket of her jeans, she lit up and took a couple of quick puffs.

Umar gestured over his shoulder, towards the entrance of the club. 'It's a mess in there, eh?'

Angela adopted the phlegmatic approach of cleaning-ladies the world over. 'Always a mess.'

'Yeah.' Sucking down another lungful of smoke, Umar watched her empty the remaining contents of her bucket onto the pavement and hurry back inside. He knew that the woman was on a deadline: she had four different cleaning jobs to do each day and even taking two minutes for a quick smoke probably threatened to derail her entire timetable.

Flicking his stub into the gutter, Umar lit another cigarette and poked at a discarded flyer for Royal Escorts with the toe of his boot. Royal Escorts was Harry's main operation – and the source of all of Umar's current woes. After almost five years, it consisted of around three dozen girls generating healthy profits on revenues of more than eight million pounds a year. A little bit of drug-dealing on the side – servicing the pharmaceutical needs of Harry's well-heeled clientele – brought in another couple of mil. The club – Bob le Flambeur, a.k.a. Bob's – was little more than a front.

Conscious of someone approaching, he looked up. Hidden behind a pair of outsized sunglasses, Karen Jansen strode past him with barely a nod of recognition. The statuesque Australian brunette, vaguely famous thanks to a couple of appearances in a series of TV beer adverts, was one of Harry's senior girls. Pulling open the door, she disappeared inside.

'Nice to see you, too.' Taking a final drag on his cigarette, Umar watched a police van pull up to the opposite kerb. It never ceased to amuse him that they were running one of London's largest brothels barely a hundred yards from one of London's biggest cop shops. And him an ex-policeman, too. He ran a hand across the stubble on his chin as he reflected on the various changes in his life over the last year or so. He had resigned from the force in anticipation of being pushed – brought low by an incontestable sexual-harassment claim – moved out of the family home and signed up to work for Britain's poshest criminal.

All in all, quite a year.

Umar glanced at the scratches on his knuckles, wondering if he should have put some antiseptic cream on the worst of them. On the other side of the road, the staff in the juice bar were getting ready to open up for the day. Zoë would appear in a second and Harry would be back on his case. Umar thought of the mound of paperwork waiting for him inside and tossed his latest cigarette stub towards the drain. Fumbling in his pocket, he retrieved the almost empty packet of cigarettes. One more and then he would start work.

Standing by the window, Harry Cummins eased open one of the shutters and stared morosely at his reflection in the glass. When did you start to look so old? he wondered.

Coming back from Goa had been a big mistake.

Organizing raves for stoned holidaymakers was a piece of cake, compared to this lark. Wistful thoughts of going back floated through his brain, setting up camp in the Caravela Beach Resort and re-establishing his Indian business empire.

Sadly, he realized that those days were gone for good. He was ten years older and his customers had grown up and moved on to more sedate pastimes – most of them anyway. These days, they were more likely to be found in Mark Warner or even, God forbid, Center Parcs.

Scoffing a second bacon roll had been equally ill-advised. Stifling a burp, he spied Zoë on the street below. After exchanging a few words with Umar, she waited for a break in the traffic before jogging across the road and disappearing inside the juice bar. Harry gestured towards the Belisha beacons barely ten yards away. 'Why can't you use the bloody zebra crossing?' he hissed. 'Someone's going to take you out one day. No amount of antioxidants will help when you go under the wheels of a bloody taxi.'

With Zoë out of sight, his attention returned to Umar, still hovering on the pavement. 'Get on and do some work,' Harry muttered, 'you useless lump.' Just how he had ended up relying on a drunk ex-copper to help run his tottering business empire was a mystery. Royal Escorts had begun losing girls at an alarming rate. Harry didn't know why, or what to do about it.

The phone started ringing. Padding over to the desk, he picked up the receiver. 'Yes?' he demanded grumpily.

'Hello, H.' The voice at the other end of the line was cool, relaxed, but with a clear thread of steel running through it.

79

'Don't call me that.' Harry snapped. 'I'm not some used-car salesman . . . or football manager or something.'

'Maybe one of those alternative lines of work might suit you better.'

'I'm doing fine.'

'Don't bullshit me, son,' Vernon Holder shot back, the sudden anger in his voice betraying his Black Country origins. 'I know that your little operation is falling apart faster than Arsenal's back four.'

'I'm doing fine,' Harry repeated, trying to believe it.

'How many girls have you got left?'

'Fuck off.'

Holder chuckled. 'Have you thought about my proposal, yet?'

'My position hasn't changed,' Harry said stiffly. 'It's still no.' There was a pause. For a moment, Harry optimistically wondered whether his unwelcome suitor might have hung up. 'Did you hear me? I said no.'

Finally, Holder spoke: 'Suit yourself. I can sit here and wait while the price keeps going down.'

'I'm not selling.'

'Soon you'll have nothing left to sell.' Holder guffawed. 'You know and I know that this isn't really a game for a nice, well-brought-up boy like you. Better to leave it to the proper professionals.'

'And that would be you, I suppose?' Harry snorted. He was sick of this low-life hoodlum hassling him. But, equally, he was tired of the fight. His business empire was supposed to be fun, easy money. Instead, he found himself in the middle of a turf war, a war that he was clearly losing.

'Get out while you can,' Holder continued, not so much nego-tiating as goading, 'with a little bit of money in your pocket and your limbs still intact, and go into something a bit more sedate, like insurance or something.' There was a pause. 'Maybe estate agency. I think you'd be good at that, presentable, well spoken.

You could flog what's left of South Kensington to the Russians and the Chinese. Better than beating up girls in alleyways at any rate.'

'Whaddaya mean?' Harry was finding it hard to keep up with this game – all the accusations, challenges and threats were coming too thick and too fast. 'What girl? I haven't beaten anyone up. I look after my people. You're talking nonsense.'

'In that case you'd better talk to your man.'

Harry started to ask another question but this time the line did go dead.

Returning the receiver to its cradle, he crawled round the desk. Slumping into his seat he began drumming his fingers on the desk, totally at a loss as to what to do next. Almost immediately, the phone was ringing again. Harry stared at it suspiciously for several seconds before reluctantly picking up. 'Hello?'

'It's me.'

'Thank God for a friendly voice.' Harry relaxed into his chair.

'Tough day?'

'No more than usual.' There was no need to be over-familiar. 'What can I do for you? Need a girl?'

The laughter coming down the line was gentle, controlled, vaguely annoyed. 'You know that's not my thing.'

'A boy, then?'

The laughter stopped. 'No. I just need some more of those tablets you got for me recently.'

Harry's brow furrowed as he tried to recall the particular order. 'The coke?' He corrected himself instantly: 'No, the H.'

'That's right. Same amount as last time.'

'No problem,' Harry said, happy to be able to conclude a piece of straightfoward business, however small. 'Gimme a day or so.'

'Need it tomorrow,' was the firm response.

'Okay, okay. Come around eleven thirty when we open up. COD.'

'Obviously. See you then.'

Putting the phone down, Harry smiled. There was nothing to beat the pleasure of honest toil.

THIRTEEN

The only word for number sixty-one Sandringham Gardens was 'nondescript'. The 1930s semi, at the end of a long street just off the Uxbridge Road, was stereotypical suburbia. As he approached the front gate, Carlyle glanced nervously over his shoulder. At this time of the afternoon, the street was deserted. Nothing moved. It was like a scene from one of those old movies where a bomb kills all the people but leaves the buildings standing.

What a place to have to live. The inspector was already pining for the vibrancy of Covent Garden. Checking his watch, he decided he was two minutes early for his appointment. Hovering on the pavement, he eyed the house warily. Everything looked well-tended. The windows were clean, the front door enjoyed a fresh coat of red paint, and the small patch of front lawn had been neatly mown. All of which seemed at odds with what he knew lurked inside.

One minute to go. His heart rate was elevated and he could feel beads of sweat forming on his forehead. How does this work? What happens if the previous client is overrunning? Do I have to wait? Do I get tea and biscuits? Off to his left, he imagined he caught a flash of movement. Twitching net curtains. The neighbours must be having a field day.

Taking a deep breath, he pushed open the gate and marched up the path. He was about to push the bell when the door swung open.

'John?'

'Er, yes.' Carlyle took a moment to consider the woman standing in front of him. Madam Monica was slim and petite, with long red hair pulled back into a ponytail. Somewhat confusingly, she was casually dressed in a blue shirt and grey trousers rather than a black latex catsuit.

'Come in.' She held open the door and invited him inside. 'You're right on time.' Her green eyes sparkled with mischief, as if she was speaking in some kind of code that he was somehow supposed to understand. 'I like a man who is punctual.' Her accentless English suggested she could have come from almost anywhere in the world. 'You have no idea how rare it is to find a client who manages to keep to time.'

At the word 'client' Carlyle felt himself blush. How the hell was he going to explain this to Helen?

'You have no idea how difficult it is to manage my diary.'

'No, I suppose not.' Stepping across the threshold, he hesitated.

'Straight down the corridor and off to the left.'

Following her directions, Carlyle found himself in what looked very much like a normal living room. On the wall a flat-screen TV was switched on, with the sound muted. Rather disconcertingly, it was tuned to one of the news channels, which was reporting the sudden death of a B-list actress.

'Please, take a seat.'

Carlyle lowered himself onto an over-stuffed sofa and waited for his hostess to take up position in an armchair opposite.

A smile crept along her lips as she contemplated his discomfort. 'Never done this kind of thing before?'

'Not really,' he admitted.

'Not quite what you were expecting?'

Carlyle tried not to squirm. 'Again, not really.'

Madam Monica pointed towards the ceiling. 'My dungeon is upstairs. I'll give you a tour later.'

'Okay.'

'This is what I like to call your introductory interview.' She gave him a warm smile. 'With all new clients, I like to have a get-to-know-you session before we get down to things. It is, of course, fully refundable against future bookings.'

Fumbling with his warrant card, Carlyle took a deep breath. 'Well, actually, I am here on business, just not that kind.' Handing over the ID, he felt himself relax slightly as he sat back on the sofa.

Madam Monica inspected it carefully. To her credit, the smile wavered only slightly. 'You're a cop?'

'Yes.'

She returned the warrant card and Carlyle shoved it back into his pocket.

'But you paid for a session.'

'Yes, well, no. It was the quickest way of finding you.' He thought of his bank balance and shivered. 'And I need to get the two hundred and twenty-five pounds back.'

Her eyes narrowed. 'I don't give refunds. It says so on the website.'

Carlyle had expected such a response. 'Maybe you could give me a receipt. For my expenses.'

Her face brightened. 'That's no problem. I do dry cleaning, psychotherapy or secretarial services. Take your pick.'

'Sorry?'

'Quite a lot of clients claim the cost of their visits back,' Madam Monica explained, 'but they can't put in a claim for BDSM, so I have to be a little bit inventive.'

Carlyle thought about it for a moment. 'A receipt just for your normal services will be fine.'

'Are you sure?' She seemed rather disappointed. 'I'm not sure I've ever done that before.'

'Well,' he grinned, 'I suppose there's a first time for everything.'

'Just as long as you don't shop my clients to the taxman.'

'Don't worry. I'm nothing to do with HMRC. Not my area of interest.'

'Okay.' She played with an expensive-looking watch on her wrist. 'Now we've got that out of the way, you've got forty-five minutes till my next booking is due to arrive. Let me go and make a cup of tea and then you can tell me precisely what you're after.'

Five minutes later, she came back with two mugs of green tea. Handing one to Carlyle, she returned to her chair. 'No biscuits, I'm afraid. I can't have them in the house. I have to watch my figure.'

'Me too.' Carlyle took a sip of the tea. 'Very nice.'

Slipping off her sandals, Madam Monica pulled her legs up underneath her backside. 'So, what can I do for you?'

The inspector flashed what he hoped was a reassuring smile. 'Don't worry, I'm not here to cause you any grief or embarrassment.'

Blowing on her tea, she raised an eyebrow. 'Embarrassment? What are you talking about?'

'Well, erm, the neighbours and stuff.'

'Pah. The neighbours know all about it.' She gestured towards the TV screen. The news was now reporting on a military coup in Thailand. 'I was on telly, for God's sake.'

'On telly?'

'Channel 4.' She mentioned the name of a fairly famous actor whom Carlyle occasionally saw hanging out in different cafés in Soho. 'He was sitting right where you are now, talking about what the clients liked to have done to them.'

Carlyle shifted uneasily in his seat. 'I must have missed it.'

'I even let him have a go at whipping one of them. I think he quite liked it, the kinky sod.'

'Sounds like the kind of thing my wife would watch.'

'You can probably still get it on demand,' Madam Monica offered helpfully. 'Check it out.'

'Erm, I don't get much time to watch TV but I will.'

'They interviewed my mum, as well.'

'Your mum?' Carlyle almost spilled the tea into his lap.

86

'Yeah, she was made up about it. She's my greatest fan.'

'That's nice.'

'It's not a bad job. Certainly a lot better than what I was doing before.'

Carlyle didn't ask.

'And the programme was great for business. The number of clients has almost doubled since it went out. I can't deal with the demand. I had to put my prices up. I'm beginning to think about franchising the brand, you know, a bit like Starbucks.'

Feeling somewhat disoriented, Carlyle struggled to remember the purpose of his visit. Finally, the name rolled across his tongue. 'Richard Furlong.'

'One of my longer-term clients.' Monica didn't miss a beat. 'What about him?'

'He's dead.'

'Oh dear.' A look of professional dismay spread across her face.

'Suicide.'

'What a shame. He was here only a couple of weeks ago.'

'He jumped out of a window after eating his breakfast.' He stifled a cough. 'The stuff you sent him.'

For a moment, she looked surprised. 'The stuff I sent him?'

'The stuff you sent him with the letter telling him what to do with it.'

'Ah, yes.' She giggled. 'I remember. Popped it in the post last week.'

'The letter was still on Mr Furlong's kitchen table,' Carlyle explained. 'That's how I found you.'

'I didn't tell him to jump.' She stared into her tea.

'I know.'

'He was a perfectly normal guy.'

Carlyle tried not to sound too sceptical. 'Wasn't it a bit strange?'

'What – jumping out of the window or eating my excrement?'

'Well, er, both,' Carlyle replied primly. 'But I was thinking mainly about the latter.'

'Well, maybe it *is* a little strange. But hardly unique. It is an established niche within the subculture. I send out maybe two or three packages a month. There's a guy in Wales and one near Birmingham. There's also a man in Cornwall whose wife buys him one every year as a birthday present. It's a nice little sideline. People do different things with it, of course. Not everyone puts it on their toast.'

Carlyle blanched. He took a deep breath and tried to cast the image from his mind.

'It's not that unusual. Anyway, I don't judge, I don't analyse, just let people indulge their desires. I certainly didn't force Richard to do anything. And I very much doubt that it had anything to do with him taking his own life.'

Without any credible points of reference, Carlyle found it impossible to disagree. 'Do you have any idea what might have been behind his death?'

'Not really. When people walk through the front door they leave their everyday cares behind. We don't talk about what's on their mind or anything like that. That's the whole point. I'm not a psychiatrist.'

'No.' For £225, Carlyle felt he could ask one more question. 'Did he ever talk to you about his pigeons?'

'Pigeons? No. I didn't know he had any.' She thought about it for a moment. 'I didn't even realize that people kept them these days.'

'It's not that unusual.'

'No, no. It's just I imagined it was, you know, the kind of thing that people did years ago.' The conversation meandered to a close and she got to her feet. 'Sorry if I've not been much help.'

'Just tidying up loose ends – all part of the job.' The inspector stood up and handed her his mug. 'Thanks for the tea.'

'My pleasure.' She started back in the direction of the kitchen. 'Let me see if I can get you that receipt.'

For a couple of minutes, Carlyle stared blankly at the TV.

When Madam Monica came back, she handed him a small piece of paper.

'Thanks.' Carlyle squinted at the logo at the top. 'Sandringham Gardens Enterprises?'

'My trading name,' she explained.

'Okay.' Carlyle tried to calculate his chances of getting this past Accounts as he shoved it into his pocket.

'It's all completely above board. It's VAT-registered and, in case you do end up speaking to the HMRC, I pay all my taxes – in full.'

'Glad to hear it.' Slipping out into the hallway, Carlyle was about to open the front door when he felt a hand on his shoulder.

'Seeing as you're here,' Madam Monica smiled, pointing up the stairs, 'why don't I give you the guided tour? It'll only take a couple of minutes. Who knows? Now that you're registered on the website you might want to come back later on, in a personal capacity.'

FOURTEEN

Back in Covent Garden, Carlyle had no interest in heading to the station. Instead, he made for the flat, via a quick detour to Tesco. At home, he found his wife vegged out in front of the TV. Alice, apparently, was at a friend's house. Helen, enjoying a little me-time, did not seem overly pleased to see her husband.

'You're home early,' was her rather muted response to his appearance in the doorway.

'I had the chance and took it. There's nothing that can't wait until tomorrow.' He gestured at the TV screen. 'What are you watching?'

'*My Granny Is An Escort.*'

'Ha.' Carlyle chortled with glee. 'Busted.' Helen's addiction to junk television was a joke that had been running for years.

'It's diverting.'

'Yeah, yeah, yeah.' Heading back down the hallway, Carlyle retreated to the kitchen. Heating a pizza in the microwave, he ate it standing by the sink, washed down with a glass of beer. After tidying away the rubbish and washing up, he made some tea and headed back to the living room just in time to see the closing credits roll.

'Good timing.' He smiled, placing two cups on the coffee-table.

'Thanks.' Helen shuffled along the sofa to make some space for him to sit down.

Lowering himself onto the cushions, Carlyle grabbed the

remote and switched to the same news channel that had been on at Madam Monica's. 'So, were the hooking grannies worth an hour of your time?'

'It was interesting,' Helen insisted. 'The stuff people get up to.'

'The crap people put on TV.'

'That's one of the sad things, I suppose. These days, you see a show called *My Granny Is An Escort* and you don't bat an eyelid. It's normal. Or what passes for normal. I mean, can you imagine if there had been something like that when we were kids? What do you think Alice makes of it?'

I don't think she'd even notice these shows if her mum wasn't watching them. Carlyle kept the thought to himself. 'For her it is, by definition, "normal". People have always been interested in the perverse, the grotesque, the demeaning. All that's changed now is that it's far easier to see much more of it. The technology changes but people don't.'

If Helen was impressed by his insight, she kept it well hidden. 'So,' she asked, reaching for her tea, 'how was your day?'

'Well . . .' Deciding that full and timely disclosure was the best policy, Carlyle took several minutes to explain about Richard Furlong and his subsequent visit to Sandringham Gardens.

'The poor guy,' was Helen's first response. 'He must have been in a really bad way.'

'Yeah.' As was often the case, Carlyle was nonplussed by his wife's initial reaction.

'I mean, what kind of person would do something like that to a bunch of pigeons?'

And her second as well.

There was the sound of the front door opening and closing, followed by the familiar thud of Alice's schoolbag landing on the hallway floor. Thinking he wasn't going to get much of a grilling on Madam Monica, Carlyle relaxed slightly. As he did so, Helen looked at him sideways. 'But I don't understand why you felt you had to run off and visit a brothel.'

'It isn't a brothel,' he responded, tensing again. 'It's a dungeon. It's been on the telly.' He explained about Madam Monica's fifteen minutes of fame. 'I'm surprised you didn't see it. It seems right up your street.'

'What was Dad doing in a brothel?' Alice stood in the doorway in a Pixies T-shirt and a pair of ragged jeans. Hovering behind her in the hallway was a long-haired creature that looked like it might be a boy. From the look on his face, he seemed as embarrassed by the question as Carlyle himself.

Realizing that attack was the best form of defence, Carlyle gestured past her shoulder. 'Who's that?'

'Jack,' Alice replied, trying to get the right mix of defiance and insouciance into her tone as the creature shrank further into the background.

Carlyle looked at Helen, who offered an expression that said, *No idea*.

'We're going to listen to some music.' Grabbing the boy's hand, she pulled him towards her bedroom. 'So you can get back to explaining to Mum what you were doing in the knocking shop.'

'Have you done your homework?' Helen shouted after her.

'Ye-es,' Alice replied wearily.

'Okay. Well, keep the noise down.'

'Ye-es.' The bedroom door slammed. A few seconds later, the sound of the Ramones filled the flat at a just about acceptable level.

'Maybe she's finally found someone who shares her interest in punk,' Helen mused. From an early age, Alice had taken her musical inspiration from her father's collection. Given that this spanned the period from 1975 to 1990, it didn't give her many common points of reference with most of her contemporaries.

'The Ramones were kind of pre-punk,' Carlyle quibbled.

Grabbing the remote control, Helen began flicking through the video-on-demand services. 'Well, whatever, it's nice if she's found a kindred spirit.'

A kindred spirit in need of a haircut. Carlyle glanced unhappily in the direction of Alice's room. 'He gets half an hour.'

'Relax.' Helen gave him a gentle punch on the arm. 'Here, I think I've found it.'

Carlyle read the text on the screen. '"*Credit Card Love*. Why people really buy and sell sex: getting behind the stereotypes and talking to sex workers and their clients."'

Helen hit the play button. 'In fact, I think I have seen this.'

'Why am I not surprised?' Carlyle groaned, snaking out an arm and gently pulling her close.

'One of them anyway.'

Carlyle shifted his position, to get more comfortable. 'There's more than one?'

'Three or four.' As the opening credits rolled Helen pressed fast-forward. 'Now, let's see if we can find Madam Monica.'

The first episode yielded nothing. As they sped through the second, Carlyle saw a familiar street appear. 'Here we go.'

Helen slowed the video in time for them to see the front door of sixty-one Sandringham Gardens being opened by Madam Monica, just as she had for the inspector earlier in the day. This time, however, she was dressed rather differently.

'Cat Woman meets the Marquis de Sade,' was Helen's verdict.

Carlyle watched as Madam Monica led the programme host on the same guided tour that he had enjoyed earlier. This time, however, the place was in use. A man, naked apart from a gimp mask, knelt on all fours before his mistress. To protect the sensibilities of the audience, his genitalia had been pixilated.

'That's not you, is it?' Helen giggled.

'Ha-ha.' Carlyle watched as Madam Monica handed the TV presenter a riding crop and invited him to administer a few blows to the buttocks of the willing supplicant. Could that be Furlong? Carlyle wondered. It was impossible to be sure, but his impression was that the poor chap having his backside whipped was too small to be the deceased pigeon fancier.

After a few lusty blows, the action switched downstairs to the kitchen, where Madam Monica explained her mail-order operation.

Helen squirmed on the sofa. 'That is so disgusting.'

'This is your kind of television,' Carlyle reminded her. 'I'm only watching it for work.'

'How much does she charge to sell . . . that?'

'Good question. No idea. I didn't ask.'

'Isn't that what you're supposed to do?' Helen teased him. 'Ask questions?'

'I ask the right sort of questions.' On the screen, a little old lady appeared at the kitchen door, smiling broadly. 'There's Mum. Proud as punch.'

'I suppose she has to make the best of it.'

'It could be worse. After all, turning shit into money is quite a talent.'

The segment came to an end. 'So,' Helen asked wearily, switching off the TV, 'what did you learn from watching that?'

'I learned that Madam Monica's real name is Harriet Whitmore.' Rather embarrassed, Carlyle remembered that was one question he should have asked during his visit. Sometimes he wondered if he was going senile.

'Anything else?'

'Not really.' Carlyle yawned. 'It was a bit of a waste of time.'

'Looks like you'll just have to go with the other angle,' Helen advised.

Carlyle tried to lever her off the sofa. 'What other angle?'

Reluctantly she got to her feet. 'The pigeons.'

Carlyle pointed towards the hallway. The Ramones had fallen silent: Alice's bedroom had gone alarmingly quiet. 'And you'll have to get rid of lover boy.'

'Jack's mum texted him to say he was late home for his tea.'

'Good old Mum.' With Alice's new friend off the premises, Carlyle felt he could relax slightly. The tumbler of whiskey in his hand also helped. After the day he'd had, the inspector thought he deserved it.

'Apparently,' Helen added, 'they bonded over a discussion of the relative merits of *London Calling* versus *Sandinista!*'

Better than photographing each other's genitals and posting them on the internet, Carlyle mused, trying to look on the bright side. 'Alice told you that?'

'No.' Helen returned to her position on the sofa. 'I had a quick chat with him on the way out. He seems like a nice enough kid. Lives in South Kensington.'

Must be a rich family, then. Carlyle's attitude to the boy softened slightly.

'I said he should come round for dinner one night.'

'Pffff.' The prospect of another painful meal with one of his daughter's would-be suitors filled him with dread. Over the last year or so, there had been a couple of proto-boyfriends. So far, none had made it to a second family dinner.

'We've got to make the effort,' she admonished him.

'You should want to see how things shape up before sending out the dinner invitations. It's too soon.'

'I'm just showing an interest.'

He took a sip of his whiskey. 'I seem to remember we had been going out for something like *two years* before I met your parents.'

'Just be grateful I didn't expose you to their withering glare earlier,' Helen chuckled, 'or you might not have survived.'

'I was lucky to survive even then,' Carlyle retorted, his voice rising slightly. 'I don't remember either of them being too impressed.'

'Don't get yourself worked up.' Leaning over, she gave him a peck on the cheek.

'I'm not getting worked up,' Carlyle replied, irritated.

Helen gestured towards his glass. 'Should you be drinking? On a school night?'

'Ach, it's just the one.' He manoeuvred himself around, so

95

that he could rest his head on her shoulder. For a short while they simply sat together, enjoying a rare moment of peace.

'Oh, by the way,' Helen said finally, 'we need to get something for Alison Roche.'

'We do?' Carlyle finished the last of his whiskey and stared at the empty glass.

'Didn't you get the text?'

Carlyle grunted. If he had, he hadn't picked it up.

'She had a baby boy. Seven pounds, three ounces. David William Alexander Roche. Mother and baby still in hospital but doing well.'

'David William Alexander.' Carlyle tried to search for clues to the newborn's father in the name. Despite considerable speculation down at the station, Roche had kept the man's identity a closely guarded secret.

'In honour of your dad.' Helen chuckled.

'Hardly.'

'She's gonna find it tough.'

'Her choice,' Carlyle grunted.

'How very sympathetic of you,' Helen said tartly.

'That's what she said herself,' Carlyle pointed out. 'The reality is that it's hard enough being a parent when there's two of you. All I'm saying is that it's going to be a lot of work.' Feeling the need for a little more booze, he padded into the kitchen in search of the bottle of Jameson's.

When he returned, Helen had her head in a copy of the evening paper. Looking up, she registered his refilled glass but said nothing before returning her attention to the paper.

'What shall we get her?' Carlyle asked, sitting back down.

'Probably a voucher.' Helen turned the page. 'Alice said she'd come with me to see her. You should come too.'

'I will if I can,' Carlyle replied noncommittally. In reality, he had no intention of going. The last thing he wanted to do was see his sergeant in such an unfamiliar setting. 'Things are really quite busy at the moment.'

Seeing straight through his equivocation, Helen tutted her disapproval.

Time to change the subject. 'I saw Dom today.'

Helen didn't look up. 'Oh, yes?'

'You know what? I think he's had a facelift.'

'You're kidding.'

'I'm fairly sure he has. I couldn't quite work it out at first but when he started talking his face wasn't moving properly.'

Laughing, Helen let the paper fall on to her lap. 'But he's always been very good-looking.'

'Eh?'

'I'll have to give Eva a call.'

'You can't ring her up and say, "I hear your old man's had plastic surgery."'

'Don't worry, Inspector. I'm far more subtle than you when it comes to extracting information from people.' Closing the paper, she folded it in half and tossed it onto the coffee-table. 'I'll give her a call tomorrow. Now, I'm going to have a bath.' Getting up, she gave him a smile. 'Finish your drink and you can come and join me.'

FIFTEEN

'I was wondering if you'd like to go?'

'Huh?' Nadine Hendricks looked up from her notes and yawned. The clock on the wall told her that her shift had finished more than half an hour ago. She had been on her feet, non-stop, since before lunchtime, and the back of her calves ached with the kind of dull pain that burrowed deep into the muscle, like some malevolent microbe. Her shoulders ached, the harsh office lighting was hurting her eyes and her brain had seized up. If she didn't get out of here right now, a complete breakdown beckoned.

'The Hoxton Tapas Festival.'

'The Hoxton Tapas Festival,' she repeated slowly. An unappealing scene full of smug, bushy-bearded hipsters and vintage-clad girls who worked in PR swam before her eyes. What she needed was a glass of cold white wine and a warm bath. What she didn't need was to be distracted by Markus Siebeck. The lovelorn German doctor was becoming increasingly tiresome. Hendricks recognized when a guy needed to get laid and Siebeck *really* needed to get laid. That didn't mean she had to oblige him, of course.

The poor sod was only fixating on her because she was just about the only woman he came across in the blizzard of their impossible working hours. Hendricks wished there was someone she could hook Siebeck up with. The reality, however, was that she met as few new people as he did. All of her long-term friends were either married or unsuitable. Or married *and* unsuitable.

Hendricks wondered how long it was since Helma had been in town. She had only met Siebeck's nominal girlfriend once, at a drinks reception held by the hospital trust in a nearby hotel. Never one to avoid snap decisions, Hendricks had come to the conclusion that the couple were uniquely mismatched. Whereas Siebeck was gentle and rather ineffectual, Helma had all the charm of a Panzer tank. She had given their relationship almost no chance of working out in the long-term, and that was before Helma had run back to Germany.

The whole mess made Hendricks feel sorry for her colleague. Not sorry enough to sleep with him, though. His attentions could – at times – be flattering: after all, he was so much younger and not bad-looking. But he just wasn't her type. Anyway, ever since some very unhappy experiences in medical school she had stuck to a firm rule: *Never date doctors*.

'It's supposed to be very good,' he said hopefully. 'I was thinking of going on . . .' he hesitated, clearly trying to calculate which day might better fit in with her shift pattern '. . . Sunday.'

'Not really my thing.' Hendricks gave him a tired smile. 'Anyway, I agreed to see Brian this weekend.' It was a shameless lie. She would rather allow herself to be ravaged by a gang of syphilitic gargoyles than spend any time with her soon-to-be-ex-husband. At the same time, the useless shit remained a useful get-out-of-jail-free card when it came to turning down unwanted invitations.

'Oh.' Siebeck couldn't hide his disappointment.

Hendricks was too tired for sympathy. On the way home she would drop into Tesco Metro for a bottle of wine. She wondered if they stocked bath salts. 'I'll see you tomorrow.' Dropping her notes into a file, she placed them in a drawer and turned towards the door.

'Sure.' Now he sounded like a sulky teenager.

'See if you can get some rest. With a bit of luck it should be a quiet night.' Without waiting for a reply, she marched out of the office and down the corridor.

Siebeck watched Nadine Hendricks disappear for the night. 'Damn,' he muttered to himself. 'You've blown it. What a stupid time to ask her out, at the end of a shift when she's dead on her feet and only wants to get home.' It had taken him the best part of three months to work up the courage to ask her out on something that could be even remotely considered a date. What should he do now?

In front of him was a pile of papers that needed to be completed before the end of the week. With a sigh, he grabbed the top form and quickly scanned its contents. Terminal patient Alexander Carlyle was being released into the hands of the healthcare trust's Terminal Palliative Care Division.

Carlyle? Which one was he? After a few moments, the doctor placed the old man amid the ever-expanding ranks of his patients. The sad-looking stoic with the policeman son. Siebeck recalled his conversation with the officer about Anne, the hapless Miss X. The woman was still in a coma down the corridor. Meanwhile, there was no visible sign of any effort on the part of the police to find out who she was or to track down the thug who had almost killed her. Alexander Carlyle's son hadn't even kept his promise to come back and talk to Nadine.

'Bloody people.' The damn cop had probably forgotten his promise before he had even left the hospital. Grabbing a pen, Siebeck signed Alexander Carlyle's discharge form with a flourish. Shoving it into an envelope, he tossed it into the internal mail tray and returned to the rest of his paperwork. With luck, he would get maybe half of it done tonight. He would have to finish the rest tomorrow. A wave of tiredness swept over him. Finding it impossible to read any more forms, Siebeck leaned back in his chair and closed his eyes.

* * *

Perversely, Siebeck was dreaming of Helma when he felt a hand on his shoulder. Blinking, he slowly came around.

'Hi.' Sonia, a.k.a. Tank Girl, stood over him, grinning. 'Were you asleep?'

Siebeck quickly pushed himself upright and crossed his legs. 'No, no.'

'Just resting your eyes, huh?'

'Thinking.' A quick glance at the clock told him that he had only been out for something like fifteen minutes. 'A difficult dilemma with a patient,' he stammered, 'not easy to resolve.'

'Well, it can wait. Get your arse out of that chair and come with me.'

He looked at her blankly. Siebeck knew that Sonia worked even longer shifts than he did. A lot of it was hard, physical labour too. Yet, even now, the girl retained a brio that he could only dream of. How could she have so much energy?

'Come on.' She made a half-hearted attempt to drag him from the chair.

'Why?'

'Miss X, your beloved Anne.'

Siebeck's stomach lurched. Instinctively, he knew that the poor girl was dead even before he heard the words.

'Hurry up.' Sonia was already out of the door and heading down the corridor. 'She's woken up.'

'You bastard. Where the fuck are you?' Overwhelmed by frustration, Umar flicked a feeble punch at his computer screen. According to Mike Difford's Facebook page, which hadn't been updated for more than a week, the accountant was still trekking in the Atacama Desert. Umar stared blankly at the heap of paperwork in front of him. 'How can you be off enjoying yourself at a time like this?'

The smiling, deeply tanned accountant grinned back at him, saying nothing.

'What a time to decide to have a sodding mid-life crisis.'

Three floors down, he could make out the dull thud of a heavy bass line. One of the DJs would be trying out some new tracks before the club opened. I really need to go downstairs and get a drink, Umar thought, before my bloody brain explodes.

Before he could get out of his chair, Harry appeared in the doorway, looking like he'd just woken up from a long nap: his hair was dishevelled and one half of his shirt had come out of his trousers. On his face was a glazed expression that suggested he was struggling to remember what his name was.

I wonder if he's on his second bottle of cognac yet? Umar thought. Harry had always been partial to a drink and his recent troubles had led him to up his alcohol intake considerably. In Harry's parlance, this was known as 'stress relief'. For his part, Umar saw it more as 'blotting out reality'.

'How's it going?' Resting against the doorframe, Harry had a dangerously full tumbler in one hand and a smouldering cigarette in the other. Bob's was a strictly no-smoking establishment but, then again, Harry was the boss.

Gesturing at the papers strewn across the desk, Umar tried to affect an air of insouciance. 'Your record-keeping is a bit, like, abstract.'

'Ha.' Harry slurped his drink.

'Mike needs to take a look at all this.'

'Mike's not here,' Harry slurred. 'That's the problem with being an accountant. You spend your whole life denying yourself any fun and then, poof, it's suddenly time to *paartay*.' He did a little jig, spilling brandy over his shirt.

Careful with the fag, Umar thought, or you could go up like a Christmas pudding. It was not such an unappealing thought.

'You just explode.' Harry did a vague impression of a man being caught up in a bomb blast in slow motion. 'That's why you should never become an accountant – you burn out.'

'I'm not an accountant,' Umar pointed out.

'Good for you.'

'And I can't make head nor tail of your paperwork. My best

guess – so far – is that the girls who have gone accounted for a quarter of clients but almost half of the revenue.' Inventing some figures, Umar had decided, was the best way of getting Harry off his back. Apart from anything else, he would end up so pissed that their conversation would be totally forgotten by tomorrow. 'In other words, you're losing the best ones.'

'I knew that.' Harry took another slug of booze.

'So,' Umar said, with the confidence of a man who was, at the very least, one step ahead of his boss, 'with the club's high cost base,' he waved a hand above his head, 'we're facing an imminent cash-flow crisis.' It was amazing how easy it was to make this crap up. Feeling a weight lifting from his shoulders, he offered up a rueful smile.

'Eh?'

'You're gonna be bust by the end of next month.'

'Hmm.' Sticking the cigarette between his lips, Harry fumbled in his trouser pocket. Pulling out a key, he tossed it towards the desk. Umar watched it bounce off the back of the computer screen and land somewhere on the carpet.

'Do me a favour, will you? Go and pick up Zoë. I'm too pissed to drive.'

You don't say. 'Sure.' Umar slipped out of the chair and began searching for the key.

'I can't afford to be stopped again.' Earlier in the year, Harry had been pulled over by the police at four one morning. Barely able to stand, he had refused to give a breath sample, had been arrested and taken to a nearby station. There, a breathalyser test had shown he was almost two times over the legal limit. 'They'd take my licence for sure.'

'Yes,' Umar agreed. Recovering the key, he stood up slowly, careful not to smack his head on the desk.

'They haven't even heard the last one yet,' Harry complained. 'It only comes to court next month.'

Umar tried to sound sympathetic. 'I thought you were going to get off?' Harry's lawyer was trying to argue that signals from Harry's iPhone had interfered with the readings on the intoximeter machine used in the police station.

'We'll see.' Harry shook his head. 'Lawyer says it's probably fifty-fifty.'

Legal speak for 'You haven't a hope in Hell'.

'How many points have you already got on your licence?'

Puffing on his cigarette, Harry stared at the ceiling, as if the answer might be written up there. 'Six? Something like. It's not fair. It's like living in a police state. It *is* living in a police state. This country's going to the dogs. The BBC, the *Guardian*, the police – they're all out to destroy our wonderful British society.'

The police? Not the sharpest tool in the box at the best of times, too much alcohol robbed Harry of his residual cognitive powers. Umar jiggled the key in his hand. 'Don't worry. I'll go and get her.'

'Thanks.' Harry gave him a drunken grin. 'She's just finishing her cardio class at Infinity.'

'Okay.' Infinity was Zoe's twenty-four-hour members-only gym and spa in Mayfair. The girl was certainly leveraging her new-found position as Harry's girlfriend to the max: her membership had cost him a £5,999 joining fee, on top of the £3,600 annual subscription. These were the kind of expenses that Harry could no longer afford. Given his current problems, Umar wondered if the boss might try to put Zoë back to work. The idea was repulsive to Umar but Harry was a man with even less of a moral compass than he possessed himself.

Harry stared blankly at the chunky Rolex weighing down his wrist. 'She should be done in twenty minutes or so.'

Umar approached the door. 'Sure, no problem.'

'Don't want to keep the little Princess waiting.' Draining the last of his drink, Harry stepped aside to let him pass.

'I'm on it,' Umar said briskly, bounding down the hallway, happy to escape the paperwork, even happier to escape Harry.

SIXTEEN

The lounge at Infinity was completely empty. A long front desk guarded the entrance to the gym proper. On the far wall, a hyperactive music video played on a large TV screen, the sound on mute. Resigned to a long wait, Umar flopped onto a long grey sofa. From behind the desk, a young receptionist eyed him warily. Tall and lean, she looked ready, indeed eager, to dance round the desk and administer a drop kick to Umar's privates at the first hint that he was set to cross an invisible line in front of the doors leading into the gym.

'You know that this is a women-only spa, right?'

Getting quickly back to his feet, Umar tried one of his winning smiles. 'I'm just waiting to pick someone up.' Holding up a hand, he waved the car key in front of her face as evidence for the defence. Unimpressed, the receptionist turned her attention to folding towels.

Friendly place.

Returning to his seat, Umar scrutinized the image that dominated the opposite wall. Two lithe blondes with well-defined stomach muscles were engaged in a vigorous exercise class under the legend 'Bionic Bullet Ballet – the latest exciting fitness trend spreading across the globe with a large celebrity following'. At the bottom of the poster, the advertising blurb talked about 'combining the precision of Pilates with the positions, moves and technique of ballet'.

Yada, yada, yada.

If the sisters are so smart, he wondered, why do they fall for all this stuff?

From a table next to the sofa, he picked up a leaflet describing the various waxing treatments on offer: 'Our technicians take the utmost care when it comes to protecting the vibrancy and elasticity of the skin.' Good to know, he thought, reviewing the price list. Deciding against a 'Brazilian Bikini Plus, at a bargain £132', he turned his attention to the in-house music channel.

After watching three indistinguishable videos merge into each other, he was hunting for a remote control when he became aware of someone approaching him.

'Sorry to keep you waiting.' Zoë wiped her face with a small towel. Wearing a pair of black Lycra shorts and a pink sports bra, she had her hair pulled back into a ponytail. She wrapped the towel around her neck and smiled. 'That class was a killer.'

This was the first time Umar had ever seen Zoe without any make-up. It made her look about ten years younger and twice as pretty.

A frown crinkled her forehead. 'Harry sent me a text. Is he pissed again?'

'Yeah.'

'He'll probably crash out in the office.' Zoë glanced at the clock above the reception desk and sighed. 'Another wasted evening.'

A male gym instructor with a sculpted torso sauntered past and gave Zoë a big smile. Umar tried not to scowl as she smiled back.

'That's Kelvin,' Zoë whispered, as the instructor disappeared through a door marked 'Staff Only'. 'He's a level-four instructor. His class is ab-so-*lute*-ly amazing. The first time I tried it, it was oh, my God, what is happening? Right now, it's my absolute fave.'

'Uh-huh.'

'Before he came here, Kelv was a dancer for Justin Timberlake and Christina Aguilera.'

'Good for him.' Umar was genuinely unimpressed.

'They have such brilliant instructors here,' she burbled, 'and it's great being able to work out without having to worry about sweaty blokes hitting on you all the time.'

The receptionist, having built a pile of towels three feet high, disappeared after Kelvin.

'Doesn't a gym for women mean all female trainers?' Umar wondered.

Zoë thought about it for a moment. 'They like to bring in the best people, regardless of gender.'

'I suppose that's what you're paying for.'

She looked at him blankly.

What *Harry*'s paying for.

'Kelvin's one of only two male trainers they use here. On a full-time basis, anyway. They're always bringing in different guest instructors.'

'Is he gay?'

'No, he's not.' She took another swig of water. 'Not according to some of the girls, anyway.'

'*That* is a perk of the job, I suppose.' Umar grinned lecherously.

Finishing the water, Zoë tossed the empty bottle into a nearby bin. 'I need a shower.'

'Okay.' Resigned to a further wait, Umar was surprised when she grabbed his hand and pulled him towards a set of double doors. 'C'mon, I'll give you a guided tour.'

Looking around, Umar saw there was no one to stop him. 'Sure, why not?'

Pushing through the doors, she led him past an empty room full of cardio machines and free weights and down a flight of stairs. As they walked along a dimly lit corridor, Umar could hear the accelerated beat of techno music coming from a nearby studio.

'Clara's dance class,' Zoë explained. 'She's really into Ecuadorian techno at the moment. You're dead after ten minutes. I just couldn't face it tonight but it'll keep everyone busy for the next half an hour or so.' Coming to a series of doors, she pushed one open and disappeared inside.

Following her, Umar found himself standing in a small changing room with an en-suite shower.

'That's another thing we pay for.' Zoë grinned. 'Individual changing rooms.'

Locking the door, she shimmied out of her shorts and stood in front of him, hands on hips.

Someone's been making full use of the waxing treatment, Umar thought.

'Thirty minutes,' Zoë repeated, blushing slightly as she swayed to the sound of the music. 'Do you think that will be enough?'

Struck down with a bad case of the munchies, Harry wondered what he should order from Bob's extensive in-house menu. After giving the matter some considerable thought, he decided on a club sandwich and fries. That was what he always ordered when he was drunk. Picking up the phone, he called down to the kitchen with his order. Job done, he refilled his glass and sat back in his chair, staring at the shadows from the streetlights outside playing on the ceiling. As the gravity of his financial situation had begun to emerge, he had taken to sitting in his office with the lights off. For reasons he didn't quite understand, the darkness soothed him.

After a couple of minutes there was a knock at the door. 'That was quick.' Salivating, Harry watched it open.

'What are *you* doing here?'

The man stepped in front of the desk.

'What are you *doing*?' In his drunken stupor, Harry refused to believe what he was seeing. The gun being pointed at his face didn't look real. Listening to his stomach rumble, he closed his eyes. 'I'm starving.'

'Not for very much longer,' the man replied, pulling the trigger.

* * *

Nadine Hendricks rubbed her temples in the forlorn hope of massaging away her throbbing hangover. One glass of wine had quickly turned into two, and the next thing she knew she'd been opening a second bottle. At least there was still half of that one left in the fridge.

Did she have a drink problem? At least, unlike Siebeck, she didn't smoke. Even so, the question of lifestyle abuse was rearing its ugly head with some regularity these days. According to government guidelines, women should limit themselves to fourteen units of alcohol a week, with at least two alcohol-free days in that period. The last time Hendricks had done the calculation, she estimated that her weekly average was closer to twenty-five. And the last time she'd had an alcohol-free day? Her memory didn't go back that far.

She made a silent vow not to have another glass of wine before the weekend, at least. The drinking was just habit, nothing she couldn't handle. Equally, there was no harm in having a couple of days off. If she could manage that, maybe she could manage a week, even a month.

A wry smile crossed her lips. The next thing you know, she told herself, the fridge will be full of Evian and you'll be training for the London Marathon.

Maybe not.

'Doctor?'

'Huh? Sorry.' Hendricks focused on the sleeping girl in the bed on the other side of the glass. 'How long was she awake?'

'I don't know,' Sonia Gavril admitted. 'Dr Siebeck sat with her for about an hour – he held her hand.'

'That sounds like Markus.' Hendricks sighed. Always compelled to play the Good Samaritan. Not for the first time it crossed her mind that the poor guy was far too soft to be a doctor. In this job, too much compassion would end up destroying you.

'As far as I know, she didn't say anything.' Sonia paused. 'Maybe she's got amnesia.'

Leave the diagnosis to me, if you don't mind. Profoundly

irritated by Sonia's interest in *her* patient, not to mention the girl's appallingly healthy glow, Hendricks turned her attention to the badly bruised face of the woman in the bed. The most annoying thing was that the kid might be right. Hendricks recalled reading a case where a hospital outside London had cared for a patient for more than five months after he had lost his complete autobiographical memory. Even after the police had managed to identify him, the man had faced a long and painful struggle to regain his identity.

Five months. Hendricks shivered at the thought. The first thing they needed to do was get their mystery patient out of this expensive room as quickly as possible. The poor woman might look a mess but many of her injuries were quite superficial and all the signs suggested that she would make a full recovery. They might try to slip her onto a general ward later in the day. The fact was they needed the room back as soon as possible: in this business demand always exceeded supply. 'What time is Dr Siebeck due back in?'

'In a couple of hours, I think.' Sonia feigned ignorance. In fact, she knew the young doctor's rota patterns as well as her own. She glanced at her watch. Markus was always at least twenty minutes early for his shift. Based on past experience, he should be walking down the corridor in about fifty minutes.

'Okay,' said Hendricks, wearily. 'I'll speak to him when he arrives. In the meantime, have the police been informed that she woke up?'

'I've been trying to get hold of them. So far, no one's returned any of my calls.'

'Give them another try. Maybe they've worked out who she is by now.'

'Maybe,' said Sonia doubtfully.

'We can dream.' Hendricks stalked off in search of some black coffee and a couple of extremely strong painkillers.

SEVENTEEN

'Is that what I think it is?' Holding up the transparent evidence bag to the light, Kelly Moss pointed at the dirty USB stick inside. 'Poo?'

The inspector felt himself blush slightly. 'I've no idea.'

Kelly knew he was lying but she didn't call him on it. 'Where did this come from?'

'We got it from a woman who was found badly beaten in an alleyway off Tottenham Court Road,' Carlyle replied, keeping things suitably vague. 'She's currently in a coma at UCH.'

'Hm.' Kelly dropped the bag onto the desk. 'Have you tried looking at it yourself?'

The persona of the technological idiot came easily to the inspector. 'I wasn't able to make head or tail of it.' He shrugged. The truth was he had forgotten about the damn thing until five minutes ago when he'd found it in his pocket. 'I thought I'd bring it to the expert.'

Kelly's face said, Don't try to butter me up, but it was clear that she was pleased to be asked to help. Two years attached to the Met's e-crime unit made her the nearest thing to a computer expert that Charing Cross police station could boast. And looking at Carlyle's file would be a welcome distraction from her current day job – organizing the station's work rotas.

'So what are you looking for?' Opening a drawer, Kelly pulled out a pair of latex gloves and put them on. With three small kids at home, she was fastidious when it came to matters of hygiene.

'I dunno.' Carlyle shrugged. 'Anything that tells us who the victim is or why she was attacked, I suppose.' Out of the corner of his eye, he saw the outsized frame of Dombey lumbering towards them.

As he came closer, the young constable waved at Moss. 'Hi, Kel.'

'Hey, Paul.'

'How're things?'

'Good. You?'

'All good.'

Glad we sorted that out, Carlyle thought sourly.

Oblivious to the inspector's irritation, Dombey asked, 'How's the family?'

'Fine, thanks.' Moss beamed. 'How about you?'

'All good. Marie's getting fed up waiting for sprog number two to drop, though – it's already a week overdue.'

'It'll be fine,' Moss reassured him.

How could Dombey have a family? Carlyle wondered, somewhat confused. The constable was just a kid himself, one with plenty of growing up to do. The inspector, who rarely showed much interest in the private lives of his colleagues, tried to keep a lid on his impatience as he waited for them to finish their chat.

'I know, but it's, like, stressful,' said Dombey, earnestly. 'Especially with her mum coming down to help.'

The Specials' 'Too Much Too Young' started playing in the inspector's head. Grinning, he turned to the young constable. 'Did you want something?'

'Er, yeah.' Dombey gestured with the phone in his hand. 'I've been trying to call you but you're not picking up your phone.'

Carlyle gave him a blank look. He had long since given up trying to work out how he managed to miss so many calls. 'What is it?'

112

'The hospital called. That girl's woken up. Miss X.'

It was clear that Dombey liked saying 'Miss X'.

'Anne,' Carlyle corrected him. 'At least, that's the name the hospital staff have given her.' He gestured towards the plastic bag sitting on Moss's desk. 'This is the girl we took the USB stick from.'

'There must be something important on there,' Dombey said earnestly. 'She ate it to hide it from the bloke who beat her up.'

Kelly's eyebrows shot up. 'She ate it?'

'They found it in her nappy,' the constable said gleefully.

'So it *is* poo.' Kelly giggled. 'Urgh.'

Well done, Dombey. Carlyle wanted to throttle the big lump. 'Who told you that?' he demanded.

'The hospital asked about it when they called,' Dombey explained. 'They wanted to know if we'd found anything on it.'

Carlyle switched his attention back to Moss. 'Will it still work?'

'Only one way to find out. Quite probably. Gavin, my eldest, ate one of his DS games once. It came out a couple of days later and it still worked. They still play with it.'

'The joys of modern technology,' the inspector opined.

'Now I know why you didn't want to do it yourself,' Moss chided him.

'Not my area of expertise,' Carlyle said lamely.

'Don't worry, Inspector.' She wiggled her fingers inside one of the latex gloves. 'I'll take a look.'

'Thank you.'

'No problem.'

'What about the girl?' the inspector asked Dombey. 'Has she told the doctors anything? Do we know her real name?'

Dombey shook his head. 'Apparently not. And, before you ask, we haven't had any relevant missing-persons reports either.'

'Okay.' The question hadn't crossed Carlyle's mind but it was good to know.

'The hospital wants us to go round.'

'Okay.' Carlyle sighed. 'Let's take a look.'

If the girl had woken up earlier, she was asleep again now. The inspector regretted not sending Dombey to UCH on his own. He stood in the corridor, eyeing the exit.

'You remember the manager at Il Grillo's?'

'The pizza restaurant Richard Furlong dropped in on?'

'Mediterranean fusion,' Dombey corrected him. 'She's suing us.'

'Eh?'

'She's suing the police for trashing her alarm system. Apparently her insurance company is saying that the alarm being out of action means that the restaurant's cover is invalid.'

'Bollocks.' Carlyle snorted. 'For a start, you only smashed it *after* the damage to the restaurant had been done.'

Dombey bit his bottom lip. 'Am I gonna get into trouble? I mean, I did trash that alarm.'

The look of concern on Dombey's face was so genuine, Carlyle felt a passing twinge of almost parental concern. 'No, no, no,' he insisted. 'You were only acting as instructed by a senior officer. If it comes to it, worst case, you might have to give a statement – just make sure your Federation rep gives it the once-over before it goes in. Even then, it's not a big deal. The Met gets sued all the time. Insurance companies always try it on. They just can't help themselves. And if there's any comeback, the buck stops with me. I was the one in charge of the scene.'

Dombey's face brightened at the prospect of someone else taking the blame. 'Thanks, boss.'

'It's nothing,' Carlyle asserted, 'we'll be fine.' The sound of leather on linoleum caused him to glance up. A tall woman in a white coat was striding towards them, a look of composed irritation on her face.

The doctor gave Dombey a curt nod. 'Where's your colleague?'

114

'WPC Granger is on leave,' Dombey explained. 'Gone fishing.'

The inspector stepped forward. 'I'm John Carlyle. I spoke to one of your colleagues previously.'

'Nadine Hendricks.' The woman gave his hand a limp shake. 'So you're in charge of this investigation?'

The doctor's breath hit him in the face. Carlyle tried not to let his discomfort show. 'That's right.' He gestured towards the glass. 'I hear that Miss X – Anne – woke up.'

'Apparently so,' Hendricks replied wearily. 'I wasn't here at the time.'

'Did she say anything?'

'Not as far as I know.' The doctor didn't seem particularly curious, either way. 'You'll need to speak to Dr Siebeck about that. He was on duty when it happened. He's on a break now but he'll be back in a while.'

'Right.' Carlyle tried to keep a lid on his irritation at the prospect of having to return to the hospital again.

'In the meantime,' Hendricks asked, 'how is your investigation going?'

'It's continuing,' Carlyle said blandly. Hendricks started to launch into a follow-up question but the inspector was spared further interrogation by the opening bars of 'The Eye Of The Tiger' blaring from Dombey's jacket. Grabbing his phone, the young constable took a couple of steps down the corridor.

'Hello? . . . Yes, that's right . . . Yes, he is. Hold on.' Extending an arm, he offered the handset to Carlyle. 'It's the front desk. They've got a call for you.'

Moving further down the corridor, the inspector reluctantly lifted the greasy handset to his ear. 'Carlyle.'

'Hold on a sec,' said a gruff voice.

There was the sound of silence, followed by a buzz of background noise.

'Hello?'

'Inspector? This is Fiona Cope from the RSPCA. Sorry to

chase you, but I couldn't get hold of you on your mobile.' She sounded hassled, in a hurry.

No one can, it seems, Carlyle reflected. Still, he was happy to hear from her. 'How goes the fight against animal cruelty?'

'Good, good. Listen, where are you right now? I've got someone I think you should meet.'

EIGHTEEN

Leaving Dombey at the hospital, the inspector ducked into Warren Street tube station and jumped on an Edgware train. Half an hour or so later, he found himself standing in a north London field. In the distance, a man was walking a dog. Other than that, the place seemed pretty much deserted. A nearby sign informed him that 'Clitterhouse Playing Fields is a park and Site of Local Importance for Nature Conservation.'

Twenty yards away, Cope was deep in conversation with a short, middle-aged man wearing a pair of dirty jeans and tatty trainers. The ensemble was completed by a replica England shirt, one of the red ones that harked back optimistically to the days of 1966, Bobby Moore and dodgy Russian linesmen. In the man's hand a smouldering cigarette never seemed to reach his lips. Every so often, he would break off from the conversation and scowl at Carlyle. For his part, the inspector pretended not to notice. Instead, he stood patiently, hands behind his back, staring off into the middle distance, in search of some nature conservation taking place.

Cope finished talking to the man and walked over. She was dressed in the same basic outfit Carlyle remembered from the other day – this time her polo shirt was lime green, but the jeans and the fleece were the same. 'Eric will talk to you,' she said quietly. 'He's not that happy about it, though, so take it slow. We don't want him running off.'

Carlyle stole a glance at the man, who was now staring at his cigarette, as if wondering what to do with it. I wouldn't worry about that, he thought. Even I could catch him. He scratched his head. 'What precisely am I asking him about?'

'Sorry,' she said. 'I should have explained better. Eric Rayner is one of our confidential informants.'

Carlyle stifled a laugh. 'The RSPCA has informants?'

'Sure.' Cope shrugged. 'We need information the same as you do and human intelligence is a vital tool in the fight against animal cruelty. Rayner's not my informant, but I know him from a previous investigation. He helped colleagues in north London a couple of years ago when they were chasing down an animal-rustling ring.'

'Animal rustling? In Barnet?' This time Carlyle did laugh.

'You'd be surprised,' Cope said glumly. 'People will nick anything.'

'True enough,' Carlyle agreed.

'This gang were quite well organized. More than two hundred animals were taken in a period of less than nine months from around Stanmore, Edgware and Southgate. You might have read about it in the paper. They called it "the worst animal-related crime spree in the history of north London".'

'Must have passed me by.'

'It should have been a matter for the police but they didn't take it seriously. So we stepped in to run our own investigation. It turned out to be three young guys who were selling the animals on to an illegal slaughterhouse near Milton Keynes. In a couple of months, they nicked thirty-four sheep, six horses, more than a hundred and twenty chickens and a couple of pheasants.'

'That's quite a haul,' was all Carlyle could think of to say.

'They were convicted and jailed last year.'

So far, so *Crimewatch*. Carlyle gestured towards the man in the red football top. 'So what's all that got to do with Bobby Charlton over there?'

Cope got the gag but failed to muster a smile. 'Eric is the

chairman of the Hendon Pigeon Racing Association. Before they were caught, the gang tried to branch out into kidnapping.'

Who knew that north London was so interesting? Carlyle folded his arms, preparing to be further entertained.

'They raided six coops on successive evenings and took a total of fifty-one racing pigeons. Good ones, too. They knew exactly what they were looking for. They sent their ransom demand to Eric. Twenty grand or the pigeons would end up in some supermarket's pies.'

'Makes a change from horse meat,' Carlyle observed drily.

'There was a big row in the local RPRA about it. Some people wanted to pay, some didn't.'

'Let me guess, Eric was not for coughing up the cash?'

'No, not at all. Eric wanted to pay up. At least, he did until he realized that paying up could leave him facing a conspiracy charge and a possible prison sentence. That was when he agreed to go undercover for us.'

Undercover? What is this? *Miami Vice*?

'He set up a meeting for the pay-off and handed over a bagful of torn-up newspapers. We caught two of the gang immediately. The third was picked up the next day.'

'And what happened to the birds?'

A pained expression crossed Cope's face. 'They were never recovered.'

'Coming to a meat pie near you,' Carlyle quipped.

'The RPRA wasn't happy with the outcome,' Cope admitted.

'At least they weren't out of pocket. Twenty grand seems a lot.' Carlyle stopped himself from adding 'for a few birds'.

'Pigeons are big business. There's gambling, semi-organized crime. Lots of murky goings-on. Since the gang were nicked, Eric's had a lot of grief. He's had a brick through his window, his car was vandalized and he's had a couple of death threats in the post. So, these days, he's a little bit nervous of talking to us.'

'I don't blame him.' A whole new world of criminality was

opening up around him but still a part of the inspector's brain was struggling to take it all seriously. 'Under the circumstances, it's a miracle he's agreed to come here at all.'

Cope nodded. 'Yeah, but he's basically a good bloke. His heart's in the right place. I've had a word with him and he'll talk with you.'

Carlyle returned belatedly to the matter in hand. 'And what's the connection with Richard Furlong?'

'Furlong was a member of the local RPRA.'

'He was?' Carlyle gestured around the wide open spaces of Clitterhouse Playing Fields. 'We're a long way from Covent Garden.'

'Furlong was treasurer of the King's Cross association until it closed down about a decade ago. The racing clubs have been consolidating since the 1970s. There's more money than ever in the sport but fewer and fewer people are interested in the hassle of looking after the birds.'

'So Eric knew Furlong well?'

'I promised him that was all you want to ask him about.'

'It *is* all I want to ask him about.' Carlyle watched as Rayner discarded his cigarette and immediately lit a new one. 'Let's have a word with him, then, before he bolts.' Taking it nice and slow, he walked towards the man with Cope at his side. Rayner watched them approach warily. Carlyle smiled as he stretched out a hand. 'Mr Rayner, thank you very much for taking the time to see me.'

Ignoring the inspector's handshake, Rayner did a pirouette, taking in a 360-degree view of the park. There was not a single soul in any direction – even the solitary dog walker had disappeared – but still he kept his voice low. 'Richard Furlong. I saw he topped himself.' Grimacing, he ran a hand through what remained of his hair.

'That's right. I understand you knew him.'

'Richard was a good lad. Loved his birds.' A look of genuine distress passed across Rayner's face. He took a long drag on his smoke. 'I hear they ended up in quite a mess. Richard wouldn't have been able to cope with that – it would have tipped him right over the edge.'

'He was already on the edge, was he?'

'They wouldn't leave him alone.' Rayner waved his cigarette in the air. 'They just kept coming.'

Carlyle tried to find an expression that suggested Rayner's remarks made perfect sense. 'Who are we talking about here?'

Rayner looked askance. 'Who do you think?'

'I don't know.' Carlyle smiled apologetically. 'All this is new to me.'

'It's the Belgians, innit?'

'The Belgians?' Carlyle looked at Cope.

'Big pigeon racers,' she explained.

'Big dopers.' Rayner snorted.

'Doping is a big problem in pigeon racing,' Cope added. 'The theory is that Furlong fell foul of the Belgians because he was doping his birds.'

'Or because he wouldn't dope them,' Rayner interjected.

'Okay, okay.' Carlyle held up a hand. This was too much information and yet not enough. 'Who are the Belgians?'

Cope looked at Rayner.

Rayner looked at Cope.

'That,' Rayner said finally, 'is hard to say.' He mentioned a couple of names. They meant nothing to Carlyle but Cope nodded sagely.

'That would make sense,' she mused.

'That's all I know,' Rayner added.

'That's very helpful.' Cope smiled. 'Thanks, Eric.'

'You mentioned some cash?'

Cope looked at Carlyle.

'For my time.' Rayner took a final drag on his smoke and flicked the butt into the grass.

Reluctantly, Carlyle fished a couple of twenty-pound notes

out of his wallet and handed them over. Rayner shoved them into his pocket and trudged off.

You're welcome, Carlyle thought. It was another expense that he was going to struggle to get past Accounts. At least he had got some potentially useful information for his cash. As he watched his money wander away, a final question popped into his head. He shouted after Rayner: 'One last thing.'

'Yeah?' Rayner half turned but didn't stop walking.

'Do you know Monica?'

'Who?'

'A woman called Madam Monica. She, er, knew Furlong.'

'Never heard of her.' Rayner continued on his way, his gaze firmly on the ground in front of his feet.

'Fair enough.' Carlyle watched him go.

'Who's Madam Monica?' Cope asked eventually.

'I'll explain later,' Carlyle replied. 'Let's go and find some coffee.' He tapped the empty wallet in his pocket. 'Looks like you're buying.'

NINETEEN

Standing on the pavement, Dominic Silver contemplated the police tape flapping in the breeze. At least I don't have to worry about holiday money, he thought, patting the envelope stuffed full of cash in his jacket pocket. The flow of cops running in and out of Bob le Flambeur had slowed in the last few minutes. Reaching for his phone, Dom became conscious of an elderly woman standing beside him. Despite the warmth of the day, she was wearing a heavy overcoat and a pair of leather gloves. One hand kept a tight hold of her shopping trolley as she stopped to watch the free show.

Professional gawker, Dom thought.

The pair of them made up part of a small group of onlookers that was steadily growing in size, people joining in ones and twos as more emergency vehicles pulled up outside the club. Off to his left, Dom saw the first TV satellite truck moving towards them. A low murmur of anticipation rippled through the crowd.

'A bloke's been shot inside the club,' the old woman said, addressing no one in particular. 'Always been trouble, that place.' She waved at a young constable, hovering on the other side of the police tape. 'Is it drugs?'

Unable to avoid eye contact, the officer grinned at her but said nothing.

'Bound to be drugs,' the woman muttered. 'They were all up to it in there. All the time. Off their heads, they were.

123

Doing all kinds of appalling things. It was a terrible carry-on. Terrible.'

A young couple standing behind her started to laugh.

'The place should have been closed down years ago.' The woman harrumphed. 'How they got a licence that last time round I'll never know.' She looked towards Dom for some endorsement of her view but he was distracted by the sight of a familiar face appearing from behind a police van on the other side of the road. Eyes trained on the pavement, the man studiously ignored the crowd as he disappeared into the building.

'Terrible,' the woman repeated. 'Isn't it?'

'It is indeed,' Dom agreed. There was no reason to linger so he turned and walked away.

Leaving the playing fields, Carlyle let Cope lead him down Golders Green Road to a promising-looking establishment called the Imperial Café. According to its advertising, the Imperial was the oldest eatery in the neighbourhood. Taking a table by the window, Carlyle scanned the menu with exaggerated care. After some thought, he ordered an omelette and a flat white. Cope restricted herself to a cup of peppermint tea.

'So,' she asked, while they waited for their order, 'who is Madam Monica?'

'Well . . .' Carlyle was not in the mood to go into the details, especially not ahead of receiving his food, so he restricted himself to an anodyne '. . . she was, er, a friend of his.'

Cope raised an eyebrow. 'Girlfriend?'

'Kind of, I suppose.'

She looked at him blankly.

'It was a kind of on-off thing,' he wittered. 'You know how fluid relationships can be these days.'

'Tell me about it,' said Cope, with feeling. 'My ex-husband—'

'What can you tell me about the Belgians?' Carlyle asked, not wishing to get into another discussion about her domestic situation.

'The Belgians. Well . . .' taking a moment to compose herself, Cope looked like a student preparing for her viva '. . . Belgium is, like, the home of the sport. Modern pigeon racing originated there in the mid-nineteenth century. Pigeons were specially bred for endurance races called *voyageurs*. The sport came to Britain a few years later. It gained a boost when King Leopold the Second gave some breeding stock to the British royal family.' Cope paused to smile at a waitress who had arrived at the table with their drinks. 'The sport reached a peak of popularity in the early twentieth century. In terms of the number of people breeding and racing pigeons, it has been in continuous decline since after the Second World War. The irony is that, now, like I said, it's become a big business – there's more money washing around the sport than ever before. And the best birds are big stars.'

Carlyle looked at her doubtfully.

'In that world, anyway. Last year, a racing pigeon called Ronaldo – after the football player – was sold to a Korean businessman for more than half a million pounds.'

Carlyle took a sip of his coffee and smiled. Sharp and hot, it was just how he liked it. 'How can a pigeon possibly be worth anything like that?'

'A combination of prize money, gambling and stud fees,' Cope explained. 'The cash involved in the sport inevitably brings problems such as theft from breeders and racketeering. Not to mention doping. Six racing pigeons from Belgium failed random drugs tests after a race organized by Eric earlier in the year. They tested positive for amphetamines and cocaine. When they were disqualified, it was thought that one betting syndicate in the Far East lost something like two million euros.'

Carlyle let out a low whistle.

'That's a fairly rough estimate. But the sums that get wagered on races is pretty staggering. People in China, Korea, Taiwan, India – all over the place – are gambling on this stuff. A lot in Europe too, and some in North America. And there is always someone trying to fix the result, just like in cricket matches or football.'

Carlyle's food arrived. He added some ketchup, then grabbed his knife and fork. 'So where does Furlong fit into all this?' he asked, and attacked his omelette.

'According to Eric, Furlong was quite friendly with a guy called Bram Deroo. And he's done some bits of work here and there for Elke Poosen.'

Deroo and Poosen. Those were the names Eric Rayner had mentioned in the park.

'Deroo is a modestly successful trainer from Arendonk,' Cope continued, 'a town near Antwerp. Small fry. Very well connected within the racing world but, by all accounts, a bit of a trainspotter.'

'Or birdspotter,' Carlyle quipped.

'Quite.' Cope groaned. 'Deroo might not know what day it is but he can tell you who won the Mons Classic in 1934.'

Carlyle looked at her blankly.

'It's one of the leading races in the calendar,' Cope explained. 'Been going since 1902. It attracted racers from twenty-seven countries last year.'

'Good to know,' the inspector responded. He could feel his brain silting up with pigeon-related trivia.

'The point is,' said Cope, cutting to the chase, 'Deroo has never been on the radar of either the BSPCA – the Belgian Society for the Prevention of Cruelty to Animals – or of local law enforcement. By all accounts, he's the kind of guy who genuinely loves his birds. The idea that he could be involved in the destruction of Furlong's pigeons seems a stretch.'

'What about the other one?'

'Elke Poosen is more interesting. She's the daughter of a guy called Eden Poosen, one of Belgium's most notorious gangsters. He was shot dead outside a Brussels restaurant five years ago. Despite having two older brothers, Elke took over the family firm. She's made a good job of running things, with a style that is described as "no nonsense".'

Clearing his plate, Carlyle stifled a burp. 'Has she got a record?'

'No.' Politely ignoring the inspector's grievous lapse in manners, Cope took a sip of her tea. 'One of the brothers is currently inside. He's doing six years for fracturing a man's skull in a brawl outside a nightclub. And the mother is under investigation over her tax returns.'

'Nice family.'

'Elke herself has never been in any trouble. Over the last few years she has been carefully cultivating a persona as a respectable businesswoman. She's even done some promotional work for the Antwerp Chamber of Commerce. From what I understand, though, it's all a bit of a façade. The pigeon racing is quite an important part of the family business, providing much of their cash-flow for everything from drugs to dodgy diamonds and people-trafficking.'

Picking up a napkin, the inspector dabbed at the corner of his mouth. 'And what kind of work did Furlong do for Poosen?'

'I don't know, sorry. According to Eric, Furlong mentioned it a few times but never went into any details.'

'Don't worry. You've come up with a hell of a lot. How did you find all this stuff out?'

'Aside from Eric, I have my own contacts.' She grinned. 'I was aware of the Belgian connection from the previous investigation. Eric mentioned it again when we were arranging your meeting, so I made a few calls.'

'Well done.' Carlyle hoped that that hadn't come across as too patronizing. 'Do you think Furlong was doping his birds?'

'If he was,' Cope laughed, 'he was giving them downers. He hadn't had a top-three finish in any race for over a year. Eric says it was his worst run for a long time.'

'Maybe he was throwing races,' Carlyle mused.

'Maybe.' Cope was clearly unconvinced. 'But you just don't get the impression that he would be the kind of guy to dope at all.'

'True.'

'I did find out something else that might be interesting, though.'

Maybe I should just let you run this investigation, Carlyle mused.

'The Belgians are here.'

He looked around the almost deserted café. 'In Golders Green?'

'No.' Leaning forward, she gave him a playful punch on the arm. 'Well, not as far as I know. But they're in the country. According to Border Control, Deroo arrived in the UK a week ago on a flight into City Airport. According to their records, he's still here.'

'And Poosen?'

'She actually lives here. She has a house in Chelsea.'

'Nice.' Finishing his coffee, he got to his feet. 'Thanks for lunch.'

'No problem.' Cope smiled. 'What are you going to do now?'

'I think I'll go and see how the other half live.'

'These days, they don't call them "the other half", they call them "the one per cent".'

'That's progress, I suppose.' He hesitated, then added: 'Want to come?'

'I'd love to but I've got to go and investigate a report of a man supposedly keeping a private zoo at his house in Arnos Grove.'

A number of questions popped into Carlyle's head. He didn't ask any of them. Instead his phone started to ring. Pleased at actually catching a call for once, he hit receive.

'Hello?'

'We've got a problem.'

Carlyle pulled open the door and walked out onto the street as he listened to Dom explain what had happened. 'Where are you?'

'Sitting in a juice bar across the road from Bob's club, watching the action, such as it is.' Dom noisily sucked something through a straw.

Carlyle grimaced at the sound effects. 'Are you sure about this?'

'Yeah. The first story has just appeared online.' Dom read aloud: '"Harry Cummins, thirty-four, celebrity club owner was found gunned down today in his office."'

'All right, all right,' Carlyle snapped. 'I get the picture. And he was the guy you were getting Dad's, er, medicine from?'

'Yeah. Harry and I go back quite a way. He was a good customer of mine when I was still in the dope business. When I decided to get out, I hooked him up directly with some of my suppliers. In effect, Harry took over a small bit of my operation. It was only ever a sideline for him, but it fitted in with what he liked to call his more-for-more business strategy.'

'His what?' Carlyle had no idea where he was going. Stopping, he tried to get his bearings.

'He has a strategy called "more for more" – hook in the rich clients and basically provide them with a broader range of services. Not exactly rocket science, but sensible enough.'

'I thought he was just a bloody pimp.' Spotting a number thirteen coming towards him, Carlyle dashed across the road and ran to the bus stop.

'A pimp who went to business school,' Dom observed. 'As well as the drugs, he had plans to expand into cars, holidays, insurance. You name it, Harry would try to flog it. Crossselling. Everybody does it.'

'A right little Richard Branson.' Flagging down the bus, the inspector fumbled for his Oyster card.

'I'm not sure whether Mr Branson would appreciate the comparison.' Dom chuckled. 'Then again, neither would Harry – he saw himself as more of a Stringer Bell-type character.'

'In his dreams.'

'At least he wasn't responsible for *Tubular Bells*.'

'Fair point.' As the bus rolled to a halt, the doors opened and Carlyle jumped on. Finding the lower deck full, he headed upstairs. 'So someone whacked him, eh?' A thought popped into his head as he slumped into a seat. 'It wasn't Umar, was it?'

'I don't think so. I saw your ex-partner arrive not so long ago.'

'He wasn't my partner,' Carlyle huffed. 'He was my sergeant.'

'One of many.'

'One of several.' When Umar had left the force, Carlyle had been relieved more than anything. What had started out as a glittering career had tailed off badly, to the point where Umar had had to quit before he was sacked. Taking a job with a chancer like Harry Cummins had just been a new low on his CV.

'He wasn't in handcuffs or anything. They're probably interviewing him at the moment, but it looked like he'd turned up under his own steam.'

Carlyle looked on as the bus trundled down Finchley Road. At this rate, he could expect to get back to Central London the day after tomorrow. 'Assuming he doesn't get nicked, he'll be looking for a new job.'

'I suppose so.'

Umar could look after himself. Carlyle returned to the matter in hand. 'In terms of getting some more stuff, what do we do now?'

'Don't worry about that. I'll sort something out. It'll have to be after I get back from holiday, though.'

Carlyle grimaced. How much longer would Alexander's existing supply last? He would have to go and check on his dad as soon as possible. 'Sure. Thanks for giving me the heads-up.'

'No worries.'

A further problem occurred to Carlyle. 'There's nothing that can tie you to Harry, is there?'

'Don't worry,' Dom replied, 'I knew Harry but so did lots of people. The bloke could network for England. What he considered his inner circle of close personal friends would fill the whole of Wembley Stadium. If the police ever get round to talking to the likes of me it's gonna be one of the longest investigations in recorded history.'

Carlyle lowered his voice. 'But the stuff?'

'It's cool,' Dom reassured him. 'It's not like I sent him an order on email.'

'No, I suppose not. Presumably it was in his office when he was shot, though? Seeing as you were going over there to pick it up.'

'Maybe whoever offed him nicked it.'

'Maybe.'

'Even if the cops find it they won't have any idea who it was for. Harry could have been selling to his girls or to the punters – or he might have been keeping it for his personal use. When you start thinking about it, there are loads of different possibilities.'

'Did he have a habit?'

'Harry liked to party.' Dom laughed. 'He was what I'd call a social user – he'd take whatever was going around at the time.'

'Doesn't sound like the kind of guy who was likely to sit at home sucking heroin sweeties,' Carlyle observed.

'Stranger things have happened,' Dom countered. 'Who knows what people get up to on their own, behind closed doors? The point is that there will be no comeback to us. It just means a bit of a delay in getting your dad sorted. Tell Alexander to sit tight and I promise I'll deal with it as soon as I get back.'

TWENTY

Inspector Ronnie Score looked at the scruff-bag sitting opposite him and shook his head. Apparently the bloke used to be a cop. And not so long ago, either. Something had clearly gone badly wrong with *that* story. The guy looked like he'd slept in a hedge. He needed a shave too. The dark rings under his eyes added to the overall impression of a man who needed to slow the fuck down. And then there were the hands.

Score had noticed the cuts on the guy's knuckles almost immediately. For the moment, however, he decided not to go there. There were various other lines of enquiry to pursue first. 'Your alibi,' he said slowly, 'is that you were shagging the victim's girlfriend at the time of the murder. Is that correct?'

'That's right.' Sitting back in his chair, Umar Sligo tried not to look too smug about it. He guessed that the inspector – middle-aged, gone to seed – probably couldn't remember the last time he'd got laid. As Score scribbled away in a small spiral notebook, Umar quickly built up a mental picture of the man in front of him: twenty years on the job, semi-detached house in Deptford, two kids, fifty-fifty whether he was divorced. Driving a second-hand Mondeo. West Ham fan, or maybe Spurs. In short, a completely bog-standard cop. Not someone who was ever going to cause Umar any problems.

On the other hand, this was no time to come across as complacent or uncooperative. Not with your boss slumped across his desk upstairs, minus the most important parts of his face.

Score looked up from his notebook. 'Name?'

Umar frowned. 'I just told you.'

'*Girlfriend*'s name.'

'Zoë Connors.'

'And where is Ms Connors right now?'

'In bed, most likely, still asleep.' Umar failed to stifle a yawn. 'Where I should be.' Leaving Infinity, he and Zoë had spent the rest of the night drinking mojitos in a bar in Soho. After dropping her off, he had finally made it home at just after three in the morning. Despite lack of sleep, his hangover was surprisingly benign. The world was fuzzy but manageable.

Score glanced at his watch. 'I suppose this is early for you?'

'Yeah.' Umar gestured at the mounds of paperwork on his desk. 'But I've got a lot of work on at the moment.'

'Gimme the girlfriend's address.'

Umar mentioned a recently built block of flats, half a mile away from the club. 'Don't send anyone round to wake her up. There's no point – she'll be here in an hour or so.'

'Protocol.' Score sniffed. Half turning in his chair, he bellowed, 'Newman . . . NEWMAN.'

After a few moments, a constable appeared in the doorway. 'Yes, sir?'

'The girlfriend.' Score repeated the address. 'Name is Zoë Connors. Go and pick her up.'

'Sure thing.'

'She has one of the penthouses,' Umar chipped in. 'It's got its own entrance, round the side of the building.'

'Thanks.'

'Bring her back here,' Score instructed. 'I'll speak to her before we go and look at the flat.'

PC Newman disappeared down the stairs.

Score looked at Umar. 'Penthouse, eh? Nice.'

'It's Harry's, actually.'

Score raised an eyebrow. 'So he was shacked up with her?'

'Well, he usually crashed at Zoë's when he was in London.' Umar pointed to the ceiling. 'Sometimes he would stay here – we have some rooms upstairs. And then he has a house in Gloucestershire, where his wife lives.'

'A wife.' Score kept scribbling.

'Yeah. Victoria. I've only met her a couple of times.'

'Kids?'

'No. Victoria prefers horses, apparently.'

Score raised an eyebrow.

'She spends most of her time riding. Doesn't like coming up to London. And that suited Harry, as you can imagine.'

'Hm.' Score rubbed his chin. 'So they had a bit of a complicated relationship, then?'

'Aren't all marriages complicated? I don't think she would have had him shot, if that's what you mean. As long as Harry paid the bills, and the horses were well looked after, Vicky was pretty happy. And Harry always made sure those bills were paid on time. He was shelling out something like ten grand a month.'

Score wrote '10' in his book and drew a circle round it. 'How do you know all this?'

'It wasn't any big secret. Harry mentioned it, now and then.'

Score contemplated the paperwork on the desk. 'Do you do the books?'

'No, no,' Umar said hastily. 'Harry has an accountant. He's off walking in the Atacama Desert at the moment.'

Score looked at him blankly.

'It's in Chile. He's on a career break.'

'We'll track him down.'

Good luck with that, Umar thought. 'You can try.'

'Back to your alibi.' Score gestured at Umar's hands. 'How did you get those scratches on your hands?'

'Eh?' Umar stared at the back of his hands. 'I was doing some, erm, DIY. Cleaning a bit of brickwork.' He gave a rueful smile. 'I should have worn gloves. It's not really my thing.'

134

Score looked at him doubtfully. 'So you weren't in a fight, then?'

A momentary look of exasperation passed across Umar's face. 'No. And even if I had been, so what? Harry was shot, not beaten up.' He held up both hands. 'Feel free to test me for gunshot residue.'

'We will,' said Score, stiffly, knowing that it would be far too late: any evidence would long since have been washed away.

'Look,' Umar groaned, 'I have a perfectly good alibi. Zoë will back it up. And there's always the CCTV at the gym.' Although, fortunately, none in the changing rooms.

'What time did you leave?'

'The gym? Not sure. Probably around nine thirty. We went just up the road to Toad Hall, a bar on Lexington Street. I paid the bill with my credit card around one in the morning. When we came out, I lit up a smoke and one of the bouncers tried to chat up Zoë. He'll remember her.' He paused to scratch at his Led Zeppelin T-shirt. 'At least, he'll remember her tits, the dirty bastard.'

'Pretty girl, is she?'

'What do you think? Harry wouldn't have been going out with her if she was a dog. The point is we're completely track-able all night. After the club, we got in a cab. I dropped her at her place and took it on home. I paid the fare with my credit card, too. Unless Harry was killed in the middle of the night – in which case, I would imagine, he wouldn't have been in his office – we're in the clear.'

'It'll all need to be checked.' Score knew he was right but was reluctant to concede the point.

'Check away. We're not hiding anything. I know how this works. I was a cop myself.'

'You could have got someone to do it for you.'

Umar conceded the point with a shrug. 'But I didn't. He was an okay guy. I had no motive to want to see Harry dead.'

'Apart from shagging his girlfriend.'

'That's hardly a motive,' Umar argued. 'I mean, I didn't need him to be dead to do that.'

'Been going on a long time, had it?'

'No, not really.'

'What if he'd found out?'

'To be honest?'

'Why not? Give it a go.'

'I don't think Harry would have been too bothered. Harry's girlfriends all had a life expectancy of about three months. Zoë was already over that time limit. It was only a matter of time before he moved on.'

'Maybe she was different. Maybe she was *the one*. Maybe Mr Cummins was in love.'

Umar shook his head. 'Harry has – I mean he *had* an extreme case of Attention Deficit Disorder when it came to girls. He was like a kid in a sweetshop. Always craving the next sugar rush. Anyway, even if he was in love, what would that have to do with him getting killed?'

'You can see how it would have pissed off his wife, for a start.'

'She didn't care. Separate lives. As long as the money flowed, Harry could do what he liked.'

'What if she thought a divorce might be looming?' Score hypothesized. 'A judge might not force Mr Cummins to keep up with the payments.'

'Vicky doesn't have any money. But she has good genes. Her mother was a duchess or something. Being married to her gives you an entrée into some very special social circles. Harry would never have passed that up. I think he would even have stopped shagging around if Vicky had put her foot down. But, like I said, she just didn't care. I think she felt it saved her a job.'

'I'll have to go and talk to her,' Score said.

'Suit yourself.' Umar shrugged. 'It's a long way to go.'

'I'll need the address.'

'We'll have it somewhere.'

'If it wasn't the wife, what about the girlfriend? Zoë could have got someone to do it for her.'

The guy was investigating by numbers. Umar shook his head. 'Hardly. I think she actually quite liked Harry.'

'Funny way of showing it,' Score observed.

'Well, I think if she thought Harry would leave his wife, she would have taken a different attitude to fucking the help.'

'I.e. you.'

Umar smiled. 'I.e. me.'

'So, if it wasn't the wife and it wasn't the girlfriend . . .'

'And it wasn't me.'

'. . . and it wasn't you, who *do* you think might have had cause to shoot your boss in the kisser?'

In the kisser? 'As you can imagine, I've been giving the matter some thought over the last hour or so.'

'And?' Score asked eagerly, pen poised over his notebook.

'And,' Umar smirked, 'I really have no idea.'

'No?'

'No.' Standing his ground, Umar could see the light in Score's eyes slowly extinguishing. He doesn't know where else to take this, he thought. Conscious of a residual feeling of professional curiosity, he asked, 'Got any clues, so far?'

'I'm not going to discuss that with you,' Score said gruffly. 'You're not a cop now.'

'Fair enough,' said Umar, amiably, refusing to take offence.

'Where were you based, anyway?'

'Charing Cross. I worked with a guy called John Carlyle. Know him?'

Score thought about it for a few moments. 'No. The name sounds familiar but I haven't worked with him. I don't think so anyway.'

'Well,' Umar yawned, 'you haven't missed much.'

'Didn't get on, eh?'

137

'You could say that.' Umar's verdict on his erstwhile boss was as short as it was brutal. 'He's a complete tosser.'

Postponing his visit to Elke Poosen, Carlyle headed down to Fulham to see his father. Letting himself into the flat with his key, he stood in the hallway, listening for signs of life.

'Dad? . . . DAD.'

'Sssh.'

The inspector was startled by the appearance of a tall, dark-haired woman in the doorway of the living room.

The expression on her face was fierce. 'Alexander is sleeping,' she hissed. 'He was very tired. Don't wake him.'

'Okay.' Carlyle lowered his voice. 'But who are you?'

The woman folded her arms. 'Who are *you*?'

'I'm John. Alexander's son.'

'Ah, yes, the policeman.' The woman's face did not soften.

'That's right.'

'I am Stine.'

'Steen?'

'Yes.' The woman spelt it out. 'I am your father's death doula.' When Carlyle looked at her blankly, she gestured towards the kitchen. 'Maybe you would like a cup of tea. We should have a chat.'

Sitting at the kitchen table, Carlyle sipped his tea as he watched Stine Hassing munching a carrot. Dressed in black jeans and a grey V-neck sweater, she had her hair pulled back into a ponytail and wore minimal make-up. He guessed she was somewhere in her mid-thirties but it was difficult to tell. 'I didn't know you were coming.'

'Today is only my second day.' Resting her behind against the sink, Stine waved the carrot in the air. 'I'm not going to be here all the time, just coming in to visit Alexander and talk with him if he wants to talk.' Her English was good, although the accent was clear. 'Maybe we will go to the park. Take a short walk – if he can manage it. It is up to him.'

How much is this going to cost? Carlyle wondered. 'Are you from UCH?'

'UCH? The hospital? No. I work for a charity called Die Hard.' Taking a bite of the carrot, she crunched it noisily.

'Die Hard? A pun on the movie name?'

'Funny, no?'

'Seems a bit, I dunno, frivolous.'

'It is a joke, yes, but also deadly serious. It is about attitude.' She pointed at Carlyle with the remains of the carrot. 'How do you want to die?'

'Well . . .' Carlyle let his gaze drift out of the window. From somewhere above the clouds came the sound of a jumbo jet making its descent towards Heathrow. 'It's not something I've given a lot of thought to, to be honest.'

'Well, you should. You have to know yourself, the type of person you are. Do you want to slip away, sick, scared and alone? Or do you want to walk into death, head held high?'

Carlyle chuckled nervously. 'Are those the only options?'

'Pretty much. Your father came to Die Hard because he wanted to go out with a smile on his face.' She swatted away his doubtful look. 'Alexander came to us because he wants to die alive, rather than die dying, stuck in a hospital bed.'

'That sounds reasonable,' Carlyle conceded.

'Good.' Stine offered him a measured smile. 'I am here to help him do that.'

'And, er, what about the cost?'

'The charity pays for the service,' Stine explained, 'but if you can help, they always need donations.'

'Okay.' Carlyle took another slurp of his tea.

'They are pioneering the use of death doulas in England,' she continued. 'The UK is quite backward when it comes to dealing with death. In other countries, it is important that people can stay in their homes to die, supported by family and the local community. In Denmark, for example, where I come from, death doulas are very common. Here they are quite new. The whole thing is seen as some great new idea. It takes time for people to get comfortable with it. Really, the NHS should be providing them.'

Carlyle didn't have anything to contribute to that particular debate. 'You're Danish?'

'I grew up in a place called Randers, north of Aarhus.'

'Ah.' Carlyle had no idea of the geography.

'I qualified as a nurse in Silkeborg and came to London about fifteen years ago.' She blushed slightly. 'I was chasing a boy. You know how it is.'

'Yes.'

'That seems a long time ago now. The boy went to Thailand. I stayed in London and became a death doula.'

'Strange job to choose,' Carlyle ventured.

'I didn't choose it. It chose me. A friend of mine was diagnosed with a brain tumour. Her daughter had a young baby and a demanding job, so she couldn't take on the role of live-in carer. I moved in with my friend until she passed away. After that, I got different jobs by word of mouth. I have been to see people all over the country – Edinburgh, Belfast and Norwich.'

'And Fulham.'

'Fulham is perfect for me. I have a flat in Acton, so it is not so far away.'

'Isn't the job a bit depressing?'

'No, why should it be?'

'Well,' Carlyle stammered, 'death and all that. It's a bit of a bugger, isn't it?'

'Are you scared of death?'

'Not scared, maybe, but I'll be pissed off when it comes, I suppose.'

'I am relaxed about death because I can't know it until it happens. And then it will completely pass me by. The idea that, one day, I won't be here any longer is rather unsettling. But then again, I haven't always existed – where was I in 1947? Or 1965? My not being here is the normal state of affairs.'

'That's one way to look at it.'

'I think it's the best way to look at it. When people are afraid, I walk with them directly into the state of fear. Almost always, the fear is not about death itself, but about something else.'

Carlyle wondered if his father was scared. He didn't dare ask. He gestured towards the bedroom. 'How's he doing?'

'Very well,' Stine said. 'Physically, he's in pretty amazing shape. For the moment, he still has quite a bit of mobility and independence. Emotionally, he is in a good place. He has a sense that all the loose ends have been tied up. Your mother pre-deceased him and he feels that you are established in your job and happy at home. He says that your wife is a strong woman, someone who can keep you running on the right lines. His job is done and he is happy.'

Christ, Carlyle thought, you got all this from one visit?

Stine sensed his discomfort. 'People like to talk. That's an important part of why I'm here. Maybe these are things that he feels unable to talk to you about.'

You can say that again.

'Your father is in a good place in here,' she tapped the side of her head with an index finger, 'but he still needs to be able to talk to someone about it. In that sense, I am a kind of middle-man between him and God.'

'Thank you.' Getting to his feet, the inspector took a final mouthful of tea. 'Well, I need to get back to work. I'll come and see him, erm, later on.'

'One thing, just before you go.'

'Yes?'

Opening a cupboard door, Stine pulled out a small transparent plastic bag. 'What are these?'

Carlyle blinked as he looked at the last of Dom's tablets. 'Erm, I'm not really sure.' Cursing his father, he took the bag, lifting it in front of his face as he went through the pantomime of carefully inspecting its contents. 'Part of Dad's prescription?'

'I don't think so.' Stine looked at him suspiciously. 'I should probably report them.' She moved to take the bag back, but Carlyle shoved it quickly into his pocket.

'Don't worry,' he said hastily. 'I'll talk to him about it. If there's a problem, I can go and see his doctor.' He took a backward step towards the door.

Stine eyed him coolly. 'Your father wants to go out fighting,' she insisted, 'not doped up to the eyeballs.'

Does he? Carlyle turned and headed for the door. We'll see.

TWENTY-ONE

The distance between Alexander Carlyle's shabby council flat and Elke Poosen's stucco-fronted Georgian pile was just under 1.3 miles and just over £7.5 million. The walk took Carlyle less than thirty minutes, during which time he went through the to-do list in his head, prioritizing the different things he had to achieve over the next few days. It was a depressingly long list.

Arriving in the rarefied atmosphere of SW3, the inspector felt like an outsider in his own city. In the 1960s and 1970s Gertrude Street, located between King's Road and Fulham Road, was a sleepy backwater, home to mid-ranking civil servants and TV producers. Half a century later, it lay at the heart of an international real-estate ghetto, with prices pushed into the stratosphere. Neighbouring postcodes – SW7, SW10, SW5, W8 – were going the same way. Once Alexander kicked the bucket, SW6 would be off-limits to his son, too. The thought depressed him, although he was well aware that there was nothing he or anyone else could do about it. It was a question of market forces, pure and simple, an unfortunate consequence of the rise of London as a 'world city'.

Number sixty-two Gertrude Street, set back five yards from the road, looked clean, fresh and, in keeping with its immediate neighbours, essentially unlived in. Carlyle approached the front door up a small set of steps and rang the bell. As he waited for a reply, he realized how hungry he was: he hadn't eaten anything since his visit with Fiona Cope to the Imperial Café.

Dreaming of a filled roll, Carlyle gave the bell a second, more insistent ring. The door finally clicked open, just as he was about to skip down the steps, and he was confronted by an aged crone with a face like a walnut. Struggling to reach a height of five feet, the woman looked up at him suspiciously from behind a pair of tortoiseshell-framed glasses. Dressed in a knee-length skirt and a beige sweater, she looked as if she could have been anything north of seventy-five. Momentarily distracted by the shocking red tint in her thinning hair, Carlyle stood like a statue, mouth agape.

'Yes?'

'Elke Poosen?' The creature in front of him was not at all what he had expected.

The woman shook her head. 'She's not in.' Her tone was firm and her voice carried no hint of a foreign accent.

'So who are you?' the inspector asked.

'Who are *you*?' The woman held the door tightly, ready to slam it in his face should he try to cross the threshold.

'Police.'

If his answer offered any reassurance, she didn't let it show. On the other hand, she didn't seem very surprised, either. 'Do you have any identification?'

Carlyle retrieved his ID and brought it up in front of the woman's face. She squinted at it for a couple of seconds, then gave a nod of assent.

'I need to speak to Ms Poosen.'

'Mrs Lamoot,' the woman corrected him. 'She uses her married name when she's over here.'

'Lam—?'

'Lamoot. The husband's family is from Ostend.'

Shoving his warrant card back into his pocket, Carlyle reverted to his original question. 'Who are you?'

The woman's eyes narrowed. 'Why do you want to know?'

'I'm a policeman,' Carlyle reminded her. 'I always want to know who I'm talking to.'

144

'Nosy, are you?'

'Not at all,' Carlyle countered, 'just a professional interest. It's a kind of protocol thing.'

'Am I in some kind of trouble?'

'Not unless you know something I don't.' Carlyle felt pleased with himself for not losing his temper with this obtuse creature.

'I'm Marjorie Peterson, the Lamoots' housekeeper.' The woman pointed towards the basement. 'I live downstairs.'

'And Ms, erm, I mean Mrs Lamoot is not in at the moment?'

'That's what I said.'

'What about Mr Lamoot?'

'Everyone's out.'

'Apart from you.'

'Obviously.'

'Obviously.' Hands on hips, Carlyle looked up and down the street. 'When will Mr and Mrs Lamoot be back?'

'I'm not sure,' the woman replied. 'They are out of the country on business at the moment.' She saw the next question form on Carlyle's lips and quickly added, 'Separately. And, no, I don't know how to get in touch with them. I can take a message, though.'

Carlyle fished a business card out of his wallet and handed it to the woman. 'When Mrs Lamoot gets home, perhaps you could ask her to give me a call.'

The housekeeper took the card, inspecting it carefully. 'What's it about?'

'I'm just after some help with one of my investigations,' Carlyle replied. 'It's nothing too important. I'd appreciate it, though, if she could give me a call.'

'Makes a change,' the woman muttered. 'Usually it's *him* that gets visits from the police.'

Before Carlyle could ask what she meant, the woman took a step backwards and slammed the door.

Walking down the street, searching for a café, Carlyle called Susan Phillips. The pathologist picked up on the third ring.

'Great timing,' she trilled. 'I've just finished with Richard Furlong. You'll never believe what I found in his stomach.'

Not wishing to spoil her cheery mood, Carlyle let Phillips explain about Furlong's unusual breakfast.

'That must have been his last meal, just before he jumped to his death. Isn't that disgusting?'

'It's certainly different,' Carlyle agreed.

'I've never come across anything like it. Have you?'

'Can't say that I have.'

'I mean, people eat all kinds of things. But that? Come on.'

'I'm sure there's some kind of explanation for it.' Focused on the needs of his own stomach, Carlyle didn't want to have to explain about Madam Monica's mail-order service right now. 'Maybe he was on a special diet or something.'

'Yeah, yeah. Clearly, the guy wasn't right in the head.'

Carlyle chuckled. 'I didn't know your area of competence extended that far.'

'My area of competence, as you put it, Inspector, extends far and wide. Anyway, you don't exactly have to be Saul Levine to know weird when you see it.'

'I suppose not.' Carlyle had no idea who Saul Levine was but didn't feel the need to go down that particular rabbit hole. 'Apart from the unusual contents of his stomach, what else did you find?'

'Pretty much what you'd expect.' Phillips outlined a series of injuries consistent with jumping out of a high window. 'The funny thing was, landing on the car, he might have survived but then it ran him over.'

'It's not cars that kill people,' Carlyle opined, 'it's people that kill people.'

'Insightful as always,' Phillips said sarcastically. 'The tox report shows he wasn't under the influence of drugs or anything like that. It looks like he just jumped.'

'Okay. Thanks.'

'Was that what you were ringing for?'

'Yes, but there was something else, too.'

Phillips laughed. 'With you, John, there is always something else.'

'At least I'm consistent.'

'Out with it then. What're you after now?' She listened patiently while he explained what he wanted, then exclaimed, 'Bloody hell. We're really pushing back the boundaries on this one, aren't we? I've never done anything like that before.'

'Can you do it?'

'I don't see why not. As long as I can log it as part of the Furlong case it should be fine. I can't see how anyone will query it.' As they both knew only too well, every use of police facilities had to be logged, so that it could be justified to the bean counters, or they could leave themselves open to the possibility of a disciplinary hearing.

'Of course. If there's a problem, you can refer them back to me.'

'And you'll have to get me the bodies.'

'How many do you want?'

'Three or four. Get half a dozen if you can.'

'Half a dozen?'

'For comparative purposes.'

'Okay. Are you around tomorrow?'

'In the afternoon. Call me before you come over.'

'Will do. See you tomorrow.'

'Ciao.'

Ciao? Carlyle wondered if Phillips might have found herself an Italian boyfriend. The last time he had asked, she had been dating a heart surgeon from Reading but the life expectancy of her boyfriends was pretty much on a par with that of a fruit fly. And the older she got, the faster she seemed to get through them. It was quite exhausting just thinking about it. Pushing thoughts of his colleague's love life to the back of his mind, Carlyle saw he was standing outside an agreeable-looking establishment called Caffè Concerto.

How did I get here? Peering at the menu in the window, he decided it was a matter of instinct.

Just like a homing pigeon.

After an hour with Inspector Ronald Score, Umar felt he needed a drink. He had some serious thinking to do. Having your boss gunned down was a fairly effective way of receiving your P45. Bob's remained a crime scene, closed for the foreseeable future. When the club did reopen, it would most likely be under new management. Umar calculated that it would take Victoria Dalby-Cummins's lawyers about a week to dismember Harry's crumbling business empire, selling off the property and closing down the rest. He was fairly sure that Vicky knew all about Harry's pimping. However, if she had been happy to look the other way when her errant husband was alive, taking over the reins now that the little sod had gone to the great whorehouse in the sky was another matter entirely. The family business had been falling apart even before the shooting. Now it would disintegrate, leaving Umar out of a job.

Umar exited the building by a fire door. Walking down the alley at the back, the phone in his pocket started to ring. He checked the screen: Zoë. 'Not now,' he mumbled. Maybe this was the moment for a clean break from everything and everyone. Stuffing his hands into his jacket pockets, he marched on, head bowed.

Moving on autopilot, he arrived at the Summer Palace, a rival club, no wiser about his future plans but at least having reduced his conversation with Score to a suitably dim memory. Inside, the gloom of the large room was cool and inviting. Nodding warily at Chris, the strip club's resident eighteen-stone bouncer, he walked over to the bar. The place was largely empty apart from a few drinkers, all of whom sat at different tables. On the wall opposite the bar, a pair of massive TV screens were showing highlights of a cricket match from some distant part of the world. At the far end of the room, a DJ sat behind a set of turntables, waiting for the action to start. Within an hour the place would be packed and the girls would be on and off the stage at regular fifteen-minute intervals, non-stop until two a.m.

The Palace had been Umar's preferred hangout for some time now. The company was better than at Bob's and the drinks were cheap.

'Hey, Nikki.'

Nikki Buckley looked up from the sink where she was washing dirty pint pots and gave him a wary smile. 'You've got quite a nerve, showing up here.' She tried to give him a stern look but the tone of her voice told him her heart wasn't in it.

Saying nothing, Umar slid onto a bar stool.

'You gonna be on your best behaviour tonight? I can't have a repeat of what happened last time.'

'No.' Umar couldn't remember much about the event in question. However, he had been assured that it had involved a physical altercation with a couple of fellow drinkers, leading to his ejection from the premises. Adopting a suitably contrite look, Umar held up a hand. 'There won't be any problems. Scout's honour.'

'Like you were ever in the Scouts.' Nikki grinned.

'I sure was.' Umar knew that he had won her over. 'For four years. Looked good in the uniform – got all the badges, too.'

'Yeah, right.'

'Well, the woodworking one,' Umar lied. 'I definitely got that. And the social work one, too.'

Nikki looked at him suspiciously. 'They don't do a badge in social work. You just made that up.'

'It was social something or other. The point is, I could be a good Scout when I wanted to be. And tonight I want to be. I'll be no trouble, promise.'

'That better be right.' Nikki dried her hands on a dirty tea-towel. 'First sign of you misbehavin' and Chris will be feeling your collar, all right?'

149

'Fair enough,' Umar agreed. 'But there's absolutely no need to worry.'

'Glad to hear it. We've got enough problems with punters as it is.' Nikki gestured at the rows of bottles lined up behind her head. 'What can I get you? The usual?'

'Gimme a double Jameson's and a bottle of Rolling Rock.'

'Something to nibble?' Nikki waved a menu at him hopefully. Umar knew she had brought in a new chef to try to boost food sales. To no great surprise, the plan wasn't working. Apart from the occasional bag of crisps, the punters did not come to the Palace to eat.

'I'm good.'

Disappointed, Nikki placed the beer in front of him.

'Maybe later.' Umar checked her out as he chugged down his beer. Dressed in a pair of distressed jeans and a vintage Cure T-shirt, with a silver nose ring in the shape of a bone, Nikki looked like a stereotypical stroppy teenager. In her head, however, she was twenty-three going on forty-five. A physics graduate from Imperial College, she had started out in the Summer Palace as a dancer, in an attempt to keep her student loans under control. Finding that stripping wasn't for her, she quickly migrated behind the bar, rising to assistant manager within three weeks and manager within two months. Despite a blossoming career in the hospitality industry, her aim was to save enough cash so that she could go back to Imperial to do a PhD in thermodynamics.

With his eye for talent, Harry had tried to poach Nikki on several occasions. Every time she turned him down, refusing to go to work at Bob's on the grounds that its owner was 'a dirty pimping bastard'. Umar thought that was fair enough. After all, everyone has their principles. He deeply regretted never having seen Nikki perform on the Palace's stage, just as he regretted her brusque rebuff the one time he had tried to chat her up. After laughing harshly, she had dismissed his approach

150

with a curt 'I don't date old men.' His pride had recovered – eventually – but he had never asked again.

'New haircut?'

Nikki shook her strawberry blonde bob. 'You like it?'

'It makes you look even younger.'

'Thanks, *Dad*.'

Ouch.

'How's the family?'

Double ouch.

'Fine.'

'Have you seen Ella recently?'

'Yeah.' Time to move on to a different subject. 'Did you hear about Harry?'

'Yeah.' Nikki reached for a glass. 'Is it true that someone shot his face off?'

'Apparently.'

'That must have been a hell of a shock.'

'It was for Harry, I would imagine,' Umar deadpanned, swigging his beer.

'For *you*, I mean.' Nikki laughed. 'I know the guy was a total bastard, but no one really deserves that, do they?'

'No, I suppose not.'

'I read about it online. Harry was trending on Twitter earlier.'

Ah, the joys of social media. A thought popped into Umar's head. 'Have the police been in here?'

'Here? No. Why?'

'Just wondering.'

'Not as far as I know, anyway. Then again, I only came on shift an hour ago.' Nikki found the whiskey bottle and proceeded to fill his glass almost to the rim. 'Here you go.'

'Thanks.' Umar tipped back his head and downed the spirit in a single gulp. 'Aaaaah.' He chased the whiskey down with the last of his beer. 'Same again, please.'

Nikki looked at him doubtfully. 'You're not going to get smashed, are you? You promised you'd behave.' She gestured

151

towards the door. 'I don't want Chris to have to throw you out again.'

'Don't worry. I'm just gonna have a couple of looseners.' Fishing a twenty-pound note out of his pocket, he placed it on the bar. 'One more round and the rest is a tip.'

Nikki's mood lightened at the sight of Adam Smith. 'Thanks, sweetie,' she beamed, coming up with another beer.

Umar pushed his glass across the bar. 'Don't need a fresh one.'

Nikki poured the whiskey – a slightly smaller measure this time – before picking up the twenty and quickly slipping it into her pocket.

Grinning, Umar glanced up at the security camera trained on the bar.

'Don't worry,' she whispered. 'I'm the one who checks the recording in the event of an issue. Anyway, everything gets wiped after twenty-four hours.'

'Good to know.'

'A girl's got to make a living, right?'

'Right.'

'You'll be pleased to hear that I made sure your last little transgression was not kept for posterity. Good job I'm the manager, or you'd have been banned for life.'

Umar saluted her with his beer bottle. 'God bless you.'

'Don't make me regret it.'

Nikki returned to her washing-up. Intending to keep to his self-imposed limit, Umar concentrated on drinking slowly. The Palace began to fill. After a while, Nikki slipped down to the far end of the bar to serve a group of students. The DJ cranked up some music and the first dancer appeared. A series of cheers went up from the students but Umar kept his back to the stage. He came to the Palace to drink, not to gawp at the naked women. And, anyway, the dancers reminded him too much of his wife.

TWENTY-TWO

The students seemed easily pleased and the first dancer left the stage to a round of applause.

'Very civilized in here, innit?'

Umar didn't look round as an older man dropped onto the stool next to him. 'I wondered how long it would take for you to turn up,' he said wearily.

'How's it going, Umar?'

'It's going.'

'Stressed?'

'Not really. I've seen a lot worse in my time.'

'I doubt that, son.' Vernon Holder raised a finger into the air to catch the attention of Nikki further down the bar. 'I seriously doubt it.'

Handing another customer his change, Nikki shuffled over. A blast of techno heralded the arrival of a new dancer on the stage.

'A gin and tonic, please, love.' Holder pointed towards one of the bottles on the top shelf. 'The good stuff, none of that unlabelled crap you smuggle in the back door.'

Nikki glowered at him but said nothing.

'And whatever my friend here is drinking.'

Umar held up his almost-empty bottle. 'I'm fine, thanks.'

'Don't be like that.' Holder placed a meaty paw on Umar's shoulder. 'Get him another beer,' he instructed Nikki. 'We have things to talk about.'

'Like what?' Turning in his seat, Umar looked past Holder as an Asian girl was hanging upside down from the solitary pole, her legs apart so that she was in a Y shape. Even at this distance, he could make out the pimples on her backside. Suddenly, his stomach lurched and he felt a bit sick.

'Business.'

'Is that what shooting Harry was? Business?'

'Don't be a prick, son. That was nothing to do with me.' Holder shifted his considerable weight on the stool, effectively blocking Umar's view of the stage.

'Yeah, right.'

'Have you spoken to the cops yet?'

'What do you think?' Umar groaned. 'I've only just got out of there.'

'Who do they think did it?'

'They haven't got a clue.'

Holder scratched his chin. 'Is that a professional opinion?'

'Yes. They're going through the basic drill. It's not like they're chasing down any particular leads.'

'Who interviewed you?'

'A muppet called Score.'

'Ronnie's a good lad. I've known him a long time. He'll sort it all out.'

So, Score was in Holder's pocket. Umar got the message immediately. The cop could leave him alone or cause him a world of pain, depending on Holder's wishes. The hand on his shoulder moved up to grip the back of his neck.

'Ow. Gerroff.' Umar tried to shake it away but Holder steadily increased the pressure, only letting go when Nikki reappeared in front of them with the drinks.

'You okay, Umar?'

'It's all fine.'

Nikki placed a glass containing a measure of gin in front of Holder, along with a small bottle of tonic water and another of Rolling Rock.

Holder looked at his drink with some dismay. 'Got any lemon?'

'Sorry.' Nikki gave him a sour smile.

'Bloody hell, what a dump.' He turned to Umar. 'Why do you come here?'

'I like it,' Umar replied, rubbing the back of his neck.

Holder turned back to Nikki. 'Loyal customer, eh?'

Nikki's eyes sought out Chris, still standing by the entrance. But the bouncer, happily chatting to one of the strippers, paid her no heed.

Holder waved a hand in front of her face in an attempt to regain her attention. 'Do you know who I am?'

Did you really just say that? Umar couldn't quite believe it.

'Yes, Mr Holder,' she said calmly, still looking towards the door. 'I know who you are.'

'Well, then, you should know I like to have some bloody lemon in my gin and tonic.' Fumbling in his trouser pocket, Holder came up with a fifty-pound note and slapped it on the bar. 'Do me a favour. Send someone round the corner to Tesco to get a couple of lemons. Can you do that?'

'Sure.' Nikki glanced at Umar, then scooped up the cash.

'Good girl. Keep the change.'

Umar watched Nikki's jaw flex as she bit down on her anger at being patronized by the old bastard. Slipping out from behind the bar, she went over and had a word with Chris, handing the bouncer Umar's twenty and sending him out to get the shopping. Meanwhile, the dancer he had been talking to pulled on an overcoat and slouched outside for a fag break.

Holder watched Nikki return to her station and begin serving a couple of lads who looked like they'd just walked in straight off a building site, which they probably had. 'Nice girl,' he said, 'if you like that kind of thing.'

Umar murmured something meaningless. The last thing he wanted to do was get into a conversation about girls with Vernon Holder – compared to Vernon, Harry had been a saint.

'Are you banging her?'

'Me? No.' Umar started on his third beer.

155

'Oh? I thought I heard something different.'

'We're . . .' Umar was about to say 'friends' but, realizing how lame that sounded, just said, 'We're not fucking.'

'That's quite a surprise.' Holder's tone was goading. 'You've got quite a reputation when it comes to shagging. I thought you'd chase anything in a skirt. Like Zoë Connors, for example.'

Umar stared at his beer. He had a nice buzz going on now and he could feel his self-control beginning to slip away. Gripping the bottle tightly he imagined jumping up from his seat and smashing Holder across the face with it. Holder was a big man, but out of shape. Once he went down he wouldn't put up much of a fight. In his mind's eye, Umar saw Holder rolling across the floor, trying to protect himself from a succession of kicks as their fellow drinkers watched with a mixture of amusement and disbelief.

And what would you do then, genius?

Lifting a hand, Holder snapped his fingers in front of Umar's face. 'Wake up.'

Instinctively, Umar tilted his head back and blinked.

'Do the cops know you're shagging Harry's girlfriend?'

'I told Score,' Umar admitted, 'but what's Zoë got to do with this?'

'Well, that depends. If I get what I need, you can both live happily ever after.' A leer spread across Holder's crumpled face. 'I might even be able to offer you both jobs in my rapidly expanding business empire.'

'Zoë's retired,' Umar said quickly.

'And what about you?'

'I'm considering my options.'

'Good for you. When you find you haven't got any, give me a call.'

'I don't think so.'

For a second, Holder looked genuinely put out by the rebuff. 'You worked for Harry,' he pointed out, 'why wouldn't you work for me?'

Because – despite being a sleazebag – Harry had never killed anyone.

Because Umar was sick of the downward spiral his life had taken since leaving Manchester.

Because everyone had their limits.

Appearing at Umar's shoulder, Chris dropped a string bag containing half a dozen lemons onto the bar.

'Good man.'

Nodding at Nikki, the bouncer retreated to his place by the door. Reaching over the bar, Holder grabbed a knife from next to the sink. Slicing open the bag, he pulled out the biggest lemon and cut in it half, then chopped one half into thin slices. He dropped a couple into his glass and added a small amount of tonic before taking a succession of careful sips. 'Worth waiting for,' he declared. 'It's always better with some lemon.'

Umar sullenly drank his beer. On stage, the Asian girl had finished her act and was remonstrating with a customer who had been taking pictures on his smartphone, in violation of the large sign behind the DJ that declared *No Photography Allowed*. The punter, egged on by his mates, was giving as good as he got until Chris appeared. With a minimum of fuss, the bouncer took possession of the phone and began deleting the offending images.

'What a place.' Holder finished his drink and signalled to Nikki that he needed a refill. 'The word "dump" doesn't begin to cover it.'

'You said you needed something,' Umar reminded him.

Holder's expression grew serious. 'Where's Isabel?'

'I don't know.' Trying to make the words sound as casual as possible, Umar glanced at the cuts on his knuckles.

'Bollocks, son.' Nikki placed a fresh glass in front of Holder and he resumed his lemon-cutting duties. 'Isabel worked for Harry. You saw her every day.'

'You know what it's like. Girls come and go.' Umar tried to remember what Harry had called it. 'Churn was always a problem at Bob's.'

'Isabel didn't just up and leave.'

Umar stared at his beer. 'No?'

'Don't try to play dumb.' Holder mimed clipping him around the ear. 'You know that Isabel was really working for me.'

Giving nothing away, Umar affected complete disinterest.

'She was my spy in the enemy camp. A smart kid. Sharp. Hard-working.' He gestured in the direction of Nikki. 'Like that one.'

'From what I recall, she seemed a nice girl,' Umar conceded. 'But I didn't know she was working for you.'

'You remember her?'

'Of course. She was from Bristol.'

'That's right.'

'Maybe she went back there, then.'

'She hasn't,' Holder said. 'Her mother hasn't heard from her for months.'

'Maybe she's hiding from you.'

'Why would she need to do that?' Holder seemed genuinely bemused by the question.

Because you're one of London's nastiest gangsters, Umar thought. 'Maybe she just wanted a change, a new start.' God knows, I do. 'Who knows what goes through the minds of these girls?'

'Isabel was smart,' Holder repeated. 'Tough. She wouldn't just run off.'

'Well, it looks like she did.' Umar tried to move the conversation on. 'What was she spying on Harry for?'

'Knowledge is power.' Holder chuckled. 'These days, it's better to fight with data than with guns or knives. Isabel was going to help me bring Harry to his knees without any of this messiness. If she hadn't gone missing, your boss might not have lost his head. The little ponce could have fucked off back to Somerset and played the country gent to his heart's content.'

'Gloucestershire,' Umar corrected him.

'Whatever. It's all the same, isn't it? Lots of sheep and berks in green wellies.'

'Why don't you just go and talk to Harry's missus?' Umar suggested. 'I'm sure she'll happily sell up in the blink of an eye.'

'Sell?' Holder frowned. 'What is there to sell? Harry's business isn't worth a penny. The club's losing money hand over fist and the girls, well, those that haven't jumped ship already will all be working for me by the end of the week, if not quicker.'

'So why are you hassling me?'

'Isabel,' Holder repeated. 'Where is she?'

'I don't know,' Umar insisted. 'Why is it such a big deal anyway?' A nasty smile spread across his face. 'Were you fucking her?' Still grinning, he watched Holder raise an arm. The fist seemed to appear in slow motion but he made no effort to duck out of the way. Taking it full in the face, he was lifted off his stool, landing on his backside.

Before he could get up, a hand grabbed the collar of his shirt. As Chris lifted him to his feet, Umar protested his innocence. 'I'm the victim here. He hit me.'

'Doesn't matter. The rule is no fights. As far as management is concerned, it doesn't matter who starts it. You gotta go.'

'Fair enough.' Umar held up a hand to signal that he would leave without a fuss. As he staggered towards the exit, he was vaguely conscious of Nikki shouting over the music that he was banned from the Palace until the end of time.

TWENTY-THREE

Standing by the kitchen sink, Helen sank her teeth into a slice of buttered toast and began chomping happily. Watching her eat, Carlyle's thoughts turned to Richard Furlong and his final breakfast.

'What's wrong?'

'Nothing, nothing.'

She waved the toast in front of his face. 'Want a bite?'

'Er, no.'

'Suit yourself.' Helen took another bite of her toast, washing it down with a mouthful of tea.

Trying to forget about the dead pigeon fancier, at least for a little while, Carlyle took a sip of his own green tea. 'I went over to see Dad earlier. There was this woman there.'

'Stine.'

'You know her?' Carlyle asked, surprised.

'I know *of* her.' Helen wiped some crumbs from the corner of her mouth. 'I haven't met her yet, but I'm looking forward to it. Alexander told me she had started her visits. She sounds a very interesting woman.'

'I suppose you could put it like that,' Carlyle grumped. 'And how did this pass me by?'

Pushing the last of the toast into her mouth, Helen shook her head. 'It didn't pass you by, sweetheart. It's more that you didn't want to know.'

Carlyle started to protest but thought better of it.

'When it comes to supplying your father with illegal pain relief,' Helen went on, 'you are the man. However, when it comes to dealing with his *emotional* needs, well, that's another matter entirely.'

'I'm a middle-aged man,' Carlyle remonstrated. 'I'm not supposed to be in touch with my emotional side.'

'Don't be such a dinosaur.' Grabbing another couple of slices of bread, Helen dropped them into the toaster. 'You should take a leaf out of your old man's book. I have to say I'm very impressed by the way Alexander's been handling all this.'

'Yeah,' Carlyle said drily. 'It turns out that he's quite the modern man when it comes to staring death in the face.'

'He's dealing with it brilliantly. He decided what kind of help he wanted and he went out and found it.'

'Danish,' the inspector commented, 'tall, slim and good-looking.'

Helen raised an eyebrow.

'Just an observation.'

'You liked her, then?' There was no edge in his wife's words.

'She was different. Then again, I've never met a death doula before. The stuff she talked about seemed sensible enough, if a bit banal.'

'Death is banal,' Helen mused. 'You've got to get your head round that.'

'The charity she works for is called Die Hard. They'll probably end up being sued by Bruce Willis.'

'It's a bit of a cheesy name but it looks like they do a good job. Anyway, why should we take all this stuff too seriously?'

Carlyle looked at his wife, wondering if she might have been snaffling a few of Dom's happy pills.

'Well,' Helen continued, 'it's not like you can do anything to change the final result.' The toast popped up, ending the conversation. Helen reached for the butter. 'Are you sure you don't want a slice?'

* * *

Ronnie Score had written so much that his notebook was almost full. His arm ached with cramp, he was dehydrated and he had a terrible headache. Apart from that, it had been a great day. Almost twenty interviews down and the inspector was no nearer to developing anything approaching a credible lead on the Harry Cummins shooting. The victim himself had long since been bagged up and taken up to Whipps Cross Hospital. Meanwhile, Score had been stuck in the same room since just after seven that morning. Massaging his wrist, he wondered about the chances of suing the Met for RSI.

'Are you okay?' The woman sitting on the opposite side of the table looked less than concerned.

'I'm fine.' Score was feeling sorry for himself. 'Just too much notetaking.' Conscious that he was staring at her too much, he focused on manipulating his hand. He had seen a lot of pretty girls today but this one was a class apart. The thought struck him that there was a touch of the Nicole Kidmans about her; Nicole Kidman twenty years ago, maybe twenty-five, back in the days when the actress made the occasional good film. 'It's been a very long day.'

'Want to leave it till tomorrow?' The woman was halfway out of her chair before he signalled for her to sit back down.

'We need to crack on. This is my golden time.' She looked at him, not understanding. 'The golden time is the first day – when we usually crack a case.'

'Usually?' The woman's amused expression was irksome.

'Sometimes.'

'And this time?'

'We're continuing with our enquiries.' Score gestured around the office he had commandeered from that total scrote Umar Sligo. 'My bosses will want to see progress before calling it a day. And this is your chance to help us.' He paused, giving her the chance to offer up some useful gobbet of information. When she didn't, he returned to the line of questioning he had been pursuing before his wrist had started hurting. 'This rumour,' he asked, 'it's true then, is it?'

'So what if I was?' Karen Jansen flicked back her head to get her fringe out of her eyes. She looked at the funny little cop with a mixture of amusement and disapproval. 'Since when has it been a crime to sleep with the boss?'

'Did he sleep with all the girls?'

Jansen played with her phone. 'One or two.'

'And that didn't bother you?'

'No – why should it bother me? If it had, I wouldn't have done it. It was just a bit of fun. Harry didn't take it seriously and I certainly didn't. I was under no illusions about him. After all, this is a man who was cheating on his *mistress*.'

'What does that make you, then?'

'It doesn't make me anything in particular. But Harry didn't "audition" all of the girls, if that's what you mean. He could be a creep but he wasn't that kind of creep.'

'Everybody loves you when you're dead,' Score observed drily.

'Harry would usually have a couple of girls on the go at any one time. No more than that.' A sly smile crossed her face. 'Apart from anything else, he didn't have the stamina.'

I can relate to that, Score thought sadly. 'So there was no one else he was, erm, seeing, apart from you and Zoë?'

Jansen looked him straight in the eye. 'I assume he probably slept with his wife now and again, when he was at home.'

'Yes.' Score realized he badly needed to get out of this room. The atmosphere had become increasingly fetid over the course of the day and he was beginning to find breathing difficult. On top of that, the woman's Australian accent was really annoying him. Worst of all, he was conscious that he smelt rather bad. He needed to get home, have a shower and a pizza, then jump into bed. A minimum of eight hours' sleep was essential if he was going to be able to face another day of this tomorrow.

His brain told him to stand up and start walking towards the door. His mouth, however, kept working. 'Why did you sleep with him?'

'What kind of a question is that?' Jansen's nose wrinkled in disgust. 'I told you, it was just a bit of fun. We liked to party. So what?'

Score shrugged. 'I'm just trying to get a handle on what was going on here.'

'How's that going to help you find Harry's killer?'

Score changed tack. 'What did Zoë think of you and her boyfriend?'

'About as much as Vicky thought of Zoë shagging her husband, I'd expect.'

'You've met Mrs Cummins?'

She shook her head. 'Nope. She made an appearance at a party once, but we were never introduced. I remember that Zoë was all over her that night, which I thought was a bit weird. That girl has a screw loose, though. She's been drinking too much kale juice.'

Score grunted in agreement. His interview with Zoë Connors had been one of the strangest he had ever conducted. The conversation had ranged from Greta Garbo to the dangers of eating deep-water fish. Harry hadn't been mentioned once. Maybe it was Zoë's way of dealing with the grief. Score was inclined to think that it had had more to do with the fact that the girl was a total nutcase.

'She's never been the same since she started eating like Gwyneth Paltrow,' Jansen observed. 'I don't think she's getting enough nutrients to her brain.' She made a mini-performance of checking the screen of her phone. 'Look, I've got to be somewhere in half an hour. Aren't you going to just ask me who killed Harry?'

Score's eyes narrowed. 'You know who killed Harry?'

'No,' Jansen grinned, 'but I've got a good idea who might be able to shed some light on the matter.'

TWENTY-FOUR

Halfway through his latest shift, Markus Siebeck began to contemplate sustenance. At this time of night, the fare on offer in the UCH staff canteen would be meagre, to say the least. On the other hand, if he stepped outside, the doctor knew he would probably end up with a kebab from the Dionysus takeaway close to Goodge Street tube station. By comparison, sticking to cigarettes and coffee would be the healthy option.

The sound of voices in the corridor caused him to look up. Sonia, the porter, was walking towards him, deep in conversation with a second woman, who was casually dressed in jeans, baseball shoes and a leather jacket. As the pair came closer, Sonia gave him a smile and pointed towards the room containing the patient still known only as 'Anne', or 'Miss X'. 'Any change?'

Siebeck shook his head. 'She was awake earlier, sleeping now.'

'Still not communicating?'

'Not a word. As far as we can tell, there is no physical problem. She is young and healthy, and is making a good recovery from her injuries. It must be something psychological.' He looked at the second woman, who was listening intently.

'Sorry.' Sonia smiled again, 'Markus, this is Rita Vicedo.'

'Hello.' Up close, he could see that Rita Vicedo was an extremely good-looking young woman. He held out a limp hand. 'Nice to meet you.'

'Nice to meet you, too.' Leaning forward, she grasped his hand and shook it firmly.

'Rita,' Sonia said brightly, 'is going to get to the bottom of this mystery. She is going to help us find out who this girl really is.'

'Is that right?'

'I will try,' Rita said. 'First, however, I could really do with a coffee.'

'I work for the Network. The full name is the International Network Against Human Trafficking.'

'Rita,' Sonia chimed in, despite having a mouth full of Cornish pasty, 'is a nun.'

Markus almost choked on his tea. 'A nun?'

'That's right.'

His jaw dropped. 'But . . .'

Sonia laughed. 'She's way too good-looking to be a nun, right?'

'N-no,' Markus stammered. 'Well, I mean . . .' He waved an arm across the table in an attempt to distract attention from his embarrassment.

'I don't look the part.' Rita smiled.

'That's what I mean,' Markus blushed, 'I suppose.'

'I work on the streets,' Rita explained. 'I have to dress appropriately.'

'You are a nun but you work for this group against trafficking?'

'That's right,' Rita said. 'We are supported by various big international organizations, not to mention the Pope. We have members in countries all around the world. In London we go out with the police when they target houses suspected of being used by people-traffickers. We have helped rescue more than two hundred kidnapped women in the last year alone.'

'And you think Anne might have been trafficked?' Siebeck was genuinely horrified at the idea.

'Anne?' Rita looked at Sonia. 'I thought you didn't know her name.'

'Markus made it up,' the porter lied. 'He felt she should have a proper name. Everybody else thought it was quite cool to call her Miss X.'

Blushing, Siebeck repeated his question. 'Do you think she might have been trafficked?'

'It's a possibility,' was all Rita could offer.

'Maybe the girl doesn't speak English,' Sonia suggested. 'You've tried in German. I've tried in Romanian. Rita can speak to her in Spanish, Portuguese and also French.'

'Nadine's not going to like it,' Markus warned.

Rita looked at him blankly.

'Dr Hendricks,' Sonia explained. 'The boss.'

'She's one of the senior doctors,' Markus added. 'She wants Anne moved out of her room into a general ward as soon as possible.'

'Pfffff.' Sonia's expression made it clear what she thought of that.

'She's just trying to juggle the competing demands on our limited resources,' Markus said lamely.

Sonia muttered something in Romanian.

'Maybe we should speak to the police about it,' Siebeck suggested.

'I will do that,' said Rita. 'We have very good relationships with the police.' She turned to Sonia. 'The officers who are investigating this are from the Charing Cross police station. Is that right?'

'Yes.'

'I know people there. I will see how their investigation is going.' Finishing her drink, Rita got to her feet.

'Are you going already?' Siebeck asked, not bothering to hide his disappointment.

'There's to be a police raid later on,' Rita explained. 'Four of us are going. They think there might be as many as twenty girls in a brothel in the East End. It will be a long night.'

Sonia jumped up and gave her a peck on the cheek. 'Good luck.'

'I will come back tomorrow.' Rita smiled at Siebeck, almost making him swoon, then headed for the exit.

'Well,' Sonia whispered, watching her leave, 'what do you think?'

'Brave lady,' Siebeck muttered.

'Yeah,' Sonia agreed, 'and a great arse.'

Siebeck frowned.

'C'mon,' Sonia protested, 'don't tell me you didn't check it out?'

'Well . . .' Siebeck couldn't quite bring himself to lie.

'A hot nun fighting for social justice,' Sonia teased. 'What's not to like?'

On the back wall there was a row of framed black-and-white photographs of famous Belgian citizens. Audrey Hepburn, Georges Simenon, Jacques Brel and Eddy Merckx, the cycling legend known as the Cannibal, all gazed down on the ill-looking man sitting alone in the middle of the empty restaurant. All of them were smiling, apart from Merckx, who had his nickname to live up to.

The man at the table wasn't smiling either. Dressed in a crumpled grey suit and a blue shirt, open at the neck, he slumped forward in his chair, breathing heavily. The skin on his neck sagged and his face was ashen. His eyelids drooped and he looked as if he was on the point of nodding off while never quite managing it.

After a while, the hum of distant traffic was interrupted by the sound of footsteps, leather soles tapping across the wooden floor. The man jerked upright.

'I need to go home.'

'You can't go home yet, Bram.'

'I'm not well.' Bram Deroo felt his heart rate tick upwards and he wondered if he might be in danger of yet another cardiac arrest. At sixty-three, he had already survived two heart attacks. The second had been serious enough to leave him in hospital for almost a fortnight.

'Have a drink.' Kevin Lamoot handed Deroo a cold bottle of De Koninck beer and returned to his seat.

'I don't feel well,' Deroo repeated.

'Neither do I.' Lamoot gestured at the half-eaten steak baguette on the table. 'I've got terrible heartburn from that sandwich. It's tougher than the sole of my shoe. I really need a new chef in this place. This is London, not Sint-Truiden. You have to be able to cook things properly or people will go somewhere else.'

Deroo wasn't interested in Lamoot's staffing problems. 'I need to see my birds,' he whined, adding, as an afterthought, 'and my wife.'

'Pauline can wait. Your pigeons can definitely wait. We need to sort this out. You can't run away from what's happened.'

Deroo's beer tasted like acid. He stared at Eddy Merckx, but the cyclist was keeping his own counsel.

'Look at me.'

Deroo struggled to make eye contact. Lamoot was a lazy man, a small-time playboy gone to seed. But he was twenty years younger than Deroo and he had a terrible temper when pushed.

Lamoot poked at his cigar, smouldering in an ashtray. 'Don't worry, Bram, nothing is going to happen to you.' There was nothing reassuring in the younger man's tone. 'But we need to agree what we're going to do next.'

'Yes.' Struggling to suck sufficient oxygen into his lungs, Deroo glanced nervously towards the kitchen. No one was watching them: the staff knew their boss well enough to steer well clear when he was conducting his 'other' business.

'We have worked together for a long time. You are almost family.'

Almost.

'We can sort this out.' Lamoot looked at the older man intently. 'What do you suggest we do?'

'About what?' Deroo scratched nervously at the tattoo on his right forearm, the name 'Edda' in Gothic script. Edda had been his first girlfriend; she had crashed her car into a lamppost on the N79 when she was twenty-one. In a coma for almost a year before she died. Funny how things turned out. Deroo had visited the Electric Wasp tattoo parlour two days before the accident. For decades he had told anyone who asked that Edda was the name of one of his pigeons. 'About the races?'

'Of course about the races. What else would we be talking about? Elke will go crazy when she finds out what's happened.'

Mention of Lamoot's wife sent Deroo's heart beating even faster. If Kevin was difficult to deal with, Elke Poosen was the worst. The woman was a force of nature – absolutely terrifying.

'Elke spent months trying to sort all this out,' Lamoot reminded him. 'The amount of money at stake is massive. And we've already been paid.'

You might have been, Deroo reflected, but I haven't.

'Elke is not going to like this. Not at all. You know how poorly she takes bad news.'

'Yes,' said Deroo, with rather more feeling than he had intended.

'In that regard she was truly her father's daughter.'

'Yes.' Even though he was safely interred in Laeken Cemetery, Eden Poosen could still put the fear of God into the pigeon breeder. Deroo would never forget the time he had watched Eden drop a man into a barrel of motor oil, head first, in a dispute over gambling debts. They were round the back of a garage on the outskirts of Uccle. It was a stiflingly hot day, July 1991. The man had been called Peter Delvaux. If he closed his eyes, Deroo could still hear Delvaux's screams as he went under the surface. Poosen himself had held Delvaux's legs until the kicking stopped. Deroo remembered thinking how Poosen enjoyed the whole thing. The body was burned on a pyre of used car tyres. On that day Deroo, burdened with ruinous debts of his own, knew that he would never be able to leave the family's employ.

Reaching into his pocket, Lamoot pulled out a business card and tossed it onto the tablecloth. 'And now we have this cop sniffing around too.'

Deroo looked at the card but made no effort to pick it up, preferring to fiddle with his beer bottle.

'What the hell were you thinking?' Lamoot demanded. His face was red and Deroo could see he was already intoxicated.

'It w-wasn't me,' the older man stuttered. 'Christian went over there and, well, things obviously got out of hand.'

'For God's sake,' Lamoot barked, 'what the hell did you send your idiot grandson for?'

'He's not . . .' Deroo didn't have the energy to argue the point. Christian had been casually abusing glue and ketamine – a horse tranquillizer – since he was thirteen. The boy must have been off his face when he'd paid a visit to Richard Furlong.

Lamoot smacked a palm on the table in frustration. 'I thought we'd agreed that Christian wouldn't get involved in any of this.'

Deroo stared at a couple passing on the street outside. 'I wasn't feeling well. My health . . .'

Lamoot dismissed the excuse with a wave of his hand. 'So where is Christian now?'

Deroo hesitated, then realized that lying was pointless. 'I've sent him back to Belgium.'

'I suppose we should be grateful for that,' Lamoot said sarcastically.

'He won't get involved in anything like this again.'

Lamoot reached for the glass of Scotch on the table. 'Dammit, Bram, it was supposed to be so simple. Just a quiet chat with Mr Furlong, to remind him of his obligations, make sure that his birds were ready and stop him trying to back out.'

Deroo stared at the table.

'And what happens?' Lamoot took a gulp of his Scotch and placed the glass back on the table. 'The bloke ends up jumping out of the window. How the hell did that happen? Christian must have scared the living shit out of him.'

'Christian says, when he left him, he was fine,' Deroo protested meekly. 'He seemed fine.'

'Fine?' Lamoot's face started to darken. 'How could he be fine? He jumped out of a bloody tower block.' Incensed, he lurched forward, grabbing Deroo by the throat and lifting him out of his seat. Struggling to keep his balance, Deroo felt his chest begin to tighten. The beer bottle slipped from his grasp. He heard it smash and watched the foamy liquid spilling across the wooden floor even as his vision started to blur.

'Kevin—' His words were choked off as Lamoot tightened his grip.

'And what about his birds, eh?' Deroo felt Lamoot's spittle on his face. Struggling for air, he felt overwhelmed by the stink of the man's breath. 'How were they going to race with their bloody heads pulled off?'

TWENTY-FIVE

Humming 'Always Look On The Bright Side Of Life', Carlyle walked past a row of street-sweeping vehicles parked by the side of the road, as he approached a large, single-storey building that looked like a rotten tooth in an otherwise set of fine molars. Westminster Council's recycling depot was incongruously situated in a block of prime real estate just south of Euston Road, close to Marylebone High Street. It had to be, the inspector mused, the most expensively located junkyard in the world.

After negotiating his way through a shabby reception area, the inspector found himself standing in what was effectively a small warehouse. The space was lined with rows of floor-to-ceiling metal shelving filled with a selection of old office equipment – everything from desks and chairs to photocopiers and computers – along with domestic household items such as fridges and cookers. On first glance, most of the stuff looked fairly serviceable.

'It's amazing what people just throw away these days.'

'Erm, yes.' Looking round, it took Carlyle a moment to locate the small woman who appeared from behind one of the distant rows. Heading towards him, she was struggling to carry a large commercial microwave.

'They just dump the stuff on the street and expect us to take it away. It costs money to dispose of stuff properly, you know. London is drowning in rubbish. And people wonder why their council tax is so high.'

'Can I give you a hand?' The inspector stepped forward, arms outstretched.

'I'm fine.' The woman swerved around him and staggered over to a long bench that ran along the wall next to the entrance. Dropping the microwave next to an open copy of the *Sun*, she turned and eyed her visitor suspiciously. 'Were you looking for something?' With a flat, expressionless face, thinning grey hair and a complexion that suggested an aversion to sunlight, she was dressed in a green uniform that made her look like a prison inmate. Over the breast pocket of her jacket, next to the council logo, a name badge bore the moniker 'Flynn'. 'Only we're not open to the public.'

The inspector explained who he was and what he was after.

'I heard about that – strange carry-on.'

'Nasty business,' Carlyle agreed.

'You'd have to be sick in the head to do something like that to some poor birds.' Flynn tutted.

'Yes.'

'But, then again, what were they doing there in the first place?'

'What do you mean?'

'Well, you're not allowed to keep pigeons like that in Westminster. It's against the health and safety regulations.'

Carlyle wondered if Furlong had ever found himself in trouble with the council. It was one more thing that would need to be checked.

'People think they can just ignore the rules when it suits them. And we have to clean up the mess, eh?'

'Yeah.' Carlyle laughed ruefully. 'That's exactly right.'

'Someone's got to do it, I suppose.' Flynn glanced at her watch. 'And you might just be in luck. They shouldn't have gone yet.' She started walking towards one of the rows, gesturing for Carlyle to follow.

'Where are they going?' the inspector asked.

'They need to be properly disposed of, obviously. That means a trip to the incinerator in Barking. According to today's schedule, they were supposed to get picked up around now. But I know that the truck hasn't been round yet. Probably got stuck in traffic. It's terrible on the roads out there today.' She led him towards a small door at the back of the building. 'God knows why they were brought here in the first place. Everything that comes in here is supposed to be recyclable. What are we supposed to do with some dead pigeons? The lazy buggers should have taken them straight to Barking but they couldn't be bothered.'

'Typical.'

'Story of my life,' Flynn continued. 'Ever since they stopped our overtime, nobody cares. All kinds of things end up getting left here that shouldn't. People don't give a monkey's about the health hazards. Just dump it and forget about it.' It sounded like an extremely well-rehearsed complaint.

'I didn't even know this place existed,' Carlyle admitted.

'It won't for much longer.' Reaching the door, Flynn pulled back a bolt and pushed on the handle. 'They're closing us down next year. Some developer is turning the site into a hotel, apparently.'

Makes sense, Carlyle thought.

Pausing in the doorway, she turned to face him. 'Everything's being consolidated on the Barking site.'

'So you're going to be working out there?'

Flynn let out a snort of derision. 'You've got to be kidding. I've been working here for seventeen years. If they think I'll start going to bloody Barking every day they've got another think coming. It would take me an hour and a bit just to get there. And if the trains aren't working, well, God knows how long it might take.'

Following Flynn through the door, Carlyle found himself in a remarkably large yard, about the size of a football pitch, with various items of junk scattered about in a seemingly random fashion. 'This is the stuff that we can't do anything with and needs to be shipped out.' His host pointed to a small mound of different coloured refuse sacks about five feet high, piled up next to the shell of an eviscerated red washing-machine. 'And then there's the stuff that shouldn't be brought here in the first place. There's a school just down the road. They regularly complain about the vermin, not to mention the smell.'

Carlyle gave the air a tentative sniff. 'It doesn't smell that bad,' he ventured cautiously.

'Wait till the sun comes out.' Flynn started back inside. 'The stuff you want should be in one of those grey bags near the top. I'm going to have a cup of tea and finish reading my newspaper. When you've got what you want, come back in and we can do the paperwork.'

Carlyle raised an eyebrow. 'Paperwork?'

Placing her hands on her hips, Flynn adopted a not unfamiliar bureaucratic tone. 'You have to sign for whatever you take and make a declaration that, once you've finished with it, you agree to dispose of it in accordance with Section 147a of the Waste Minimisation Act of 2008.'

Carlyle had never heard of the Waste Minimisation Act. 'That's fine,' he lied.

'Good. Just make sure that you open the bags carefully and make sure it's all closed up properly afterwards. You also accept responsibility for any injury you may incur on site – you'll have to sign a disclaimer.'

'Of course.' Watching the woman disappear inside, the inspector retrieved a pair of latex gloves and a plastic bag from his pocket. Pulling on the gloves, he walked gingerly over to the pile of rubbish to begin his search.

Up close, he could see what Flynn had meant about the smell. To his relief, he found what he was looking for in the second sack he opened. With a squeal of triumph, he retrieved a selection of dead birds and retreated inside to complete the necessary paperwork.

Back on the street, the inspector came face to face with a shabby bloke in a crumpled green shirt and a pair of dirty jeans.

'Are you Carlyle?'

'Who are you?'

The man offered a quick flash of his warrant card. 'Inspector Ronnie Score. I work out of Bethnal Green. The desk sergeant at Charing Cross said I'd find you here.' Sticking the ID back in his pocket, Score considered the Tesco bag in Carlyle's hand. 'What's in there?'

'Evidence.' Carlyle didn't feel the need to explain further.

Score nodded. 'I wanted a quick chat.'

'Sure.' Carlyle let Score lead him to a nearby Starbucks. Restricting himself to a small bottle of sparkling water, he eyed Score's venti caramel latte with something approaching dismay. I couldn't manage one of those, he reflected, even with my sweet tooth.

Oblivious to his colleague's opprobrium, Score sipped his drink. 'Ah.' He wiped his mouth with the back of his hand. 'I'm gonna need a few of these to help me get through the day.'

'What can I do for you?' Carlyle asked. Conscious that the bag at his feet had to be breaking various different health regulations, he was keen to be on his way.

'Umar Sligo.'

'Ah, yes. My former sergeant.'

'His boss had his face shot off.'

Carlyle stared at the bubbles in the bottle. 'I heard about Harry Cummins. Poor old Umar must be looking for a new job.' A horrible thought popped into his head. 'Umar didn't shoot Cummins, did he?'

'You worked with him.' Sticking out his tongue, Score licked a bit of froth from the top of his latte. 'You think he could do something like that?'

Carlyle considered the question. 'As much as anyone could,' he said flatly. 'Same as you or me.'

'That's hardly a ringing endorsement,' Score pointed out.

'When it comes to Umar, I have no particular reason to

lean one way or the other. He wasn't the greatest cop I've ever worked with, but he was okay. He probably didn't live up to the reputation he arrived with, but he had his moments. Would he be daft enough to shoot someone? No, not normally. But shootings happen when you're outside normal circumstances, don't they?' Carlyle was conscious that he was wittering. 'Bottom line is I don't know.'

'He originally came down from Manchester, didn't he?'

'That's right. He was running away from a girl or something. I never really knew the background but it had caused some kind of family bust-up. That was the thing about Umar – he was a real ladies' man.'

'Skirt-chaser.'

Carlyle laughed. 'He was a lover, not a fighter, which, I suppose, would make it seem unlikely that he might shoot his boss. When I worked with him it was like he was operating on automatic pilot. Even after he had a kid and got married it was like he felt compelled to chat up just about every pretty girl who crossed his path.'

'He hasn't changed in that department,' Score remarked. 'His alibi for when Cummins was killed was that he was banging Cummins's girlfriend.'

'Umar, Umar.' Carlyle shook his head sadly. 'Christina will have your balls this time.'

'He split up from his wife about four months ago, apparently.'

'That's a shame but not much of a surprise.' Unscrewing the top of the bottle, Carlyle drank a mouthful of water. 'Have you spoken to her yet?'

'No. His alibi holds up, so I probably won't bother for the moment. Got too much else on my plate.'

'You could see his life spinning out of control even before he left the force,' Carlyle mused. 'He was the author of his own downfall.'

'Why did he get kicked out?'

'He resigned. But it was a case of jumping before he was

pushed. He was facing a misconduct charge and would almost certainly have been booted out.'

'What did he do?'

'Have you not checked his file?'

Score shook his head. 'Not yet. I thought I'd come and talk to you first.'

'It was a sexual-harassment thing. The stupid boy was taking pictures of his willy and sending them to some of the women at work.'

'Taking pictures of his knob?' Score exploded with laughter.

A woman at the next table gave them a disapproving look.

'That kind of thing,' said Carlyle, lowering his voice, 'appears to be what passes for courting, these days. Some people complained, though, and he was going through the disciplinary process when he left.'

'They'll have your balls for that, right enough. You can't be too careful.'

'It's fair to say he made a right mess of things. And I wouldn't have thought that working with Harry Cummins was the best way to get back on the straight and narrow.'

'No,' Score agreed. 'Sligo's personal life is a complete mess but that seems to be the case for everybody connected with Cummins, including the man himself.'

'Harry Cummins was a right waster, a playboy, club-owner and . . .' Carlyle was about to say 'drug-dealer' but managed to correct himself in time '. . . party animal. He was never going to surround himself with what might be described as "normal" people.'

'He was also running one of London's biggest high-end brothels out of his nightclub.'

'A pimp, too?'

'Yeah. The whole thing is quite an embarrassment, considering it was all taking place just across the road from a police station.'

Bloody hell, Umar, what were you playing at, hooking up

with a guy like that? 'So,' Carlyle said, 'apart from commenting on my ex-colleague's various character defects, what can I do for you?'

'You know Umar, how do I get under his skin? I don't think he shot Harry but I'm pretty sure he knows more than he's letting on. I just need him to open up a bit.'

'Umar knows exactly how the game is played.'

'That's the trouble with trying to deal with an ex-cop,' Score agreed.

'He's not going to give you any more than he needs to.' Carlyle was distracted by some movement at his feet. A small dog, a poodle, was sniffing interestedly around his bag. Shooing the mutt away, he grabbed the bag and gestured towards the door. 'I need to get going.'

Score finished his latte and got to his feet. 'Have you ever heard of a woman called Isabel Corey?'

Carlyle thought about it for a moment, then shook his head. 'I don't think so. Why?'

'It's a name that came up in one of the interviews I did at the club. One of Harry's girls – she seems to have disappeared off the face of the planet.'

'Not uncommon,' Carlyle observed, sliding off his seat and moving towards the door. 'People come and go all the time.'

TWENTY-SIX

After dropping the birds off with Phillips, Carlyle returned to Charing Cross. Arriving at the police station, he found Kelly Moss at her desk on the first floor. Surrounded by empty paper cups, the computer whizz was peering at tightly packed rows of numbers on a large screen. As he approached, she sensed his presence at her shoulder.

'I've been trying to get hold of you.' Not looking up, she continued scanning the data. 'This is what's on that dirty USB stick of yours.'

Carlyle squinted at the spreadsheet. 'Lots of numbers.'

'And you say you're not an expert.' Moss laughed.

'Do they mean anything? Is there anything in there that can help us identify the mystery girl at UCH?'

'It's a set of business accounts, basically.'

'Do we know whose?'

'Nope. But I can tell you that, whoever it is, they're in deep trouble.' Moss tapped the screen with her finger. 'The figures go back eighteen months. Things are okay for the first nine months – steady growth, respectable profits – then they start to go awry. Costs keep going up, while income remains flat, tails off and falls through the floor.'

'No way to run a business.' Carlyle did not have an entrepreneurial bone in his body but he had a basic grasp of economics, thanks to Charles Dickens.

'Annual income twenty pounds,' as Mr Micawber pointed

out in *David Copperfield*, 'annual expenditure nineteen pounds nineteen and six, result happiness. Annual income twenty pounds, annual expenditure twenty pounds nought and six, result misery.'

'It certainly was misery for someone,' he murmured.

'What?'

'Nothing.' What did this have to do with a girl beaten up and left for dead in an alley off Tottenham Court Road? The inspector suspected that Mr Micawber wasn't going to be much help with that one.

'Whatever the business is, it's going bust at a rapid rate of knots,' Moss concluded. 'The numbers are very up-to-date – they go up to last month. On current trends, unless the owner has taken some pretty drastic remedial action, the losses should have reached almost fifty thousand a week by now. In three months' time, that could spiral almost to a million.'

Carlyle let out a low whistle. 'Wow.'

'Bankrupt.'

'Yeah. Maybe it's closed already. You might want to check on businesses that have gone bust recently.'

The inspector wondered how many firms closed down every day. 'Maybe,' he said doubtfully.

Clicking on her mouse, Moss brought up another page of the spreadsheet. 'And then there's this.'

Leaning forward, Carlyle looked at rows of email addresses and mobile phone numbers.

'A contact list of some sort. Clients, maybe.'

'Do we have any names?' Carlyle asked hopefully.

Moss shook her head. 'No names. But you can trace them, surely, from the information we have here.'

Yeah, Carlyle thought, if I had a warrant, a budget and the necessary manpower. He knew that none of these things would be forthcoming for the investigation into a mere assault case, however violent. The most likely outcome was that the investigation would be quietly dropped once the girl left hospital. Given the way things were going, he regretted giving Moss the USB stick in the first place. All he seemed to be doing was generating work for the sake of it.

'Does that help?' Moss asked.

Not really. 'Yes, thanks.' He tried to sound sincere. 'Very helpful.'

'I'll drop hard copies of everything on your desk, so that you can take a look at it all at your leisure.'

'That's great.' Carlyle knew that the papers would go unread for several weeks before being filed in one of the confidential shredding bins that were dotted about his floor upstairs.

'No problem,' said Moss, cheerily.

'Thanks.' Out of the corner of his eye, Carlyle saw Adam Palin walking towards him. The sergeant's cheeks were flushed, as if he had just jogged up the stairs. Following him was a poised young woman with jet black hair and striking cheekbones. Clipped to the breast pocket of her jacket was a visitor pass.

The sergeant greeted Moss before turning to Carlyle. 'Inspector, this is Rita Vicedo. She wanted to meet you.'

'John Carlyle.' He extended an arm and they shook hands. Carlyle was surprised by the firmness of her grip.

'Ms Vicedo,' Palin explained, 'is a—'

The woman cut the sergeant off with a casual brusqueness that stopped just the right side of being rude. 'I am part of an organization that works with the police to try to stop people-trafficking and abuse against women.'

'Ms Vicedo is trying to help us identify the unidentified woman at UCH,' Palin added.

Carlyle stifled a groan: civilian help was more of a hindrance than anything else. Not wishing to appear too churlish, he forced himself to smile at the young woman. 'That's great,' he managed to say. 'We're very grateful for any help you can possibly give us.'

'I am going to the hospital this afternoon,' Vicedo explained, 'to try to talk to the woman – if she's awake, obviously. In the meantime, I was wondering, have you made any progress in the investigation into the attack?'

Carlyle glanced at the information on Moss's computer screen and scratched his head. 'Not really. Until we can work out who she is, I fear we're going to struggle.' The girl standing in front of him was attractive enough to take your breath away, even though she was clearly exhausted. Belatedly he remembered his manners. 'Would you like some coffee?'

Vicedo shook her head. 'Thank you but no. I've had too much caffeine already. It was a long night.'

'Ms Vicedo and her colleagues,' Palin explained, 'took part in a Grandmother raid on a house in Hackney last night.' Operation Grandmother was a long-running campaign involving the police and various other government agencies, aimed at organized immigration crime. 'They picked up a dozen women and made three arrests.'

'Well done,' said Carlyle, genuinely impressed. Fighting people-trafficking was grim work. Someone had to do it, he was just glad it wasn't him.

'We thought there might be more women there,' Rita shrugged, 'but it is something.'

'Yes.' Carlyle stared at his shoes.

'I think the girl in the hospital may be an illegal, too. Perhaps that is why she doesn't talk. Maybe she is worried about being deported by the authorities.'

'It's possible,' the inspector agreed. 'What do the doctors say?'

'That she is making a good physical recovery. They cannot see any reason why she is not talking. She must be really scared.'

'The doctors need the bed back,' Palin chimed in.

'She'll have to say something, sooner or later,' Carlyle pointed out. 'They won't discharge her until they know who she is.'

Rita shot the inspector an enquiring look. 'Maybe if I

184

could give her some reassurance that she is not in any kind of trouble . . .'

'That may not be a bad idea,' the sergeant put in. 'I mean, it can't do any harm, can it?'

It might not be a bad idea if you were to make some progress on the Furlong investigation, Carlyle reflected, irritated at Palin's attempt to bounce him into making a promise he couldn't keep. Letting sleeping pigeons lie, he addressed his remarks to the saintly Ms Vicedo. 'I'm sure you know as well as I do how it works when it comes to immigration matters. Anne, Miss X, whatever we want to call her, was the victim of a very serious assault. We need to talk to her so that we can try to catch her attacker and put him behind bars. That is my primary, indeed sole, interest here. However, if what you might call incidental issues come up in the course of the investigation, we'll have to deal with those as they arise. If they are issues that are primarily the responsibility of other agencies, I cannot promise that the police will be able to do anything to intervene on the victim's behalf.'

The scowl on Vicedo's face told him he was sounding like the worst kind of bureaucrat.

'All I can promise is that if we can help, we will help. But these matters are not always down to us.'

'Of course.' Vicedo's scowl remained.

'I have to be honest. I don't want to mislead you. And I don't want to mislead a girl who has been badly hurt, either. We will find out who she is sooner or later – the sooner the better when it comes to trying to catch her attacker. That is my only job here. I have absolutely no interest in kicking people out of the country just for the sake of it, believe me.'

Vicedo narrowed her eyes and pursed her lips, as if she was trying to work out what she made of the cop standing in front of her. Finally she offered a hand. 'Thank you for your time, Inspector. I will let you know if I find out anything useful for your investigation.'

'Thank you.' Carlyle shook the woman's hand for a second time before watching Palin lead her back towards the lifts on the far side of the room.

'Pretty girl,' Moss murmured, once they were out of earshot.

'Yeah,' Carlyle agreed.

'I reckon Sergeant Palin's smitten,' she added. 'Did you see the way he looked at her? Like a little puppy, he was.'

'Good luck to him,' Carlyle said, 'but I think the poor bloke's trying to punch way above his weight.'

TWENTY-SEVEN

Retreating upstairs, the inspector flopped into his chair and fired up his computer. The third floor was deserted – a cycle race taking place on the Embankment: like everybody else, he was supposed to be on crowd control. No matter, they would cope without him. Logging on, he checked the latest football news before deleting a few hundred unread emails. Confident that he was fully up to date with his electronic communication, he turned his attention to the pile of receipts that had collected in the top drawer of his desk over the last few months. The next forty minutes were spent agonizing over his expenses. How best should he characterize the costs incurred in the course of his visit to the House of Pain? In the end, he settled on 'incidental expenditure incurred while interviewing a supportive witness in the course of an ongoing investigation'. Burying Madam Monica's invoice in the middle of a small bundle of uncontroversial taxi receipts, he stapled everything to the claims form and said a silent prayer in the hope that the Accounts Department would refund him the £225 without further investigation.

He placed the form and the receipts in an envelope, then got up and walked over to a set of pigeonholes on the wall that served as a collection point for the station's internal mail. Dropping the envelope into the hole marked 'Accounts', he was startled when his desk phone started to ring. Skipping back across the room, he grabbed the receiver.

'Yes?'

The desk sergeant at the other end of the line was all business. 'There's someone down here who says she needs to see you. She says it's important.' His tone suggested that he doubted that last point very much.

'Who is it?' Carlyle asked, irritated by his colleague's brusqueness.

There was a momentary pause, while the sergeant considered whether he might not have established this basic fact before picking up the phone, followed by the sound of a hand going over the mouthpiece and a few seconds of muffled voices.

'A Mrs O'Brien.'

'Ms,' a voice hissed in the background.

'Miss O'Brien,' the sergeant corrected himself.

'*Ms.*'

Carlyle's heart sank. 'Christina O'Brien?' A.k.a. Mrs Umar Sligo.

'That's right.' The sergeant lowered his voice to a whisper. 'And she's got a kid with her.'

'Urgh.' You should have known this might happen, Carlyle admonished himself. You should have bloody known. Eyeing Umar's former desk, he loudly cursed his former sergeant. Unoccupied since his departure, covered with old newspapers, empty coffee cups and discarded food packaging, it had become the chosen dump of the office fly-tippers. 'When I catch up with you,' the inspector promised, 'I'm going to wring your scrawny northern neck.'

'Shall I send them up?' the sergeant asked, clearly impatient to get back to whatever it was he had been doing.

'No, no,' Carlyle said quickly. 'I'll come down.'

Picking up his unwelcome guests, the inspector led them to the basement canteen. There, he bought a coffee for Christina and an orange juice for Ella, her daughter, along with another bottle of mineral water for himself. The little girl took the juice with a bright 'Thank you,' while her mother restricted herself to a cautious nod.

'My pleasure.' Carlyle smiled, warming to the child. He pointed at the book in her hand. 'What are you reading?'

'It's a selection of fairy stories,' Christina said flatly, shooing her daughter towards an empty table at the far end of the room. 'You take a seat over there, sweetheart, while I have a conversation with Mr Carlyle. I'll only be a few minutes.'

Carlyle wandered over to a table where they could talk out of earshot. 'I wish Alice had been as well behaved when she was that age.'

'Ella has her moments.'

'They all do.'

Beneath a veneer of tiredness, Christina looked tanned and healthy. Dressed in a pair of crisp jeans, a plain white T-shirt and an expensive jacket, she looked far removed from the outrageous young woman the inspector had first met not so many years ago. Placing her coffee on the table, she sat down. 'You know why I'm here?'

'I can guess.' Carlyle unscrewed the cap on the water bottle and took a swig.

'Umar is a real shit magnet.'

'I heard about Harry Cummins.'

'Is Umar in trouble?' Christina looked more irritated than annoyed by the prospect.

Carlyle looked around. The canteen was largely empty and nothing he might say within the confines of Charing Cross had much chance of getting back to Ronnie Score but it was better to be paranoid than to be sorry. Pulling his chair in close to the table, he kept his voice low. 'I don't think so. As far as I understand, he's not in the frame for the shooting.'

A look of utter disdain passed across her face, one that he remembered from the old days. 'That's not what I meant.'

Carlyle waited for her to explain. 'What did you mean?' he asked, when nothing more was forthcoming.

'Is anyone going to try to shoot him, too?' She snorted, as if it was the obvious issue they needed to address.

'Sssh. Keep your voice down.' Even if no one was eavesdropping, he didn't want the child to hear her mother's fears. He glanced over at Ella. Happily, she seemed totally engrossed in her book.

'Is Umar in trouble?' At least Christina managed to keep the decibel levels down this time.

Carlyle had to admit – at least to himself – he hadn't even considered the question.

'Will you go and speak to him?'

Noooooooooooooo. Carlyle tried to appear to be giving the matter some thought.

'He could be in serious trouble this time.'

This time.

'I don't see how I could do much good,' he offered limply.

'You might be able to talk some sense into him,' Christina persisted. 'He always listened to you.'

Yeah, right. Carlyle's brow furrowed. He was about to protest but he realized that it would only prolong the conversation unnecessarily. 'Where is he living, these days?' he asked reluctantly.

Christina mentioned an address in a particularly grubby part of east London. 'He's got a bedsit there.'

Lovely.

'But, knowing Umar, he won't be there. He's more likely to be hanging out with one of his girlfriends.' She shook her head in disgust.

You married him, love, Carlyle thought, not me. 'Anyone in particular?'

Christina's expression darkened further. 'There's a girl called Zoë – Zoë Connors. She was supposed to be dating Harry Cummins but Umar . . . Well, you know. He probably got an additional thrill from screwing the boss's girlfriend.'

The depressing thing was that Christina was probably right.

190

'And you know all this because?'

'I have my own sources,' Christina offered cryptically.

'Have you got an address for this Zoë?'

'No, but I know someone who will.' She stuck out her hand. 'Give me your phone.'

Carlyle obliged, watching as she typed a number into it, added a name and saved it to his contacts list.

'Karen Jansen's a good mate,' Christina said, handing back the phone. 'We worked together for a while at Everton's.' A crooked smile played across her lips. 'You remember Everton's, don't you?'

'Yeah.' Carlyle would never forget the first time he had seen Christina O'Brien, naked, on stage at the now defunct Holborn strip club.

'Clive's retired to Marbella, apparently.' Clive Martin, Everton's owner, had been a mini-celebrity in the fleshpots of midtown.

'He'll be back.' Carlyle grinned, happy at the digression.

'I wouldn't have thought so. Once you drop out, it's a hard business to get back into.'

'I'm sure Clive'll be fine.'

'Yeah,' Christina agreed. 'He could always look after himself.'

'So,' Carlyle asked, 'Karen'll know where I can find Umar?'

'She worked for Harry. Or, at least, she did until he was shot.'

'She isn't another of Umar's girlfriends?'

'No, no.' Christina looked offended at the question. 'She has too much class for that.'

Interesting definition of 'class', Carlyle thought, given that the woman had been working in a knocking shop, in the employ of Britain's poshest pimp. He let it slide. 'When I get to speak to Umar, what do you want me to say?'

Christina had obviously given the matter some thought. 'Tell him that he needs to get a proper job,' she said sharply. 'And he needs to catch up with his child support.'

TWENTY-EIGHT

Elke Poosen looked down at the bemused expression on the face of Bram Deroo. Placed inside one of the restaurant's freezers, the man was still clearly visible beneath bags of frozen chips and packs of finest English beef. 'How long has he been in there?'

'Not that long.' Red-faced under the harsh strip-lighting of the storeroom, Kevin Lamoot tried to look vaguely sober. 'Since last night.'

'At least he's not going to smell,' Elke observed. 'Unlike you.' The stink of booze coming off her husband made her want to gag. 'What the hell happened?'

'I think he had a heart attack,' Lamoot said ruefully, hoping his wife wouldn't notice the marks that were clearly visible on the dead man's neck. 'One minute he was drinking a beer and we were chatting away. The next thing I knew he had just kind of keeled over. He hadn't been well – a history of heart trouble.'

Well aware of her husband's temper, Elke raised an eyebrow. 'And you were just talking?'

'Yes.' Lamoot meekly continued with the lie. 'We were talking about how to deal with the Furlong situation. Bram knew he'd fucked up. But, again, it was his health. He had been ill on the day, which was why he sent his grandson, Christian, to do the job. The youngster, well, he just let things get a bit out of control. When you understand the background, you can see that it wasn't really Bram's fault.'

Elke had to resist the urge to batter her spouse about the head with a frozen steak. 'And you put him in there? You're talking to a guy with a history of heart trouble who falls down dead, so you stuff him into a *freezer*?'

'What else could I do?' Lamoot protested. 'We had to open up for service.'

'If it was a straightforward heart attack,' Elke let the freezer door drop shut, 'why didn't you just call an ambulance?'

'It was just . . .' a constipated look passed across Lamoot's face '. . . *too* complicated. With everything else that's going on at the moment, I thought it was the sensible thing to do.'

'Sensible?'

'I thought you'd be pleased.' He was swaying slightly. 'Aren't you?'

'What do you think?' Folding her arms, Elke took a moment to ponder the relative merits of divorcing her idiot husband, as opposed to having him 'disappeared' by one or more of her father's ex-colleagues. It pained Elke to admit it, but Eden Poosen had been one hundred per cent right in his judgement of Kevin Lamoot. From their first days of courting, her father had dismissed him as 'lazy, stupid and a risk to the business'. With the benefit of hindsight, it was a perfect summary.

Sometimes Elke felt she had spent the last fifteen years trying to prove the old man wrong. Now it was finally time to give up the job as hopeless. She had little doubt that a divorce would be wearisome, not to mention expensive. Given his complete lack of self-awareness, Kevin might even try to get custody of the kids. The thought of the potential legal fees alone made Elke shiver. There was no doubt that the other option would be far simpler, cleaner and massively cheaper.

First things first, however. She gestured towards the door. 'What happens if one of the staff comes in looking for some *frites* and finds Bram in the freezer?'

'I've changed the code for the lock,' a self-satisfied smile crossed Lamoot's lips, 'and told them that the storeroom is off-limits for the moment.'

The idiot thinks he's being clever, Elke thought wearily. She tried to massage the back of her neck with a hand. Straight off the flight from Warsaw and having to deal with this nonsense – it really was too much. She should have been at home by now, relaxing in a hot bath with Marjorie bringing her a glass of Krug and a chicken sandwich while she listened to Radio 4. 'You've got to get rid of him. Immediately.'

Lamoot's smile grew wider. 'Don't worry, I'm on top of it. We're going to—'

'I don't want to know,' Elke said sharply. 'Just make sure that this whole place is completely clean of any trace evidence that Bram was ever here. And the body can never be found. That's never as in *never*.'

'No.' Lamoot stared at his shoes – eight hundred pounds from Savile Row, if Elke remembered correctly. She started calculating in her head how much she could save each month, as a widow, stopping when she reached ten thousand. Dead, Kevin would pay for himself in less than six months. It really was a no-brainer.

Lamoot lifted his gaze but didn't make eye contact with his wife. 'What about Mr Biswas?' Bob Biswas was an Indian diamond trader and bookie based in Antwerp, a long-time business associate of the Poosen family.

'What about him?'

'Well, you know . . .'

'First, I'm not waiting for Mr Biswas to find out about this from someone else. We have to keep him properly informed.'

Lamoot's face brightened slightly as his wife took control of the situation. 'What are we going to say?'

'Just leave Bob to me,' Elke said firmly. 'I'll speak to him alone. That will underline that we're taking the situation seriously. Bob's a pragmatist. He understands that these things can happen occasionally in business. The important thing is to be open and transparent. Trying to cover things up will only back-fire in the end. If we deal with it now, there's still time to sort things out and limit our losses.'

'But the race?'

'The race will go ahead, just without Richard Furlong's birds. No one will notice. Biswas will be able to cancel most of his losing bets. We'll just have to take the hit for his lost winnings.'

'That's still going to cost us a lot.'

'It is the unavoidable price of your *grotesque* incompetence.'

Lamoot bit his lower lip. 'It was just bad luck. Bram was unwell and he decided to use his grandson and—'

'You know what my father used to say. "Bad luck is for losers."'

'But—'

'But nothing. Don't whine, Kevin. You know I hate it when you whine.' Those words were also her father's. She could hear his voice in her own. Sorry, Papa, Elke thought sadly. You were right all along.

She placed a hand on her forehead. Despite the coldness of the room, it felt hot and clammy. She was running a tempera-ture, maybe going down with a virus. The idea of being ill was profoundly annoying, further darkening her mood. Illness was also for losers. She would not succumb. 'We're done here. I need to go home.'

'Sure.' Lamoot followed her out of the storeroom, making a show of checking the lock before shuffling into the restaurant and going straight to the bar. Picking up a bottle from the back shelf, he poured himself a large cognac. 'Do you want one?'

Elke waved away the offer. 'Go easy on the alcohol while you deal with this issue.'

'It's all right. I can handle it.' Tipping back his head, he downed his drink in one, then poured himself another. 'You know I could always hold my drink.'

Elke made no attempt to hide her disdain. From the kitchen

came the sounds of the staff getting ready for the evening service. She caught the sound of a pair of chattering female voices, followed by laughter. Which one of you is he fucking at the moment? she wondered. Or maybe it's both. Her husband's infidelity was the thing that bothered her least. Not interested in anyone's pleasure but his own, Kevin had never been much to write home about in the bed department. Indeed, after fourteen years of marriage and two children, Elke had only managed to orgasm after swallowing her prudishness and visiting a sex shop on Charing Cross Road to buy a vibrator. Nowadays she supplemented that with the occasional use of a discreet and expensive internet service that would supply the man of her choice at the time of her choice, then take him away again. As for servicing Kevin, that was a grim chore she was more than happy to leave to someone else.

He tilted the neck of the bottle towards her, his face flushed. 'Are you sure you don't want one?'

'I'm going home,' she repeated. 'I need a bath and a good night's sleep. Make sure you don't wake me when you come in.' Grabbing her travel bag, Elke gestured towards the ceiling. 'Better still, why don't you stay in the flat upstairs tonight?' She was about to add, *And you can fuck the help if you can manage to get it up*, but buttoned her lip.

'All right.' Lamoot seemed quite content at the prospect.

'Just make sure that Bram's gone by tomorrow. And think about what we're going to say to the poor man's family. They're bound to come asking what's happened to him.'

Lamoot downed his second drink. 'I can deal with them.'

'I think you've done more than enough already. No more brandy. No more using your own initiative. Just focus on the matter in hand. Bram has to disappear completely. Get that done and we'll speak in the morning.'

'Yes, boss.' The resentment in his voice was clear.

'In the meantime, I'll speak to Bob Biswas. And to that cop.' Holding out her hand, Elke waited for Lamoot to recover the policeman's business card from his pocket and hand it over. A couple of waitresses appeared from the kitchen and began setting tables on the far side of the room. She was pleased to note that they were plain creatures. She lowered her voice: 'You deal with our frozen friend. We'll talk in the morning.'

TWENTY-NINE

The look of defiance on Miss X's face was clear. '*No voy a hablar con la policía*,' she whispered, her voice barely registering above the hum of the machines surrounding her bed. Propped up by a couple of plump pillows, the girl formerly known as Anne looked as if she was on the way to recovery. Her bruises were fading and she could breathe without pain. She had also started to talk, but only when the doctors were not around.

Rita Vicedo patted her gently on the arm. 'Don't worry, Isabel.' Her tone was soothing but, at the same time, business-like. Once they had established the girl's name, the rest of her story had come quickly. Now it was just a question of working out what to tell the cops and the hospital authorities.

'The doctors say you are well enough to discharge yourself,' Sonia added, 'if you want to do so. If you stay, they will move you to a general ward for a few days.'

Holding Rita's gaze, Isabel Corey easily switched languages. 'But what about the police?'

'I can give them the relevant details,' Vicedo offered, 'but at the same time we will make sure that they respect your privacy.'

'The police will probably come back,' Sonia ventured, 'but they are always very busy – they have other things to take care of – so maybe not.'

Isabel pushed a stray strand of hair behind her ear. She shifted uneasily in the bed. 'If leave here, can I go home?'

Sonia looked at Rita.

'That might not be such a good idea,' the nun pointed out.

A pained expression crossed Isabel's face. 'Then I have nowhere to go.'

'We can take care of that,' Vicedo assured her. Lifting a plastic bag from the floor, she placed it carefully on the bed. 'Sonia's brought you some clothes. I can get you a place to stay until we can work out what is going to happen, longer-term.'

'Somewhere in London?'

'Yes,' Vicedo replied. 'I can get you a room in one of our safe houses in Kentish Town. You'll be safe from the man who attacked you.'

'And the police,' Sonia added.

'And the police,' Vicedo agreed. 'You'll have a place to stay, good meals and a little spending money, if you need it.'

'All right.' Isabel pushed back the duvet. 'Let me get dressed.' Gingerly swinging her legs over the side of the bed, she placed her feet on the floor and began inspecting the contents of the bag.

'We'll wait outside.' Sonia led Vicedo out of the room. Stepping into the corridor, she closed the door gently behind her. 'This is the best way.'

'Yes,' Vicedo agreed, 'but I will have to speak to the police in the morning.'

'She told you who did this to her?'

'Not yet. But I think she will. It just takes time to build up a rapport. I think she knows the guy who attacked her.'

'Okay. Let me go and find Markus. He will want to say good-bye to her. And he'll need to sort out the necessary paperwork.'

Leaving Rita hovering outside Isabel's room, Sonia headed down the corridor in search of Dr Siebeck. She found him having a cigarette in the ambulance bay outside A and E.

'Hey.'

'Hey, yourself.' Shifting nervously from foot to foot, the

German braced himself for another lecture on the evils of smoking.

'Quiet night?'

'So far, so good.' Siebeck gestured towards the entrance to A and E. 'The drunks haven't started arriving yet.'

Sonia glanced at her watch. 'It's still quite early.' A couple of nurses walked past. Sonia waited until they were out of earshot before saying, 'Isabel's leaving.'

'What?' The doctor looked genuinely shocked. Sonia knew that, apart from everything else, he was still getting used to the fact that Miss X, the girl he had christened Anne, now had a real name.

'She's leaving,' Sonia repeated. 'She's talked to Rita about it and she's going to discharge herself.'

Flustered, Siebeck took a long drag on his fag. Not for the first time in recent days, he contemplated Rita Vicedo. To his surprise, the nun had driven all thoughts of Nadine Hendricks from his brain. It was clear that he had a new madonna to fixate upon. How was it that he only ever fell for completely unattainable women?

Sonia tugged at his coat. 'Come on, you need to get the papers sorted.'

The doctor took another drag on his cigarette, watching the tip flare in the gloom. 'She can't leave yet,' he said finally. 'She's a long way from being fully recovered.'

'She's doing well,' Sonia countered. 'You need to write her a prescription for some painkillers, but she'll be fine.'

Siebeck looked at her doubtfully. 'She took quite a beating.'

'She's tough, Markus. You're going to kick her out of her room anyway. Better that she's able to go home than get stuck on a general ward with a bunch of sick people. That'll really do her head in.'

'She's going home?'

'She's going somewhere safe,' Sonia said carefully. 'Rita's organizing it. You don't need to know.'

'But Anne – Isabel still needs to speak to the police about the man who assaulted her.'

'She doesn't want to speak to the police.'

'She has to speak to the police,' Siebeck insisted.

'Isabel has spoken to Rita about what happened. Rita will pass on all the relevant information to the police. She is the only one who can get Isabel to give up the name of the man who attacked her.'

'But she's probably an illegal immigrant.'

'How do you know?' Sonia asked defiantly. 'And, anyway, so what if she is? It's not that long ago I would have been an illegal immigrant.'

'Yes, but—'

'It's not that long ago that *you* would have been an enemy alien. That's even worse.'

'Me?'

'Yes.' Sonia grinned. 'During the Second World War they would have put you in a camp.'

'Hardly.'

'Yes, they would,' Sonia insisted.

'That's not the same thing,' the young doctor huffed. 'You are just being silly. It's completely different. That was a long time ago. It's not the same thing at all.'

'Why not?'

'It just isn't.'

'Markus, for God's sake.' Standing on tiptoe, Sonia reached up and pulled the cigarette from his mouth. Holding it as far from her body as possible, she closed her eyes and planted a kiss firmly on his lips. Shocked, Siebeck slumped against the wall. Grinning and blushing at the same time, Sonia handed him back his cigarette. 'Just finish your smoke and sort out the damn papers,' she started back inside, 'and there'll be more where that came from.'

THIRTY

The voice at the other end of the line was the very definition of stressed. 'Why are you hassling me?'

'I was just—'

'You were just chasing me,' Susan Phillips snapped, 'for the results of the tests on your damn pigeons.'

'Yes.' The inspector understood he needed to let his colleague vent. He knew better than to enquire as to why she was in such a bad mood. Surely it couldn't be anything to do with him. Standing in front of the Royal Opera House, he watched a steady stream of commuters heading across Covent Garden piazza towards their offices.

'They only came in yesterday,' the pathologist complained. 'Do you think I just sit around all day, drinking tea and reading the paper, waiting for you to bring me things to do?'

'Of course not.' He tried not to sound too irritated by her bad mood. 'I was—'

'Do you think I'm just a bloody vet?' There was the sound of voices in the background. 'I know, I know,' Phillips shouted to someone. 'I'm coming right away. Give me one minute while I finish my call.'

'Tough day?'

The interruption seemed to have taken the edge off her frustration. 'I'm sorry, but it's absolute chaos here this morning. Frozen body parts have been turning up in waste bins all along Euston Road. So far we've got half a torso, both hands, an arm

202

and a foot. There are uniforms going through all the bins between Marylebone and King's Cross looking for the rest of him.'

'Him?' Carlyle knew he shouldn't ask, but couldn't resist.

'The genitalia were found in a Waitrose bag.'

'So we're looking for an upmarket killer?' the inspector quipped. Waitrose, Helen frequently reminded him, was rather too rich for the Carlyle family budget.

'It's a shame you're not investigating this one,' Phillips said drily. 'It would probably have been solved by now.'

'Who is in charge?'

'Barney Helenius.'

Helenius was a veteran detective inspector working out of the Holborn police station. Carlyle had always considered him a good guy. It appeared that Phillips took a different view. 'I'll look out for him on the evening news,' he said. 'The media will love this.'

'Won't they just?' Phillips agreed. 'In the meantime, I'm supposed to defrost what they've got and try to work out what happened to the poor sod,' she laughed mirthlessly, 'apart from being chopped up, of course.'

Carlyle had to admit that it sounded more interesting than his pigeons. 'Was he chopped up before he was frozen?'

'That's one of the things we need to ascertain.'

'Either way,' Carlyle observed, 'you hope he was dead first.'

'Quite. Not a nice way to go, however you look at it. Anyway, I have to run.'

'Sure,' said Carlyle, resigned to a long wait for news about Richard Furlong's birds. 'No problem.'

'Fortunately for you, though, I *did* manage to take a look at those carcasses yesterday. Otherwise they could have ended up getting kicked into next week. Bottom line, some birds were doped, others weren't. I've sent you an email with the details.'

'That's great.' Carlyle wondered why she hadn't just told him that in the first place. 'Thanks.'

'If you've got any questions, give me a call, but not before tomorrow at the earliest. Speak later.' The pathologist clicked off before he could wish her luck in dealing with the mystery of the dismembered man.

'For once,' he muttered to himself, 'it looks like you dodged a hospital pass with the human ice cubes.' Pulling up Phillips's email on his phone, Carlyle found himself looking at a column of ID numbers; two had an asterisk next to them, signifying that the bird in question had tested positive for cocaine, while the other four were clean.

So Furlong had fallen in with a bad crew and was doping his birds as part of a betting scam. There had been some kind of falling out – doubtless over money – and the birds were killed. Furlong, overcome with grief, took his own life.

'Nice theory,' Carlyle said to himself. 'All you've got to do now is prove it.' Heading back to the station, he forwarded the email to Fiona Cope. When he arrived at his desk, he called her mobile.

The RSPCA inspector picked up on the second ring. 'I was just thinking of you,' she said cheerily. 'I thought you might call.'

'Furlong was doping his birds,' Carlyle said, by way of introduction. 'I sent you an email.'

'I haven't seen it yet. What does it say?'

'Basically, just that. We checked six birds and two of them tested positive for cocaine.'

'It's not as uncommon as you might expect.'

'I thought you said Furlong's birds hadn't been doing very well in races recently?'

'They haven't.'

'Maybe that's why he started doping.'

'Could be,' Cope agreed. 'Or maybe that was the plan all along – do badly in a few races, then dope the birds and clean up with the bookmakers next time around.'

'Could you have a word with your guy?' Carlyle struggled to recall the man's name.

'Eric?'

'Yeah. It would be good to know if he could shed any further light on what was going on.'

'I'll see,' Cope said doubtfully, 'but I think we pushed him about as far as we can. He's already done a lot.'

'Of course. Don't push him too hard. But see if he can tell us if the doped birds were scheduled to race any time soon. There are ID numbers for them on the email. Presumably he can check those to get a name.'

'Yes,' Cope agreed. 'These guys usually keep very good records. I'll speak to Eric, see what he says.'

'Thanks.'

'How's the investigation going overall? Are you making much progress?'

'Well,' Carlyle felt uncomfortable at being put on the spot, 'it's still a work in progress. There are one or two things I still have to chase down.'

'Like the Belgians?' Cope laughed.

'Yeah, the Belgians.'

'Well, good luck with that. I'll let you know as soon as I've got hold of Eric.'

'Thanks again.' As he ended the call, the phone rang in his hand. Without checking the number, he hit the receive button and lifted it back to his ear.

'Carlyle.'

'Inspector, my name is Elke Lamoot.' The woman's voice was calm and composed. 'You came to my house.'

'Ah, yes.' Carlyle smiled. The Belgians – one of them at least – had finally shown up. For some reason, he had a clear picture of the woman in his imagination: five foot seven, blonde, well-dressed, well-preserved, lean, toned by a personal trainer – hard on the outside, and on the inside.

'My housekeeper said you wanted to speak to me.' The background noise suggested that the woman was sitting in a public space, probably a café or a restaurant.

'Quite a woman,' the inspector recalled.

'Indeed, eighty-two and still going strong.' Chit-chat over, Lamoot got down to business. 'What did you want to see me about?'

'I'm investigating the death of a man called Richard Furlong.' Carlyle quickly ran through the back story, trying to make the guy jumping out of his kitchen window sound as humdrum as possible.

'I heard what happened.'

Carlyle waited for the usual expressions of shock or sympathy but none were immediately forthcoming. Instead the woman said, 'I don't suppose you see things like that every day, huh?'

'Thankfully not. There was quite a mess at the scene.'

'It must have been horrible, having to deal with it.'

'It comes with the job.'

'Have you been offered counselling?'

'What?'

'Isn't that what happens, these days? People get counselling for everything.'

Was she mocking him? Carlyle ignored the question. 'I've been a policeman for a long time and, as I said, it comes with the territory.'

'I suppose it does. Poor Mr Furlong. Why do you think he did it?'

'That's what I'm trying to work out.' Carlyle paused. 'I believe that he worked for you.'

'No.' The response was both immediate and firm.

'No?' the inspector repeated, trying not to sound flustered. 'Are you sure?'

'Of course I am sure,' she said coolly. 'Mr Furlong may have done some odd jobs for my husband, but he did not work for *me*.'

To Carlyle's ear, the words sounded carefully rehearsed. Most people were fairly nervous when being questioned by the police, even if they had nothing to be nervous about. Elke

Lamoot sounded relaxed and very much in control. This is a woman who knows a thing or two about dealing with cops, Carlyle reflected.

'It seems you have been given some incorrect information, Inspector.'

'But Mr Furlong did work for Mr Lamoot?'

'I believe so. As you can imagine, however, I don't pay close attention to the comings and goings of the help.'

The help.

'And what did Mr Furlong do for your husband?'

'Various things around the restaurant.'

'The restaurant?'

'Kevin has a restaurant.' She mentioned an address in a part of town Carlyle didn't know particularly well. 'It's a kind of hobby of his. It's doing all right at the moment, but these things are so very transitory, aren't they?'

'Yes,' Carlyle agreed. 'I suppose they are. What kind of things did Mr Furlong do in the restaurant?'

'Odd jobs, as I understand it, a bit of DIY, some deliveries. He didn't work in the kitchen.'

'When was the last time he worked there?'

'I really wouldn't know.' Somewhere in the background came the sound of crashing dishes, followed by raised voices. Lamoot waited for the kerfuffle to die down, then added: 'You'd have to speak to Kevin about that.'

'I will. Marjorie said that your husband is out of London at the moment, travelling. When will he be back?'

'He's in London.'

'He's back?' Carlyle felt he was being toyed with and didn't like it.

'You should be able to find him at the restaurant. He spends most of his time there. The bar's well stocked and the novelty hasn't worn off yet.'

Carlyle realized he had overlooked one rather important detail. 'What's it called?' he asked.

'Kaplan's, with a K. You'll find the details on the website. When you're there, make sure that he feeds you. We've got an Australian chef at the moment who's really quite good. Get Kevin to put the bill on my account. I can recommend the beef stew.'

'You're not there yourself, are you?' Carlyle asked.

'Me?'

'I just thought, with the noise in the background, it sounds like you're sitting in a restaurant.'

'No, no. Funnily enough, Belgian food isn't really my thing. I'm somewhere else today. And my guest is here, so I must go. Good luck with Kevin. If you need anything else from me, you should have my number on your phone.'

Carlyle moved the phone from his ear and glanced at the screen. 'Yes, thanks.' The woman, however, had already hung up.

THIRTY-ONE

Dropping the phone into her bag, Elke Lamoot carefully calibrated her smile as she pushed back her chair and rose to her feet. 'Bob,' she said, 'thank you for making time in your diary at such short notice.'

Reaching the table, Bob Biswas smiled graciously as he shook her hand. 'It is my pleasure.' The man's grasp was weak and clammy. Lamoot had to resist the temptation to reach for her napkin to wipe his fingerprints from her skin before she sat down again.

'You're looking well.' It was a lie. The Indian bookie looked like he'd just rolled out of bed after a wild night with a couple of hookers and copious amounts of cocaine. Elke knew that was a perfectly credible scenario. She tried not to stare at the crisscross of scars on the man's face, the legacy of an old shrapnel wound, incurred when a former business partner tried to terminate Biswas's interest in all things temporal with a parcel bomb. Despite extensive plastic surgery, the guy still looked like a walking pineapple.

'So are you.' Biswas sat down. 'I swear to God, Elke, you become a more handsome woman with every passing year.'

Did she imagine it or did he just lick his lips? Lamoot ignored the sensation of her flesh crawling and upped the wattage of her smile. 'You are such a charmer, Bob.'

He acknowledged the obvious truth with a slight bow. 'It was lucky that you caught me in London. I was visiting my art dealer when you called. The Molby-Nicol Gallery on Cork Street, do you know it?'

Lamoot shook her head. 'No.'

'They have some very interesting stuff there at the moment.' He mentioned the names of a couple of artists. 'Very interesting indeed.'

'Art has never been a passion of mine.'

'I can take it or leave it most of the time. But it's proven to be a good investment over the years – a safe haven in these troubled times.'

Good for money-laundering, you mean, Lamoot thought. Biswas knew nothing about art and cared even less. If he couldn't snort it or fuck it, he wasn't much interested. 'Sounds like a good tip,' she said blandly. 'I'll check it out.'

'You should. Anyway, I was planning to visit a couple more galleries this afternoon so I'm not on a flight until tonight, which is good. I think it's always much better to do these things face to face.'

'Yes, indeed.' Lamoot looked around for some service. 'And what brought you to London? Apart from the art, of course.'

'Business. And a bit of fun.'

'Of course.'

'You know my motto: business and pleasure go hand in hand.'

'Well,' said Lamoot, drily, 'I suppose that depends on the kind of business you're in.'

It was an old joke and they chuckled politely as a waitress appeared with the menus. She handed one to Lamoot and offered the other to Biswas. He waved it away. 'I'll have chicken salad and a bottle of sparkling water. No dressing.' The waitress acknowledged the modest order with a grim nod.

From behind her menu, Lamoot raised an eyebrow. 'Are you watching your weight?'

Biswas wistfully patted the small pot of his belly. 'All the time.'

'It's a constant struggle, isn't it?'

'For some of us, I'm afraid it is.'

Lamoot closed her menu and handed it back to the waitress. 'I'll have a salad, as well, please. And a large glass of the New Zealand Riesling.'

The waitress couldn't have looked any less impressed if they had ordered some stale bread and two glasses of tap water. Tapping the details of the order into her handset, she turned and stalked off.

Now it was Biswas's turn to look unimpressed. '*New Zealand* Riesling?'

'I like to try different things,' Lamoot said airily.

'I always stick to Old World vintages.'

'It's just a glass of wine, Bob. Don't be such a snob.'

'I'm sure that Kevin doesn't stock any New Zealand wine in Kaplan's,' Biswas teased.

'Kevin doesn't do a lot of things.' Lamoot gazed around the room. She would get to the matter of her troublesome husband in due course. Bringing her attention back to the table, she gave Biswas some good eye contact. 'Look, Bob, I have to apologize for what's happened.'

'The pigeon guy.' Biswas rolled his eyes. 'How did that happen?'

'Never subcontract.' Lamoot groaned. 'But I will never pass the buck. The buck stops with me.'

'A commendable attitude. Your father was the same.'

'My father would never have got into this mess in the first place.'

'Yes, well, there is that.'

'Anyway, we are where we are. I take full responsibility for what happened. And I want to assure you that—' She was interrupted by the reappearance of the waitress with their drinks. Placing a rather ungenerous volume of wine in front of Lamoot, she filled two glasses with mineral water and placed the bottle in the middle of the table.

Biswas drank some water. 'To be honest, I wasn't that surprised when things went a bit astray. London has never been a lucky city for me. When I try to do business in his city, things never go according to plan or I get ripped off or whatever. The people here are such poor quality, really atrocious, present company excepted, of course. How you manage to live here, even part-time, is beyond me. I really don't know why I keep coming back.'

Lamoot smiled indulgently. For all his alleged misfortune, she knew that Bob Biswas made a lot of money in London, through gambling, diamonds and, increasingly, drugs.

'The place is just such hard work,' he added.

'People can be hard work anywhere.' Lamoot fiddled with the stem of her wine glass. 'But what happened here, it was entirely my fault – a lack of management oversight, if you will.'

'It wasn't your fault,' Biswas countered, 'but it was your responsibility. You've never run away from your responsibilities, Elke. Neither did Eden. He was a man of honour and you have his deep sense of ethics and propriety. That's one of the reasons that our families have done business together for so long. Honour, decency, trust. When things go wrong, as they inevitably do from time to time, we fix them, whatever the cost. I know that you will not leave me out of pocket.'

'No.' Lamoot took a gulp of her wine, waiting for her guest to propose a suitably outrageous settlement. When no figure was forthcoming, she checked that the waitress was not poised to reappear with their food, then asked 'Is Manny with you on this trip?'

'Manny?' Biswas frowned at the mention of Emmanuel Bole, his long-term bodyguard and enforcer. Then he laughed. 'No. London might be a dump but at least I can wander around unmolested. I don't need security when I'm here. I gave the man mountain some time off so he could go back to India for a reunion with some of his army pals. It's the anniversary of some hush-hush mission they did along the IB.'

'The IB?'

'The International Border between India and Pakistan. Before he came to work for me, Manny was in the Indian army, special forces. Those guys deal with some really brutal shit, I

212

can tell you. Manny doesn't like to talk about it much but, from what I can gather, he killed a lot of the enemy up in the mountains – some with his bare hands, too.'

'His bare hands?' Now it was Lamoot's turn to lick her lips. 'I was wondering,' she said quietly, 'if you might be willing to lend your Mr Bole to me for a couple of days. There's a little job I'd like him to take care of.'

Sitting in front of his computer screen, Carlyle spell-checked an overdue report on a long-running investigation into a gang of petty criminals who had been caught selling counterfeit handbags to gullible tourists in Covent Garden piazza. Job done, he hit send and dispatched it to the great cyber-filing cabinet in the sky. Grabbing a pencil, he crossed the report off the depressingly lengthy to-do list scribbled on the top sheet of a pad of yellow Post-it notes on the desk. Any sense of satisfaction at finally completing a routine task was more than offset by the knowledge that there was plenty more where that had come from.

'One report down,' he muttered to himself. 'Four to go.' What to do next? The husband-battering lawyer? The shoplifting vicar? No need to rush things, Carlyle told himself. The next report could wait, it was time for a cup of tea.

The inspector was just about to get to his feet when he spied Adam Palin coming towards him, with the same attractive young woman he had brought to the third floor on his last visit. Carlyle tried to recall her name, but came up blank. As she moved closer, he could see that she looked exhausted.

'Inspector,' Palin said, 'you remember Ms Vicedo?'

I do now. Carlyle smiled. 'Of course.'

Vicedo stared off into the middle distance. This time there was no handshake.

'She wanted to speak to you,' Palin added. 'She talked to the girl at UCH.'

'Miss X?' Forgetting about his tea, Carlyle gestured towards an empty meeting room. 'Let's go in there.' Grabbing the Post-it

213

notes and the pencil, he jumped up and led the way over to a small glass cubicle at the far end of the office. The tiny room contained four chairs and a circular table that was barely bigger than a large dinner plate. After some manoeuvring, they each took a seat. Once she was confident that she had the inspector's attention, Vicedo launched into her carefully rehearsed speech. 'The woman's real name is Isabel Corey.'

She waited while Carlyle scribbled it down, correcting his spelling of both the first and second names.

'Isabel has left the hospital and is staying at one of the Network's safe houses in London.'

Carlyle looked at Palin.

'The International Network Against Human Trafficking,' the sergeant explained. 'It's an organization run by the Sisters of Mercy to work with the police and other agencies.'

Carlyle pondered this latest piece of information. 'The Sisters of—'

A look of intense irritation flashed across Rita Vicedo's face. 'Yes, I am a nun. Didn't your colleague explain that?'

'No,' said Carlyle, ignoring the blushing sergeant. 'I don't think he did.'

'Is it a problem?'

'No, no. Not at all.' Carlyle bit his bottom lip, in an attempt to stifle a grin. Poor old Palin. Not only was the object of his desire way out of his league, she had devoted herself to a Higher Being.

The Lord giveth, and all that.

Vicedo scowled. 'Why does everyone in England think it's funny that I'm a nun?'

'I don't—'

'It's almost as if no one here has ever heard of religion.'

'It's just . . . unusual,' Carlyle offered, trying to calm her down. 'I'm not sure I've ever met a nun before.'

'I'm not a freak.'

'Of course not.' Just a bit thin-skinned, perhaps. 'Anyway, you were saying about, er . . .'

'Isabel Corey.'

'Yes.'

'She is making a good recovery and she is safe. But she needs time to make a full recovery. Rest.'

'Of course.'

'She wants to be left alone. She doesn't want to speak to the police.'

'That is going to be a problem,' Carlyle said evenly.

'It is not possible.' Vicedo folded her arms and pouted. It made her look about twelve. The inspector caught a glimpse of the girl who had become a woman.

'I'm afraid,' he said, as gently as possible, 'I must insist that I have the opportunity to speak to her.'

'Isabel needs a little time.' Vicedo leaned forward in her chair, then played her trump card. 'Let me build up a relationship with her and I am sure she will tell me what happened.'

'I don't have time to wait,' Carlyle protested.

'You don't really have any choice,' Vicedo countered.

'I thought you worked *with* the police?' Carlyle tried to glare but he was coming to like the young woman. He could see why Palin might be smitten. She had spirit as well as beauty. Very few civilians, in his experience, could walk into a police station and try to lay down the law.

'This is me working with the police. I think that Isabel knew her attacker. But she isn't ready to talk about it yet. If you push her too hard, you will get nothing.'

'We've waited this long,' Palin pointed out.

'Very well.' Carlyle sighed, glancing at his watch. The day was slipping away from him and he had nothing much to show for it. Getting up, he pulled open the door. 'I will take your advice on this but don't let this situation drag on for too long. I'm going out on a limb here, so don't let me down. Let me know as soon as you get anything.' Speech over, he headed for the canteen, leaving Palin to show their guest out.

THIRTY-TWO

His plan to drop in on Kevin Lamoot at his restaurant – and perhaps scam a free lunch into the bargain – had been derailed, first by the visit of Rita Vicedo and then by a long and fractious telephone conversation with Christina O'Brien. Umar's wife seemed to be under the impression that the inspector was her personal private detective and was dismayed by the lack of progress in tracking down her errant husband. More amazed than outraged by her attitude, Carlyle promised to get on with it.

Rather than the beef stew that Elke Lamoot had tempted him with, lunch was a limp cheese sandwich that was two days past its sell-by date. Convinced that all best-before advice was a total con aimed at wasting good food, the inspector paid it no heed. Finishing, he wiped the crumbs from his lap and swept the packaging into a plastic bag. Grabbing his mobile, he made a couple of calls in quick succession. The first, to Inspector Ronnie Score, went straight to voicemail. Leaving a message, Carlyle quickly moved on to Karen Jansen, Christina's friend from their Everton's days.

Jansen did not appear at all surprised to get the call and provided him with an address for Zoë Connors with a minimum of fuss. 'It's Harry's apartment,' she advised, 'one of the penthouses. They have their own entrance round the side.'

The inspector scribbled down the details. 'Presumably, Zoë will have to vacate the property once Harry's estate gets hold of it.'

'Presumably.' In the background, he could hear a thumping techno beat – it sounded like Jansen was in a gym. 'Knowing Harry, the place'll be mortgaged to the hilt.'

Carlyle repeated the address back to her.

'That's right.'

'Harry had money problems, did he?'

There was a pause. 'He certainly knew how to spend it.'

Carlyle noted the cautious response and moved on. 'And what's *she* like?'

'Zoë?' Jansen let out a cool laugh. 'She's as dumb as a box of rocks, but sexy as hell. In other words, just Umar's type.'

Carlyle reflected that he had never come across a woman who *wasn't* Umar's type.

'I have never known a man more driven by his dick in my whole life,' Jansen added, 'and God knows that's saying something. He was even worse than Harry in that regard.'

A vaguely sympathetic noise rose from the back of Carlyle's throat. He was about to end the call when something deep in his brain told him to fish a little more. 'You don't sound too upset about what happened.'

'It wouldn't do much good if I was, would it? I'm just glad I wasn't there when Harry was shot. Otherwise I'd be dead now, too. That's quite a scary thought, you know.'

'Yes.' It suddenly occurred to the inspector that he might as well ask the obvious question. 'Who do you think shot him?'

'Look,' she said, tiring of his questions, 'I spoke to the other cop for ages.'

'Which one?'

'Who do you think? That little shit Ronnie Score. I had to sit there watching him drool at me for more than an hour. Don't you guys compare notes?'

'Yeah,' Carlyle lied. 'Sorry, I didn't mean to waste your time.'

Jansen's mood softened immediately. 'It's okay. Do you know if he's found Isabel yet?'

'Isabel?' Carlyle looked at the name he'd scribbled down on the Post-it note earlier and felt adrenalin surge through his body.

'Isabel Corey. I told Score that she would be the best person to speak to about Harry's unfortunate demise.'

'Why?'

There was another pause.

'I thought you said you guys spoke to each other,' Jansen said coolly.

'We – we do,' Carlyle stammered. 'It's just, I don't think he's found her yet.'

'Well, make sure you do. Isabel's a good kid. It wasn't her fault that she got caught in the middle of Harry and Vernon's turf war.'

'No, I suppose not.' Who was Vernon? Carlyle decided not to ask any more questions. He could always return to Ms Jansen later, if need be. Instead he scribbled down the name and added a question mark. 'As soon as I speak to, erm, Ronnie, I'll let you know what's going on.'

'Thanks.'

Once the call was over, Carlyle spent several minutes trying to join the dots on the puzzle that Jansen had laid out for him. Unable to sketch out a coherent picture, he redialled Score's number. Again it went to voicemail. This time he didn't leave a message.

What did he know about Inspector Ronnie Score? Deep in thought, the inspector headed towards Holborn tube station and the Central Line, which would whisk him directly to the East End. A little more than twenty-five minutes later, he reached the address Jansen had given him. The development, located in the middle of a particularly grungy part of Stratford, was only a few years old but already possessed an air of neglect and disrepair. One of the windows in the main entrance was cracked and the brickwork had been tagged with graffiti in a couple of places. In a decade or so, the inspector reflected, it would probably be one of the most expensive slums in the world.

Tailgating into the building behind a couple of Chinese girls, Carlyle realized he had used the wrong entrance. 'Idiot.' Retracing his steps, he found the side door that Jansen had told him about. Three buttons indicated three apartments. The top one said *Cummins*. Carlyle held it down with his thumb for three seconds. When no one responded, he tried again, this time for six. The third time, he kept his finger on it until there was a click and an angry voice jumped out of the speaker. 'Whaddaya want?'

'It's me,' Carlyle said grimly. 'Open the fucking door.'

The lift went straight to the top floor. Carlyle found the apartment he wanted and rang the bell for another extended period. Eventually, a groggy female voice piped up from the other side of the door. 'Who is it?'

Carlyle responded with another blast of the bell.

'All right, all right.' There was the sound of locks being released, followed by the door opening a crack. A sleepy face inspected him from behind a thin chain. 'Do you know what time it is?' she croaked. 'Who are you?'

Carlyle held his ID up to the door. 'Police.' He kept his voice low, just in case any of the neighbours were home. 'Are you Zoë?'

'What do you want?'

'I'm looking for Umar.'

'He's not here.' Even allowing for her semi-comatose state, Zoë Connors wasn't a great liar.

'He just buzzed me into the building.'

'Ah.'

Jansen's voice played on a tape in his brain. *Dumb as a box of rocks.* Carlyle stuffed the warrant card back into his pocket. 'I used to work with him. This is not a formal visit, I'm a friend.' That last bit was a stretch, but never mind.

She looked at him through half-closed eyes for several more seconds, then shut the door.

Standing in the hallway, Carlyle stuck his hands behind his back, telling himself to be patient. 'You've come all this way,' he told himself, 'just be cool.'

After what seemed like an age, there was the sound of the chain being released.

The door opened.

Confronted by the sight of Umar Sligo in nothing but a pair of grubby boxer shorts, Carlyle took an involuntary step backwards.

For a moment, the two men stared at each other, caught up in a mutual sense of disappointment and mistrust.

'Did I wake you up?'

'What does it look like?' Umar turned and headed back inside. 'Come on in,' he muttered over his shoulder. 'You still like your coffee hot and strong?'

'Yeah, black.' Carlyle followed him down a narrow hallway into a large living room and kitchen area. Despite the overcast conditions outside, light flooded in from the floor-to-ceiling sliding glass doors, which opened onto a small balcony. The room itself was all wooden floors, white walls and spot-lighting. In the middle of the living room two large cream sofas sat on either side of a coffee-table. One wall was dominated by a huge flat-screen TV, another by a framed black-and-white photograph of Jimi Hendrix playing his guitar on stage. The only splash of real colour came from a bunch of sunflowers, standing in an elegant red vase in the middle of the coffee-table.

'Very chic,' was the inspector's verdict. Looking round, he considered the books lined up neatly on the coffee-table, the cushions plumped up on the sofas and the bottles of olive oil and balsamic vinegar organized by height on the kitchen work surface. The place was very carefully ordered, not to mention spotless.

'Zoë's got OCD. A cleaner comes in for a couple of hours

every day and she still spends most of her time going round tidying everything up.' Umar retreated back down the corridor. 'I'm just going to grab a T-shirt. Take a seat.'

Ignoring the invitation, Carlyle stepped over to the glass doors. Sliding one open, he let in some refreshing pollution. Stepping onto the balcony, he leaned against the parapet and took in a view of nothing in particular.

After a few minutes, Umar appeared with a mug in each hand. 'Here you go.' He placed one on the parapet in front of the inspector and kept the other for himself.

'Thanks.' Carlyle took a cautious sip. Surprisingly, the coffee wasn't too bad.

'Ugandan blend.'

'Hm.'

For a short while, they drank in silence.

'How did you know where to find me?' Umar asked finally.

Carlyle stared at the dregs of his coffee. 'I had a visit from Christina.'

'Great.' Umar's face fell.

'She says you have to get a proper job and catch up with your child support.'

Umar nodded. 'Anything else?'

'Not really. She's not over-impressed by your shagging around, but that's not exactly new, is it?'

Not interested in a lecture on morality, Umar asked, 'How did she know I'd be here?'

'I dunno. She has her sources, I suppose.'

Umar laughed. 'What sources?'

'Everyone has a network.'

'The stripper network?'

'Why not?'

Umar was clearly not satisfied with the answer. 'But Zoë and I, well, I mean, we've only just got it together. She couldn't have known—'

'Does it matter?' Carlyle snapped, irritated by his

221

ex-colleague's self-obsession. 'Maybe people just assumed you were at it, even before you were. The point is you need to get your act together. When was the last time you saw Ella?'

'Fuck off.' Umar waved his mug angrily, spilling coffee onto the parapet. 'Haven't you got work to be doing?'

'Yeah, I have, as it happens. But I promised Christina I'd have a word.'

Umar let out a snort of derision. 'Always trying to play the knight in shining armour.'

'What?'

'Nothing. Bloody Christina, she should leave me alone.'

'She is your wife,' Carlyle pointed out.

'Not for long. I wish she'd go back to America and stop snooping on me. I bet she spoke to Score – that'll be how she got the address.'

Carlyle's gaze fell on a pair of pigeons getting frisky on the roof of the next-door building. 'I don't think Ronnie's spoken to her. He's got too much on his plate at the moment.'

'But he's spoken to you?'

Carlyle left the birds to it and turned back to face Umar. 'He came and asked me about you.'

'And what did you tell him?'

'Not a lot.' Carlyle made a face. 'What could I say? It's not like we hang out together. This is the first time I've seen you since you left Charing Cross.'

Umar looked at him suspiciously. 'But why pass up the chance to stitch me up, right?'

'For Christ's sake, why would I care about stitching you up?' Carlyle brought his mug down so hard on the parapet it smashed into a dozen or more pieces. Umar burst out laughing.

'Bollocks.' The inspector threw the handle at the copulating pigeons, missing by miles. The birds continued about their business undisturbed. Carlyle waited for his host to finish laughing, then waved his coffee-stained sleeve. 'Have you got a towel?'

After cleaning himself up as best he could, the inspector flopped down on one of the sofas.

'Be careful!' Umar warned him. 'Don't make a mess, or Zoë will go mental.'

Before he could reply, the woman herself appeared in the hallway. Glaring at each of them in turn, she fought her way into a jacket. 'I'm going to get a smoothie. Do you want one?'

Assuming the question was not directed at him, Carlyle did not respond.

'I'm fine.' Placing his mug in the sink, Umar proceeded to make a performance of washing it under the tap.

'Make sure you put that away in the right place this time. And don't leave a stain on the draining-board.' Zoë disappeared down the hall. After a moment, they heard the door open and close.

Carlyle looked on, amused, as Umar dried the mug with a tea-towel and carefully returned it to its allotted place in a cupboard above his head. 'Don't you have a dishwasher?'

'Zoë doesn't like me putting dirty dishes in it,' Umar said ruefully.

'God almighty,' Carlyle said. 'If things are like this at the beginning, what hope is there for the relationship?'

Umar gave him a withering look.

Then again, Carlyle thought, you don't do long-term, do you?

'She'll go mental when she finds out you've broken one of her mugs.'

'Sorry.'

Umar stepped back into the living room but didn't sit down. 'So, other than passing on a message from my ex-wife . . .'

'Your wife,' Carlyle corrected him.

'Other than passing on a message from my *wife* and fretting about my relationship with my current squeeze, was there anything else you wanted to discuss while you were here?'

'Isabel Corey.'

Knowing better than to try to bluff his ex-boss, Umar asked, 'What about her?'

'Why did you beat her up?' Carlyle kept his tone even.

Umar's eyes narrowed. 'How did you know about that?'

Lucky guess. 'Isabel told me.'

'I don't think so.' Umar took a step forward. For a moment, the inspector thought he was going to get a thump for his trouble. Instead, the former sergeant flopped backwards onto the opposite sofa.

'She ended up in UCH. A couple of officers from Charing Cross took her statement.'

'She's on the mend?'

'Yeah. You gave her quite a beating, though.' Carlyle looked at his former colleague with a mixture of bemusement and dismay. 'What the hell were you doing?'

'Pfffffff.' Ignoring his own warnings about not making a mess, Umar lay back on the sofa, stuck a couple of cushions under his head and stared up at the ceiling. 'The whole thing was a hell of a mess.'

'You're lucky she's not going to press charges.'

'She's not?' Umar pushed himself up into something approximating an upright position, rubbing the cuts on the knuckles of his right hand.

'No. She's done a runner. Gone underground. She thought she'd get deported.'

Umar chewed his lower lip. 'That would make sense. She's Cuban, so I guess she'd be deported pretty quick.' He looked at Carlyle. 'And what about you? Are you going to pursue a prosecution?'

The inspector hadn't considered the question but that didn't stop him coming up with a snap decision. 'Not if you tell me everything you know. And I mean *everything*.'

'Always with the quid pro quo,' Umar replied. 'Such a pragmatist.'

224

'Always.' Carlyle waited patiently while Umar weighed up the pros and cons.

'I picked up a few things from Harry, but I don't know it all.'

'Just tell me what you *do* know and I'll fill in the blanks.'

Umar thought about it for a while longer. 'Fair enough,' he said finally. 'I'm going back to Manchester anyway, I've decided, so it's no skin off my nose.'

THIRTY-THREE

It took Umar less than ten minutes to run through the whole sorry tale. Harry Cummins had been in the middle of a turf war with an old-school gangster called Vernon Holder. Score worked for Holder. So, too, did Isabel Corey, who had been his spy in the enemy camp, working undercover at Bob's. When Harry found out, he went mental, ordering Umar to 'take her out'. Umar saw himself as too much of a gentleman to kill a woman, but he was happy enough to send her on her way with a serious beating. Isabel then disappeared, which may – or may not – have prompted Vernon to take his revenge on Harry. As for who actually pulled the trigger on the posh pimp, Umar was adamant that he did not know.

Feeling more like a shrink than a cop, the inspector listened carefully, committing the salient points to memory rather than taking notes. From experience, he knew he would have to let the information marinate in his brain for an indeterminate amount of time before he could decide what to do with it.

Umar was just finishing when Zoë reappeared in the doorway. She had a large plastic cup in her hand and an unhappy expression on her face. 'Umar . . .' Taking a sip of her juice through a pink straw, she glared at her new boyfriend.

'Sorry, sweetie.' Umar sat up and began to reorganize the cushions on his sofa.

Carlyle jumped to his feet. 'Thank you for your time,' he

said to no one in particular, 'and sorry for interrupting you so, erm, early in the day.'

'Don't worry about it,' Umar muttered.

'Good luck back in Manchester.' The expression clouding Zoë's face suggested to the inspector that he had put his foot in it. Not waiting for confirmation of that fact, he tiptoed towards the door.

'Manchester?' Zoë huffed, ignoring the fact that their visitor had not yet gone. 'If you think I'm going to Manchester, you've got another think coming.' Umar started to say something, but she rode straight over him. 'Are there any juice bars up there? Do they even know what a mango ginger smoothie is?'

Grinning, Carlyle saw himself out. On the street, he ordered his thoughts. Nothing that Umar had told him was a massive surprise. However, it did present him with at least one tricky problem. Pondering how best to deal with it, he didn't notice the man watching him from the opposite side of the road.

Carlyle seemed such an aimless cop. The feedback on him was mixed to say the least. Not many people liked him. A few were prepared to acknowledge that he worked hard and was capable of getting results. Others just hated his guts. But here he was, at least one step ahead of where he should have been, all things considered. Standing in the shelter of a vandalized telephone kiosk – a relic from an almost prehistoric era – the man watched as the inspector sauntered down the road and took up position at a bus stop fifty yards away. After two or three minutes a number eight appeared, to take him back towards the centre of town.

As the bus drove out of sight round the corner, the man dropped his paper cup into a nearby bin. Waiting for a break in the traffic, he jogged across the road. Letting himself into the side entrance of the building with a key fob, he took the lift to the top floor. Arriving outside the Cummins apartment, he gave two short blasts on the bell. After a few moments, the door flew open.

'Back already?' Zoë was too busy sucking the last of her juice from the cup to notice the fist that connected with her jaw and sent her sprawling to the floor. 'Awwww.' A swift kick to the stomach made sure she stayed down while the man went in search of Umar.

Getting the bus was a little indulgence he felt was his due. It was significantly slower than the tube but offered a much pleasanter travel experience, not least because you could look out of the window. Sitting on the top deck, the inspector enjoyed a spot of people-watching before calling his father. After what seemed like an eternity, Alexander picked up the phone and greeted his son with a weary 'Hello.'

Carlyle felt a familiar stab of guilt. 'How are you doing today?'

'So-so.'

'How's the death doula getting along?'

'Stine's very nice.' The old man's tone brightened somewhat. 'But she's not here today. We might go out tomorrow, if I'm up for it.'

'Good.'

'She wants to ban my sweeties, though.'

Oh, Christ. Carlyle patted his pocket, only to find that he'd left his father's tablets in his other jacket. 'Don't worry, I've got them.'

'I only had a few left,' the old man said.

'I know,' Carlyle said. 'Dom's trying to get you some more.' He was about to launch into the story of Dom's chosen drug supplier getting shot but decided it wasn't the time or the place.

'I need them,' Alexander told him. 'The pain's getting worse again.'

Carlyle gritted his teeth. 'Let me speak to Dom. He's on the case. I'll come over as quickly as I can.' If nothing else he could quietly return the tablets that Stine had tried to confiscate.

228

Hopefully, his father could do a better job at hiding them this time.

'All right,' Alexander replied, apparently mollified.

'Let me speak to Dom now.' Cutting off his father rather abruptly, he pulled up Silver's number and hit call. After a pause, he heard the international ring tone, which served to remind him that Dom was currently on holiday.

'Shit.' The call went to voicemail, prompting a further slew of curses. A woman sitting on the opposite side of the aisle gave the inspector a dirty look. Ignoring it, he left a pathetic message imploring his mate to call him back. Dropping the phone into his pocket, he squinted at the line of almost stationary traffic ahead. At this rate, it was going to be a very long journey back to Charing Cross.

Sitting at a table by the bar, Kevin Lamoot sipped a glass of beer as he flipped through a computer printout listing the restaurant's bookings for the next few days. If his calculations were correct, Kaplan's was on course for its best week of the year so far. Takings were up fifteen per cent week-on-week, thirty-five per cent year-on-year. If the restaurant wasn't quite making a profit yet, it was getting close. To his surprise, the idea of being a legitimate businessman was quite appealing. Maybe his bloody know-it-all wife would start to believe that the restaurant was more than just a hobby or a convenient way of laundering some of their ill-gotten cash. Maybe they could even open a second. Somewhere in the City, perhaps, or Chelsea. Kaplan's could become a chain known across London. He could build it up and sell it at a ridiculous price to some private equity outfit, dump Elke and retire to Florida.

His idle musings were interrupted by the front door opening and shutting. Lamoot became aware of someone hovering in the doorway. He cursed Sasha, the waitress, who was responsible for closing up. Bloody hell, girl, didn't you lock the door? The last lunchtime diner had left twenty minutes ago. They wouldn't reopen now until the evening. Looking up, Lamoot gave the new arrival an insincere smile. 'I'm sorry, but lunch service is now over. We're closed.'

The man standing in the doorway said nothing.

Bloody tourist. Tossing his papers onto the table, Lamoot fell into the English habit of speaking to foreigners slowly, in a loud voice. 'Lunch is finished.' The man was a giant, easily six foot three. For a moment, Lamoot thought he looked vaguely familiar, then remembered that almost everyone in London seemed vaguely familiar, for one reason or another.

A sudden burst of laughter rose and fell from one of the private rooms at the back where the staff were having a break. 'I'm sorry,' Lamoot repeated, 'we're closed.'

Remaining mute, the man gave no indication of understanding English. Neither did he give any indication of interest in the menu as he stepped in front of the table. Instead, he thrust out an arm and clamped a massive paw around Lamoot's throat.

'Eek.' Making a sound like a trapped mouse, the restaurateur was lifted out of his chair as the remains of his beer and his spreadsheets were sent flying. Squirming in the man's grip, Lamoot tried to swing a left hook, making contact with nothing but air. For his trouble, he was rewarded with a smack to the head and frogmarched towards the back of the room. A cry for help died in his throat as he was pushed through the kitchen doors. His knees buckled and his attacker jerked him upright, like a rag doll. Looking around frantically for some means of escape, Lamoot's terrified gaze fell upon a row of kitchen knives lined up on a workbench. But his attempt to reach for one was feeble, only encouraging the giant to increase the pressure on his neck to the point where he thought he might pass out. A voice whispered in his ear, its English so heavily accented that it took him several moments to decipher what he was being told.

'Be still,' was the instruction. 'Do not try to fight me or this situation will become worse for you. Much worse.'

* * *

230

Kaplan's wasn't quite what he had expected. Situated on a dingy side street near Bayswater tube station, it looked less like an upmarket restaurant and more like a transport café. One thing it didn't have, however, was transport-café prices. Pausing to inspect the menu displayed by the front door, the inspector felt a sharp pain in his wallet that more than matched the self-pitying rumble in his stomach. Everything in this city was so expensive, he sometimes felt as if he was holding on by his fingertips. Trying not to think about the parlous state of his personal finances, he pulled open the door and stepped inside.

At first glance, the place seemed completely deserted. The lights were dim and the air-conditioning had been set to a chilly but not unpleasant sixteen or seventeen degrees. Carlyle stood by the maître d's greeting station, letting his eyes adjust to the gloom. In front of him, he counted twenty tables, many of which had yet to be cleared after the lunchtime service. To his right a set of double doors with porthole windows, leading to the kitchen. To his left, a corridor led towards the back of the building. In between there was a small bar area, along with a cloakroom and a flight of stairs heading up to the first floor.

The inspector cleared his throat. 'Hello?' His gaze fell to the floor. A smashed beer glass and some papers lay between two tables. 'Hello?' He raised his voice a couple of notches. 'This is the police.' Still there was no response. Careful not to step on the broken glass, he retrieved the nearest sheet of paper. It was a list of reservations for later in the week. Placing it on one of the tables, he moved deeper into the room, catching a reflection of his own image in a large mirror hanging on the far wall. He took a moment to consider the man staring back at him, then raised his voice still further. 'Is anyone around?' His phone started to ring. Keeping a wary eye on the back of the room, he pulled it out of his pocket and inspected the screen.

Dom.

He hit the receive button and lifted the handset to his ear.

'Thanks for calling me back.' Realizing his voice was too

loud, he dialled it down a couple of notches. 'Sorry for calling you on holiday.'

'No problem,' Dom said cheerily. 'Eva's reading by the pool. I'm just back from my jog.'

Jog? Carlyle exchanged a quizzical look with himself in the mirror. He had never known Dom to engage in exercise of any sort. First he has a facelift and now this. The boy must be having a mid-life crisis. Carlyle wondered if a Porsche and a twenty-two-year-old mistress would be next. He hoped Dom would be above all that, but you never knew.

'I'm in training for a ten K run next month. For charity.' Dom mentioned the name of a very worthy cause. 'I'll put you down for fifty quid.'

'Sure,' said Carlyle, relieved that he hadn't asked for a hundred.

'How's it going?'

'Messily, as per usual. You ever been to place called Kaplan's?'

'Don't think so. What is it?'

'A Belgian restaurant in Bayswater.'

'That's a fail on both counts.' Dom laughed. 'Tell me you didn't ring for a restaurant recommendation.'

'No, no,' Carlyle said hastily. 'I was calling about my dad.'

'Don't worry, I'm still on it. As soon as I get back, it'll get done. I'm trying to sort out a painting for an important customer, so I'll be back a few days early. Tell Alexander to hold on. Has he got any of his original order left?'

'A few, but the poor old bugger's beginning to struggle.' Carlyle was about to explain about the death doula when there was a sharp noise from the kitchen. 'Look,' he said quickly, 'I've got to go. I'll call you back.'

Peering through the porthole, the kitchen looked deserted. 'Mr Lamoot?' The inspector stepped cautiously through the door. In front of him was a passageway maybe fifteen feet long and three feet wide, illuminated by harsh strip-lighting, with stainless-steel workbenches running along either side. An extractor fan hummed ineffectually on the far wall. The temperature was maybe ten degrees higher than out front and the atmosphere was stale.

'Is anyone around?' Carlyle cautiously made his way towards the back of the room, listening to the soles of his shoes squelching on the sticky tiled floor.

'This is the police.'

Reaching the end of the passage, he turned to his right, finding himself in a food-preparation area. Boxes of fresh vegetables stood piled on the floor. An impressive set of knives lay on a draining-board next to a row of sinks.

'It's like the bloody *Mary Celeste*,' he muttered, retracing his steps.

On the other side of the passage, hidden behind a row of floor-to-ceiling freezers was a phalanx of six gas-burning ovens. Not quite believing what he was seeing, Carlyle did a double-take. 'Oh, bollocks.'

As he came closer, a sickly smell caused him to put one hand over his mouth as he reached for his phone with the other. As he did so, he was conscious of movement at the periphery of his vision. Turning his head, Carlyle saw the bottom of a copper pan rear up towards him. He let out a low cry just as it smacked him flush in the face. Staggering backwards, he felt his head bounce off the edge of a workbench, giving him the opportunity for a further, extended howl of pain before the lights went out and he was plunged into darkness.

THIRTY-FOUR

Even with an ice pack wrapped around his neck and four para-
cetamol dissolving in his stomach, the inspector felt nauseous
as he struggled with one of the worst bastard headaches he had
ever known in his entire life. All around him, Kaplan's was now
abuzz with activity. An endless stream of crime-scene technicians headed in and out of the kitchen. On the far side of the
room, seven members of staff, four girls and three boys, sat
in silence, clustered around a trio of tables. To Carlyle's eyes
they all looked incredibly young. Each one stared vacantly into
the middle distance with their hands wrapped around a mug of
steaming tea and a blanket around their shoulders. The police
had found them locked into a walk-in freezer, shaken but basically unhurt.

Ignoring the disapproving look from the pretty young paramedic who had been patching him up, Carlyle popped another
couple of painkillers from the foil packet and dropped them
into his mouth.

'You need to go easy on those.'

The paramedic was called Bella. She was originally from
Derby. Her boyfriend had a job training kids at Spurs. In less
than five minutes Carlyle had come to know far more about her
than he could ever want or need to. Grunting, he washed the
pills down with some carbonated water.

'I know it hurts,' Bella said gently, 'but you have to pace
yourself. No more for the next four hours, okay?'

'My head feels like it's falling off.' The inspector let out a small moan by way of supporting evidence. 'Are you sure you haven't got anything stronger?'

'This is the good stuff. Anything stronger than those and you'd be arrested.'

Carlyle wondered about requisitioning some of his father's pills. The idea was very appealing but he pushed it away as he watched a tall guy in a sergeant's uniform appear in front of him and sit down at the table.

'Jesus, you look a hell of a mess.'

'Thanks, Joe.'

Working out of the Notting Hill station, Joe Woods was a skinny Glaswegian who looked about seventy. The reality was that he was seven years younger than Carlyle. The two men had previously worked together on an investigation into a series of smash-and-grab raids at top West End hotels. Woods placed a phone on the table. 'We found your mobile under one of the work benches.'

'Thanks.' Carlyle hadn't even registered he'd lost it.

'Does it hurt?'

'Just a bit.'

'He's got a fractured cheek,' Bella said perkily. 'Other than that, there's no real damage. He just has to be careful and not take too many pills.' Ignoring the inspector's baleful stare, she wandered off to check on the frozen kids.

'What happened?' Woods asked.

Carlyle took another sip of water. 'I came looking to speak to the owner, a guy called Kevin Lamoot. The place was deserted. I went into the kitchen and someone smacked me in the face with a pan. The next thing I know, Florence Nightingale there was leaning over me with the smelling salts.'

'You didn't see who hit you?'

'All I saw was stars.' Lifting a hand, Carlyle pressed the ice pack against the base of his skull. 'What about the CCTV?'

Woods shook his head. 'They didn't have any.'

Carlyle frowned.

'I know. Unusual. We'll get images from the main street but it'll take time to go through them.'

'What about the human ice lollies?'

Woods chuckled. 'They're all too traumatized. All we've got from them was that a massive bloke with a gun forced them into the freezer.'

'That narrows it down, then.'

'They think he was Indian. Maybe.'

'Very helpful.'

'You've got to cut them a bit of slack, John. They thought they were going to die in there.'

'Good point,' Carlyle conceded. Things had developed so quickly that he hadn't had time to contemplate his own fate, never mind that of anyone else.

'At least,' Woods observed, 'we're only looking at one murder.'

'I know.' The inspector flicked a switch inside his brain, turning his professional detachment back on. 'Quite an interesting one, though. Have you ever seen anything like that?'

'Never.' Woods scratched his head. 'Drowning a man in a pot of stew takes some doing.'

Carlyle closed his eyes and brought up just about the last picture his brain had recorded before the lights went out: the man bent over the stove, his head stuck in a massive pot. It was a surreal image, really quite funny – assuming you weren't the hapless Kevin Lamoot. He thought back to Elke Lamoot's lunch recommendation. 'She did say that the stew was very good.'

The sergeant's weathered features crumpled still further as he tried to make sense of the cryptic remark. 'Sorry?'

'Nothing.' The inspector opened his eyes again. 'Presumably that *was* the restaurant owner in the stew?'

'Looks like it. His wallet was still in his jacket pocket. He'll have to be formally identified but it's almost certain that he's

Kevin Lamoot.' Woods ran his palm across the stubble on his chin. 'Lucky for you there was only one pot on the stove. Otherwise you could have become a Met legend.'

Carlyle grimaced. 'Doesn't bear thinking about.' The last thing any copper wanted to become was the source of tasteless jokes and sniggering across the city's police stations – especially for the way they died. As he contemplated his narrow escape, another question crawled across the inspector's battered brain. 'How did you find me so quickly?'

Woods pointed to the phone. 'You must have accidentally redialled the number of your last call before you dropped the handset. A Mr Dominic Silver called nine-nine-nine to say that you were in a bit of trouble. Or, as he put it, "It sounds like he's having the shit kicked out of him."'

Carlyle gave silent thanks for Dom's quick thinking.

'It was very lucky that the gentleman was able to tell us where you were,' Woods pointed out.

'We'd just been talking about it.'

The sergeant stared at his shoes. 'I know Dominic Silver, at least by reputation. He was a cop, wasn't he?'

'That was a long time ago now.' Carlyle took a deep breath, then gave the briefest possible explanation of their relationship. 'We started out together but Dom packed it in pretty quickly. He must have left a few years before you came down to London.' Jumping straight over the intervening decades, he brought things to the present. 'He's an art dealer now.'

Woods looked up, surprised. 'Is he indeed?'

'He's got a small gallery on Cork Street.'

'Must be doing well for himself.'

'I think he does okay,' said Carlyle, cautiously, not wishing to get drawn into speculation about the extent to which the not-so-small fortune Dom had built up over the years dealing drugs was being used to bankroll his current endeavour. 'Clients come in from all around the world, you know the sort of thing.'

Woods's expression suggested he didn't have a clue about the top echelons of the art world.

'The prices some of these people pay,' Carlyle shook his head, 'you'd be amazed.'

'I'm sure I would,' Woods said amiably. 'So, Mr Silver, what does he have to do with this little drama?'

'Nothing at all,' Carlyle said hastily. 'I'd called him to talk about something else. It was nothing to do with Lamoot. A personal matter.'

'Personal.' Woods repeated the word, making it sound highly dubious.

'It was nothing work-related.'

Taking the hint, Woods moved on. 'So why were you here?' he asked. 'And why do you think Mr Lamoot was killed?'

Looking past the sergeant's shoulder, Carlyle spotted a familiar figure hovering by the stairs. 'These are all very good questions, Joe, but doesn't Maria want to ask me them herself?'

Catching his eye, Superintendent Maria Lockhead walked over. 'You look a right mess,' she said, making little effort to hide her grin.

'You're not the first person to point that out.' Carlyle gestured towards an empty chair and waited for her to sit down. 'Joe here was just about to give me the third degree.'

'Hardly.' The sergeant got to his feet. 'I'll go and see how the pathologist is getting on, leave you two to it.'

Carlyle watched Woods disappear into the kitchen before turning his attention back to the superintendent. 'Long time no see.' He tried to remember the last time their paths had crossed and concluded that it had to be three years ago, at least. 'How's the family?'

'Fine. Growing up fast. How about yours?'

'All good.' Carlyle remembered that he hadn't called Helen to tell her about his latest mishap. Probably better to have the conversation face to face. He slipped the phone into his jacket pocket. 'Same as always.' He smiled. 'As long as I behave myself and do what I'm told, they put up with me.'

'I know what you mean.' Lockhead laughed. 'We're both very lucky. It's a total bugger trying to juggle a family with this job.'

'Very true.'

'So, anyway,' preamble over, she was suddenly all business, 'what happened here?'

A trickle of water escaped from the ice pack and began a slow journey down the length of Carlyle's spine. It was soothing and disconcerting at the same time. 'You know me,' he offered, 'I wouldn't like to speculate.'

Lockhead bit her lip. 'You wouldn't be trying to hinder a police investigation, would you, John?'

'Of course not.' Taking the leaking ice pack from his neck, he placed it on the table. A fresh wave of nausea swept over him and he pitched forward in his seat. Pushing back his chair, he got unsteadily to his feet. 'You'll have to excuse me, but I think I'm going to be sick.'

THIRTY-FIVE

By the time the inspector finally reappeared from the bathroom, a rather dumpy middle-aged woman dressed in a grey sweatshirt and black jeans was sitting at the table. Holding a small bottle of water, she listened, stony-faced, to a briefing from Lockhead. As Carlyle returned to his seat, the woman scrutinized the mess of his face.

Lockhead placed a hand on his forearm. 'Are you feeling better?'

Carlyle nodded. Another couple of painkillers seemed to have taken the edge off his headache, although he still felt like he might throw up at any moment.

Lockhead gestured to the woman in front of them. 'This is Mrs Lamoot.'

Not quite what I had in mind. 'John Carlyle.' He offered a limp handshake.

A look of anxiety descended on Elke Lamoot's heavily lined face. 'We spoke on the phone.'

Lockhead gave Carlyle a quizzical glance but he kept his eyes locked firmly on the not-so-grieving widow.

'I'm sorry for the loss of your husband.' He tried not to sound mechanical.

'Inspector Carlyle was the first officer on the scene,' Lockhead explained. 'He interrupted the presumed killer and was violently assaulted for his trouble.'

Lamoot gazed at him. Suddenly there was a sparkle in her

eyes that he found vaguely disconcerting. 'You didn't catch him?'

'No,' Carlyle admitted.

'Shouldn't you be in hospital?' There was no concern behind the widow's question.

'I'll be fine.'

Lockhead gave an exasperated tut. 'Mrs Lamoot . . .'

Elke Lamoot kept her eyes fixed on the inspector. 'Does your boss not know who I am?'

Carlyle declined to point out that Lockhead wasn't really his boss. Instead he turned to the superintendent, speaking in a low, urgent voice, keen to get the words out before he had to rush back to the bathroom. 'Mrs Lamoot is Belgian criminal royalty. Her dad was a big-time gangster in Brussels.'

Lamoot glared at him but said nothing.

'She lives in London. I spoke to her recently about the death of a man called Richard Furlong.'

'Suicide.'

Carlyle acknowledged Lamoot's clarification with a nod. 'I came to ask Mr Lamoot about Furlong's suicide. According to Mrs Lamoot, Furlong occasionally worked for her husband. When I arrived, the dining room was deserted but a bunch of papers was strewn about and beer had been spilled on the floor. When I went into the kitchen, I found Mr Lamoot but then got whacked in the face.'

'Is it true that he was found face down in a pot of stew?' Elke Lamoot looked as if she was trying to stifle a smile. 'Such a waste of a good carbonnade.'

'Can you think of who might have done this?' Lockhead asked.

It was the wrong question. A knowing look passed between Carlyle and Lamoot.

'As the inspector implied,' Lamoot said, by way of reply, 'I am not the type of person who can be messed with. Whoever did this to my husband has made a big mistake – and they will pay for it.'

Carlyle didn't believe her manufactured outrage.

'Mrs Lamoot,' Lockhead said sternly, 'if you have any information that may assist in this investigation, you must let us know immediately.'

'Kevin was an idiot,' Lamoot said grimly, 'but he was untouchable because he was my husband. I do not know of anyone who would be so stupid as to do something like this or, indeed, what their motivation might be.' Reaching for an expensive-looking blue handbag, she rummaged around inside before pulling out a business card and placing it on the table. 'This is my lawyer. Anything else you need from me, you go through her.'

Lockhead reached across the table and picked up the card. She looked at Carlyle but the inspector was already back on his feet. 'Excuse me.' He lurched back towards the bathroom.

Locking himself in one of the stalls, he bent over the bowl, almost dropping his mobile into the water. As he saw the phone slip out of the breast pocket of his jacket, he stumbled forward and saved it from a watery grave. 'Phew. Good to know the old reflexes are in working order.' Gripping the phone tightly, he felt it start to vibrate in his hand. Leaning against the side of the stall, he hit receive.

'Yes?'

'It's Ronnie Score.'

Hearing the name, Carlyle forced himself upright. 'What can I do for you?'

'I'm just with your boy, Umar Sligo.'

My boy? Trying to remove any trace of irritation or suspicion, Carlyle tried to keep his tone light. 'And what does he have to say for himself?'

'Not a great deal,' Sligo deadpanned, 'but that's probably got something to do with the fact that he's been shot in the face. Just like Harry Cummins.'

Carlyle closed his eyes, trying to ignore his somersaulting stomach. 'Dead?'

'Just a bit.' Score sounded remarkably cheery. 'The girl-friend too. It looks like someone is clearing up the loose ends.' Score started to say something else but Carlyle wasn't listening. Dropping into a crouch, he grabbed the toilet seat with his free hand and vomited noisily.

Back in Zoë Connors's living room, he watched another set of crime-scene technicians go about their business. As the sickly smell of death tickled his nostrils, Carlyle gave silent thanks that he had already relieved his stomach of its contents. The red vase he had admired on his last visit lay smashed on the floor, the sunflowers lying in a pool of drying blood alongside one of the sofa cushions. Squatting, he pulled back the sheet covering one of the bodies and looked into Umar's shattered face. 'You stupid sod.'

Dropping the sheet, he struggled back to his feet, thinking about what needed to be done next. First and foremost, he should speak to his union rep at the Police Federation. As probably the last person to see Umar and Zoë alive – other than their killer – there was no way he could avoid being dragged into this investigation. Like any sane person, he would need legal representation at his side before he opened his mouth. After that had been sorted out, he would have to speak to Christina. If nothing else, he should be the one to tell her that Umar was dead. She and Ella deserved better than to learn the news from some hapless uniform with all the empathy of an empty crisps packet.

'You look like shit.' Ronnie Score eyed him suspiciously from the doorway.

Carlyle gestured towards the body at his feet. 'Better than him, though.'

'That's a matter of opinion,' Score grunted.

'What happened?'

'No sign of forced entry.' Score gestured to the sliding doors, which were still open, leading towards the balcony. 'So, unless someone came up the fire escape – unlikely, because it's locked at the bottom – they opened the door to someone they knew and . . .' he made a pistol with two fingers of one hand and pointed it at Carlyle '. . . blam, blam.'

Carlyle nodded. 'Where's the girl?'

'They took her away already.' Score mentioned the name of the pathologist in charge of the scene. 'He runs a very efficient operation. We'll all be out of here by teatime and the estate agents will be able to have the place back on the market the day after tomorrow.'

'They'll have to do a bit of cleaning first.'

'There is that.' Score headed back down the hallway. 'Come and look at something with me.'

Carlyle followed him into a small bedroom that appeared to be used as an office. The room was empty apart from a chair and a cheap desk, pushed against the back wall underneath a small window. On the desk stood an open laptop. Reaching forward, Score tapped once on the keyboard. Almost immediately, a video filled the screen. Leaning against the frame of the door, Carlyle folded his arms as he watched it run. He was well aware of what he was watching. The question was, why was Score showing it to him?

After less than twenty seconds, the video came to a close and the screen went blank.

'That's the CCTV from outside the building.' Score scratched his nose. 'You were here this morning.'

'I was.' Carlyle shifted his weight uncomfortably from one foot to another. This was not really a conversation he wanted to have before speaking to his Police Federation rep. At the same time, he knew that refusing to comment was simply not an option. 'I came to see Umar.'

'Why?'

'His wife asked me to speak to him. She came to see me

at Charing Cross with their daughter. Umar was behind in his child-support payments. She wanted me to mention it to him.'

'Is that all?' Score looked professionally doubtful. 'Are you sure she didn't want you to lean on him a bit?'

'Hardly.' Carlyle vowed to try to keep things light. 'Anyway, there's a big difference between, quote-unquote, "leaning on someone a bit" and shooting them stone dead, wouldn't you say?'

'Things can get out of hand,' Score offered philosophically.

'We had a perfectly civilized chat.' Carlyle thought about the smashed mug – no need to go there. 'He was alive and well when I left him.'

'Child support – was that all you talked about?' A sheen of sweat appeared on Score's brow. He wiped it away, using the palm of his hand. 'What about Harry Cummins?'

'Harry came up in passing,' Carlyle acknowledged. 'It would be a bit of a surprise if he didn't.'

'He didn't talk to you about who might have killed Cummins?'

'Umar wasn't exactly delighted to see me. Anyway, I thought you had interviewed him at length, no?'

'I did.' Score scratched his belly. His green T-shirt looked as if it hadn't been washed in months. 'He didn't say much, though.'

Catching the unmistakable whiff of body odour, Carlyle took a step backwards. 'That sounds like Umar,' he reflected. 'He was always a stubborn little shit.'

'Is that why you killed him?'

'Eh?' Carlyle laughed nervously.

'Is that why you killed him?' Score repeated. He lifted his head, meeting Carlyle's gaze. 'Was it a row about money? Wouldn't he pay up?'

'Don't be stupid, Ronnie,' Carlyle stammered, trying not to sound panicked by the turn the conversation had taken. 'What are you talking about?' He recalled what Umar had told him about Score and cursed himself for walking so blindly into a waiting trap.

'What was going on? Were you banging the ex-wife?'

I'm going to be banging your fucking head against the wall in a minute. Marshalling every ounce of self-control at his disposal, Carlyle concentrated on his breathing, slow and deep. 'They're still married.'

A sickly grin crossed Score's face. 'I hear she's quite a looker.'

Carlyle was never going to compete in the Met's boxing championships, but he was more than a match for Ronnie Score. Moving onto the balls of his feet, he was just about to unleash his right fist on Score's jaw when two large uniforms appearing in the doorway caused him to rethink his strategy.

'You've got some explaining to do,' Score continued, oblivious to his lucky escape. 'I thought you were a family man, as well.'

Carlyle's latest protest died in his throat as he watched Score whip out a pair of handcuffs. The inspector had to accept that he had been done up like the proverbial kipper. A period of quiet reflection was called for; doubtless he would have plenty of time in the coming hours to plot his revenge.

Biting his tongue, he allowed Score to snap the cuffs onto his wrists.

'John Carlyle, you are under arrest on suspicion of the murder of Umar Sligo and Zoë Connors.' Score enunciated every word slowly, clearly, with obvious relish. 'Anything you say—'

'Save it,' Carlyle snarled. 'This is bullshit. You'll never make it fly.'

'They all say that.' Score placed a hand on his shoulder. 'You should know that as well as I do.'

A list of all the miscarriages of justice he'd come across in his career started scrolling across Carlyle's brain. He, more than anyone, knew how easy it was to get lost in the system. Lifting his hands to his mouth, he coughed, twice, trying to remove the doubt from his voice. 'You're delusional if you think that you can somehow manage to get away with this.'

'I guess we'll just have to see how it plays out, won't we?' After patting down Carlyle's pockets, he relieved the inspector of his warrant card and his mobile phone. 'Maybe by the time we get through this, I'll have you for Harry Cummins as well.'

Carlyle tried not to gulp. The bigger the lie, the more likely it was to succeed. One thing at a time, he told himself. Focus on getting through the next few hours. 'I'm allowed a call, aren't I?'

'When you get to the station,' Score grunted.

'Where are you taking me?'

'You'll find out when you get there.' He gave Carlyle a gentle push towards the uniforms. 'Time to go.'

Grim-faced, Carlyle allowed himself to be escorted out of the flat. Taking his time, he headed down the stairs and onto the street. A few passers-by gave him an odd look as he was unceremoniously shoved into the back of a police van waiting by the kerb. Otherwise, the world went about its business without giving him a second thought. At least there aren't any photographers on hand to capture the moment, Carlyle thought, trying to look on the bright side. *Cop arrested for murder* was a story in anybody's language. It wouldn't be a surprise if Score, still upstairs, was already tipping off some tame journalist. In the press he would be guilty until forgotten about. By the time his innocence was confirmed, the media would have moved on.

The vehicle's only other occupant was a female PCSO – Police Community Support Officer – sitting behind the steering wheel. The woman was listening to a U2 song on the radio, elbow on the windowsill, singing along tunelessly until one of the uniforms appeared at her door. After a whispered conversation, she switched off the radio and started the engine.

'Where are we going?' Carlyle asked.

'You'll find out when you get there,' the PCSO said dully, as she checked her wing mirror and pulled out into the traffic.

'Isn't Ronnie coming with us?'

This time the woman, concentrating on finding a way through the traffic, didn't grace him with a reply.

THIRTY-SIX

He was woken by footsteps in the corridor outside, followed by hushed voices and the sound of a key turning in the lock. By the time the inspector had wiped the sleep from his eyes and swung his legs off the bed, the door had opened and a familiar figure was standing in front of him. She was wearing a blue waterproof jacket and a small rucksack. In one hand she held a cardboard coffee cup and a small paper bag.

Carlyle eyed the coffee hopefully. 'Is that for me?'

'Nice to see you too.' Stepping into the cell, Alison Roche handed over the refreshments. 'I thought you might be in need of sustenance.'

'Too right.' Carlyle ripped open the bag and licked his lips.

'It was the biggest pastry I could find,' his sergeant explained.

'Thanks.' The inspector took a greedy bite from the bun, washing it down with the lukewarm coffee. As dining experiences went, it was a pretty tasteless one, but he wasn't in a position to be choosy. 'Just what I needed.'

'Good.'

'Dinner has yet to be served,' he quipped. 'In fact, I have yet to see a menu, never mind the wine list. Maybe you could have a word with the management for me.'

Hovering by the door, the duty sergeant muttered something that sounded to Carlyle very much like 'wanker'.

Shaking her head, Roche turned to the man in the doorway.

'Thanks, Dan. I'll give you a shout when I'm done. No need to lock the door.'

'Don't take too long.' The sergeant gestured at Carlyle with his keys. 'He's not supposed to see anyone till Score gets here.'

Roche shot him her best smile. 'I'll be quick.'

'No more than ten minutes.' The sergeant disappeared, closing the door behind him.

'Don't forget the menu,' Carlyle shouted after him.

'Nice to see you're taking things in your stride.' Gesturing for the inspector to shift up, Roche dropped her backpack onto the floor and sat down on the end of the bed.

Carlyle demolished the last of his snack. 'What are you doing here, by the way?'

'What do you think?' Roche snorted. 'Riding to the rescue. What happened to your face?'

So much had happened since his battering in the kitchen of Kaplan's, Carlyle had almost forgotten about his even uglier than usual mug. He lifted a tentative hand to it. 'Police brutality,' he joked.

A look of genuine concern passed across Roche's face. 'They did that to you in here?'

'No, no.' The inspector beat a hasty retreat. 'It's nothing to do with me being in here. Another case entirely.'

'You should have been given access to a doctor.'

'Nah. I'm fine. Just a couple of cuts and bruises. You should see the other guy.' He forced out a low chuckle. 'I wish I had.'

'You're not making much sense. Maybe you've got some kind of brain trauma.'

'My brain's fine,' Carlyle said. 'It's a long story. I'll explain later. Nothing to do with this palaver.'

'Okay.' Roche decided not to probe any further. 'At least you've managed to make yourself at home. Did you have a good nap?'

'Very nice.' It was true enough. Once processed and in his cell, Carlyle had surprised himself by going out like a light. A couple of hours' deep sleep had left him feeling refreshed and weirdly relaxed about his situation.

By contrast, a look of profound dismay settled across Roche's face as she looked around. The brick walls had been painted a depressing shade of battleship grey and the smell of damp mingled with various other even less appealing odours. 'How the hell can you manage to sleep in here?'

'There's not a lot else to do, is there?' Finishing his coffee, the inspector crumpled the paper bag into a ball, dropped it inside the cup and placed the cup on the floor. 'It's not like they're going to offer me a selection of newspapers or Sky Sports, is it?'

'I'm sure Dan will be only too happy to oblige.'

'Dan?' His pillow had fallen on the floor. Reaching down, Carlyle picked it up and placed it carefully back on the bed.

'Daniel Philpott, the duty sergeant. He's a decent bloke, a really good mate. I've known him for ages. We worked together for a couple of years. Lucky for you he was the one who booked you in. Thank God he gave me a call.'

'Small world.' Carlyle – who had wasted his own phone call on Dominic Silver's voicemail – tried to look grateful. 'Thanks, Dan. I owe you one.'

'What goes round comes round,' Roche said cryptically. 'He owes me a few favours, as it happens.'

Carlyle looked her up and down. 'He's not—'

'No.' The sergeant blushed. 'Dan didn't get me up the duff.'

'The mystery remains. The pool at Charing Cross has still to be claimed.'

Roche raised an eyebrow. 'What pool?'

'Erm . . .' How best to explain to his saviour that her colleagues had a pool of five hundred and forty pounds riding on the identity of the baby's father?

'I would have thought,' Roche admonished him, 'you had more important things to worry about than that at the moment.'

'Yes, indeed.'

'You were extremely lucky that Dan was on duty today. He's off on holiday tonight, a fortnight in Cyprus. If you'd have been brought in tomorrow, I would never have known about it until I saw you on the news.'

'Very funny.' Wiping a crumb from his chin, Carlyle belatedly discovered his manners. 'It's very kind of you to come. You didn't have to do it. I really appreciate it.'

'To be honest,' Roche admitted wearily, 'it's a bit of a break from the childcare.'

'You look knackered,' Carlyle blurted.

'I *am* knackered,' his sergeant shot back. 'But thanks for pointing it out.' Leaning against the wall, she closed her eyes. 'I could do with a couple of nights in here myself.'

'I wouldn't go that far.'

'Spoken like a man. I don't suppose you remember what it was like just after Alice was born?'

Carlyle tried to recall the early days of parenthood. After so many years, all he had was a rosy glow. 'Not really. It was so long ago. And Helen did most of it.'

'Speaking of Helen, does she know where you are?'

'No.' He wondered how long he could leave it before informing his wife about his latest adventure.

'Want me to give her a call?'

'No. I'll be out of here soon enough.'

'Let's hope.'

'I will,' Carlyle insisted, pleased that Roche took his innocence as read. 'Better that I speak to her face to face.'

'I suppose.'

There was a pause. Then he asked. 'Don't you need to get home? Who's looking after the baby?'

'I've got a bit of time. My mum's down to help at the moment.'

'Uh-huh.'

'Which is great,' Roche yawned 'but it's still completely knackering.'

'It gets easier,' Carlyle offered. 'Assuming you only have the one.'

'Don't worry, there are no plans for another.' She shuddered at the prospect. 'But, matter in hand, what the hell happened to you?'

Carlyle took a moment to order his thoughts. 'Do you want the long version, or the short version?'

Roche raised an eyebrow. 'There's a short version?'

'Well, the long version or the longer version?'

Tutting to herself, Roche opened her rucksack and recovered a notebook and pen. Flipping the book open, she flicked to a blank page and scribbled the date at the top. 'Why don't you just give me the relevant facts and we'll see about getting you out of here?'

'Even by your standards, you've been a bit of a berk,' was Roche's initial verdict, after he had taken her through the story of Umar, Harry Cummins and Ronnie Score. 'If Umar told you that Ronnie Score was working for this guy . . .' she paused to consult her notes '. . . Vernon Holder, why didn't you do something about it?'

'I had a lot on my plate,' was all the inspector could offer by way of response. 'It was on my to-do list.'

'Obviously not high enough up it.' Roche was well aware of her boss's sometimes strange way of prioritizing things. 'Why do you think Score parked you in Forest Gate?'

Before taking his nap, Carlyle had given some consideration to precisely that question: why had Score sent him to an out-of-the-way police station in the depths of east London? The only conclusion he could come to was that Score wanted to try to lose him in the system before anyone could cry foul. 'He's trying to buy some time so that he can fabricate enough evidence to keep this farce going.'

Roche closed her notebook. 'Score must know that this whole thing is going to blow up in his face, sooner or later.'

'I think he's lost the plot. Maybe the stress of the whole situation has just got to him.'

'Do you think he killed Harry Cummins?'

Carlyle hadn't considered that possibility. 'Why not? Maybe he shot Cummins on Holder's orders, then had to shut Umar and Zoë up.'

'It's all very thin.' Roche dropped the notebook and pen into her bag. 'Circumstantial at best.'

'No thinner than the completely *non-existent* evidence that's got me sitting in here,' Carlyle pointed out, just as the door reopened.

Daniel Philpott stuck his head inside the cell. 'Time's up.'

'Okay.' Roche waved him away as she got to her feet. 'I'll be out in one minute.' Waiting for the duty officer to retreat down the corridor, Roche picked up her rucksack and hoisted it onto her shoulder. 'I haven't got much time. Like I said, Grandma is looking after David at the moment but she can only cope for so long. So, this is what I think we'll do . . .'

'Oh, good. I really like Rich Tea.'

'Huh?' Not really listening, Vernon Holder looked blankly at the SPA in his hand. The Sale and Purchase Agreement for Bob's nightclub had conveniently been sitting in his office safe, awaiting a significant development in the tortuous negotiations with Harry Cummins. The talks had dragged on for over seven months – until Harry had come a cropper.

'Getting shot in the head,' Holder remarked to himself. 'That's a fairly significant development.' He tossed the contract onto his desk and looked up at Ashley Cotterill, who was sitting opposite.

Concentrating on dunking the biscuit into his coffee, the lawyer was not focused on his client.

'Have you spoken to the wife?' Holder asked.

'The widow.' The lawyer gave one dunk too many and watched in dismay as the bottom half of the biscuit collapsed into his cup. 'Technically speaking, she's his widow.'

And, technically speaking, you are a twat. After almost twenty-five years, Holder found Cotterill at least as irritating now as he had on day one of their working relationship. It wasn't as if Cotterill was a particularly good lawyer. His one saving grace was that he knew how to keep his mouth firmly shut. Holder watched the remains of the biscuit floating on the surface of the coffee and looked away in disgust. 'Have you spoken to her?'

Cotterill nodded. He chewed the last of his biscuit and quickly swallowed. 'Mrs Cummins wants more money.' A spray of crumbs shot from Cotterill's mouth and landed on the carpet. Holder reached forward and moved the remaining biscuits beyond the lawyer's reach.

'Obviously.'

'She can't sell the club until the estate is wound up, anyway.'

'I know, but she can still sign this.' Holder tapped the SPA with an index finger. 'We can complete the formalities later. I don't want to let things drift for another six months, then find out that the place has been bought by Starbucks.' He gestured around his office. 'I've had enough of Wanstead. We're going to move into town.'

The lawyer nodded. Personally, he had nothing against Wanstead but he knew better than to disagree with the boss. When Vernon Holder set his mind on something he would not be dissuaded. He eyed the plate of biscuits, wondering if he could snaffle another. 'So, what do you want to do?'

'I want you to sort it out,' Holder said gruffly. 'What does she want?'

'Another thirty-five per cent. Plus a performance-related fee after three years.'

Holder gave a derisory snort. 'She's got to be kidding. We're paying top dollar already.'

Deciding to leave the biscuits alone, Cotterill folded his arms in an attempt to look vaguely professional. 'You know what it's like. Everyone thinks London property is like a fruit machine that pays out every time. And she knows Harry turned us down a couple of times before.'

'Does she?' Holder was disappointed by the news that Harry had talked to his wife about their business. According to the man himself, Harry's London interests had been kept completely separate from his wife's life in the countryside. That didn't seem to be the case. Then again, why should it be a surprise? Harry was one of the biggest bullshitters Holder had ever met – and that was saying something: you simply couldn't trust a single word that came out of the little shit-weasel's mouth. 'So Vicky knew that the club was basically a knocking shop?'

Cotterill nodded. 'I got the impression that Mrs Cummins was very well informed.'

'In that case, she must realize that this is a good deal. Tell her the price is the price. She's had our final offer.'

'She won't like it.'

'She'll like it even less if the place were to burn down while it's in probate.' Holder wondered if he might not need to pay Mrs Cummins a visit himself.

Cotterill looked less than enthused at the prospect of another trip to deepest, darkest Gloucestershire. 'Shall I send Ronnie to have a word? That might help concentrate her mind a bit.'

'No, no.' Holder swatted away the suggestion. 'That's not a good idea. Ronnie's more than busy enough already.'

'Yes.' Unable to resist the temptation any longer, Cotterill got out of his seat and, ignoring Holder's disapproving glare, helped himself to another biscuit.

'I don't want him spreading himself too thinly. After all, he does have a day job to do as well. I don't want to dump too much on his plate.'

'Quite.' The lawyer sat down again. 'The last time I saw him, I thought he was looking rather ill.'

'He always looks ill,' Holder observed.

'He might be depressed.'

256

'Ronnie's a complete slob. He needs to pull himself together and start looking after himself.'

'The stress might be getting too much for him.' Cotterill inspected his latest biscuit before taking a cautious nibble.

'The thought had crossed my mind.' An anaemic smile crept across Holder's face. 'Don't worry about it, though. I'm going to make sure he takes a good long rest.'

The lawyer blanched. 'Yes, well, why don't I get going? I can get right on with seeing Mrs Cummins.' He mentioned the name of a town that Holder had never heard of. 'It's quite a trip out there. Terrible roads.'

'I can imagine.' Holder couldn't have cared less. The lawyer was on a monthly retainer, rather than hours, so he could spend as much time pissing about in the English countryside as he liked.

'Good.' Getting to his feet, Cotterill skipped to the door, biscuit still in hand. He had just reached for the handle when the door flew open. The lawyer jumped backwards, dropping his Rich Tea on the carpet.

'Pick it up,' Holder growled.

THIRTY-SEVEN

'What's going on here?'

'Nothing.' Vernon Holder watched in dismay as Ashley Cotterill, on his knees, scrambled around on the carpet, picking up bits of biscuit. 'Ashley was just leaving.'

'Oh.' Ronnie Score held the door open as the lawyer retrieved a final crumb and struggled back to his feet.

'You missed a bit.' Holder pointed at a fragment of Rich Tea that was located perilously close to the heel of Cotterill's shoe. 'I don't want it mashed into the carpet. It's antique, apparently. Turkish. Vera bought it when we went to Marmaris on holiday one year. Cost a bloody fortune. When we got it home she decided she didn't like it that much after all.' He shook his head at his wife's random spending habits. 'So it ended up in here.'

Cotterill carefully picked up the last piece of biscuit. 'I'll get going.'

'Good.' Satisfied that the mess had been properly cleaned up, the boss waved him away. 'Keep me posted.'

'I will.'

Holder waited for the lawyer to slip through the door before inviting Score to take the seat in front of his desk. 'What a bloody idiot,' he said. 'He's a grown man and can't even eat a biscuit properly.'

'I always wondered why you kept him on.'

'Because, Ronnie old son, there are only two types of people in this world – idiots and functioning idiots. Ash might be a berk, but at least he can perform to a certain level, most of the time. As long as I don't try to get him to perform outside of his comfort zone, he won't let me down. He doesn't try to be too clever and he keeps his mouth shut. That's all I can ask for.'

Score smiled weakly. 'And what about me? 'What kind of an idiot am I?'

'You?' Holder smiled. Cotterill was right: Ronnie didn't look well at all. 'You are the exception that proves the rule. A cut above. That's why I pay you so much.'

Score felt a vague stab of pain in his chest. When it came to Vernon Holder, flattery was far more troubling than criticism. 'What did you want to see me about? Things are crazy busy at the moment. It's hard to get away.'

'I appreciate you making the time to come over,' Holder said graciously.

'It's okay.' Score stared at his hands, as if he was surprised to see them sitting in his lap. 'Things are progressing well.'

'That's good,' Holder agreed.

'Yes. We'll soon have all this done and dusted. I'm tying up the loose ends.'

All except one, Holder thought. All except one.

After Roche had left, Carlyle stared at the ceiling, thinking about Umar, Ronnie Score and Vernon Holder, what tied them together, the connections that would help him bring down Score and perhaps Holder as well. One thing seemed clear. By putting him in handcuffs, Score had confirmed that he was in this mess up to his neck. It was perfectly plausible that Score had shot Umar and Zoë, perhaps even Harry Cummins as well. For that, Holder would have to be paying big bucks. Carlyle was genuinely surprised that he had never come across Vernon Holder, or at least heard of the guy. Then again, London was a big city. It had lots of cops and there were more than enough crooks to go round.

Chasing theories from his mind, the inspector tried to focus on what he actually knew. Cummins and Holder were embroiled in a turf war. Holder was winning, aided by his spy – the woman Umar had beaten up in the alleyway off Tottenham Court Road. Bleeding cash, Harry had been left facing a stark choice: he could either sell up or face impending bankruptcy.

After the facts, came the supposition: Harry, unable to stomach being bested by an old-school villain like Holder, wouldn't gracefully concede defeat and vacate the field. So Holder was using Score, and maybe others, to close out the game.

The twist appeared to be that Score was now leading the investigation into crimes he was involved in himself. If that was indeed the case, evidence that would implicate the bent cop would be extremely hard to come by.

Where did all this mess leave him? Carlyle was still pondering that question when the cell door finally reopened. A lanky bloke stepped inside. The new arrival had a gormless expression on his face and sported an ensemble consisting of green trainers, frayed jeans and a T-shirt proclaiming the merits of Jake's Café, which appeared to be an establishment in San Francisco. There was a couple of days' worth of stubble on his chin, and his hair, falling over his eyes, looked like it hadn't seen a comb in months. On first impression, he reminded Carlyle of a cartoon character from kids' TV.

'Hey, Shaggy,' Carlyle quipped, 'where's Scooby Doo and the rest of the gang?'

The dirty look he received by way of reply told the inspector that it wasn't an original observation.

'You're not my cellmate, I hope. There's only one bed in here and it's mine.'

'Mr Carlyle?'

'Inspector Carlyle.'

'Yes, yes.' The man waved away that incidental detail. 'I'm Alex Marrow, your legal representative. Alison—'

'You're not another of Roche's little helpers,' Carlyle demanded, 'are you?'

'No, no,' the man stammered. 'The Federation sent me.'

'About bloody time.' Energized, Carlyle jumped to his feet. 'Let's get going.'

A nervous look spread across the union man's face. He held up a hand. 'Not so fast, I'm afraid.'

Carlyle looked beyond the lawyer towards the uniform hovering in the hallway. Going stir crazy, he was minded to make a break for it, regardless of what the lawyer had to say for himself. 'What do you mean?'

'Well, these are very serious charges that have been laid against you. It will take some time until we can see about the possibility of your, erm, release.'

Carlyle planted his feet apart, as if he was getting ready to take a swing at Marrow. 'They are very serious *charges*, for which there is no actual *evidence*. Which probably has something to do with the fact that, although I was arrested, I haven't formally been charged with anything.'

'Yes, but—'

'Are they going to charge me?'

'Well . . .' The lawyer clearly didn't have a clue.

'If you don't get me out of here right now,' Carlyle hissed, 'I will sue every bugger from the commissioner downwards, including the Federation, including *you,* for wrongful arrest, defamation and everything else I can think of. Your miserable career will be over before you've even had the chance to have a shave and put on a suit and tie.' It was unfair to take out his frustration on the unfortunate Shaggy but, hey, guess what, life wasn't fair. It wasn't every day that you found yourself facing a multiple-murder charge, and Carlyle knew that the longer he spent banged up the less likely he was ever to get out.

There was some activity in the hallway. After a quick conversation with the uniform by the door, Dan Philpott appeared at Marrow's shoulder.

'There's been a development.' He addressed Carlyle, ignoring the lawyer. 'Let's go and talk upstairs.'

'Let's do that.' Carlyle lurched towards the door before the sergeant could change his mind.

'Whoa.' Philpott stepped in front of him, blocking his path. What now? Carlyle wondered.

Philpott pointed towards the paper cup sitting on the floor. 'Pick up your crap,' he commanded. 'You're not at home now, you know.'

Doing as instructed, Carlyle followed Philpott out of the cell, with Marrow bringing up the rear. On their journey through the building, he managed to find a bin for his rubbish and – thanks to a cash handout from his lawyer – acquire a can of Coke from a vending machine. Once they reached the top floor, Philpott ushered them inside a large meeting room with floor-to-ceiling windows, which offered an expansive view of a small park on the far side of the road.

Darkness had descended outside. As Philpott flicked on the lights, Carlyle took a seat at the table. A clock on the far wall told him that about nine hours had passed since he had been hustled out of Zoë Connors's flat in handcuffs. Should he call Helen? The inspector was far more worried about his wife's reaction to his latest adventure than anything the Met could throw at him. His assessment remained that it would be much better to explain things face to face. Assuming he got out of here, of course.

Cracking open the Coke, Carlyle took a long swig. Marrow took a seat reasonably close to his grumpy client. Philpott remained standing.

'Ronnie Score's dead.'

Result, Carlyle thought cheerily. Keeping his mouth shut, he waited for Philpott to go on.

'Someone shot him in his flat a couple of hours ago.'

'Well, I think I've got a pretty good alibi for that one, don't you?'

'They haven't done any tests yet, obviously,' Philpott continued, 'but it looks like it may have been the same gun that was used to shoot Umar Sligo and Zoë Connors.'

'And Harry Cummins?' Carlyle asked hopefully.

'Dunno about that. The point is that you're in the clear.'

'I always was in the clear,' Carlyle said churlishly, 'seeing as I was totally innocent.'

Philpott didn't argue. 'You're free to go. You'll remain on administrative suspension until this gets sorted out but you know what it's like – Internal Affairs will want this whole thing swept under the carpet as quickly as possible. If not quicker.'

'Excellent.' Carlyle stood up. 'I'll be off then. Thanks for your hospitality.'

Philpott gestured at the can still sitting on the table as he reached for the door handle. Resisting the temptation to leave it, Carlyle picked it up and emptied the last of the Coke down his throat before crushing the empty can in his fist. 'Just be grateful that Ali was looking out for you.'

Ali? It took Carlyle a moment to realize that he was talking about Roche.

'She's a great girl,' Philpott ventured.

'Yes, she is,' the inspector agreed. 'By the way,' he grinned, 'you don't know who the father of her kid is?'

'No idea. I hear you've been running a book on it at Charing Cross.'

'Yeah. There's more than five hundred quid in the pot but no winner can be declared until we have the name.'

Marrow stared at his reflection in the window.

'Ah, well,' Philpott reflected, 'if she doesn't want you to know, she doesn't want you to know.'

'I suppose that's right,' Carlyle agreed.

'Maybe it was IVF or something. You know, one of those donor banks.'

Starting to cough, Marrow jumped to his feet and slipped out of the room.

Philpott shook his head as he watched him go. 'Lucky for you this all got sorted out. I wouldn't want him for a lawyer if I was in serious trouble.'

'I know,' Carlyle said. 'What are we paying our union dues for, eh?'

Out on the street, he found Marrow fumbling with a packet of Silk Cut. 'Are you mad?' Carlyle admonished the youngster. 'Those things are bad for you.'

The lawyer dropped the cigarettes back into his pocket. 'Didn't like you very much, did he?'

'Who? Philpott? He's just pissed off because I buggered up his day. Extra paperwork, longer hours.' He dropped the crushed Coke can into a nearby waste bin. 'No cop likes that.'

'I suppose not.' Marrow pointed towards a battered VW Golf parked across the road. 'Can I give you a lift?'

Carlyle considered the offer. 'Where are you going?'

'Dartmouth Park.'

The inspector decided he had spent enough time with Shaggy for one day. 'If you're heading up to north London, I don't want to take you out of your way,' he said diplomatically. 'I can get the tube.'

'Suit yourself.' The lawyer wasn't going to offer twice. 'I'll give you a call tomorrow and we can try to get you reinstated straight away.'

'Sounds good.' As Carlyle watched the lawyer cross the road, he shouted after him, 'Hey, Dartmouth Park, isn't that where Roche lives?'

Reaching his car, Marrow turned to face Carlyle. Even in the gloom, the flustered look on his face was unmistakable. 'Somewhere round there,' he stammered, 'yeah.'

Carlyle stepped off the kerb. 'You guys know each other?' he asked, his question innocent and probing at the same time.

Marrow hesitated, then offered another limp 'Yeah,' as he stared at the tarmac.

The truth suddenly hit Carlyle like a smack in the face. I've cracked it, he thought. The mystery of young David Roche's father has been solved. Roche's choice of sperm donor left something to be desired but, then again, there was no accounting for taste. On the plus side, no one back at the station had ever heard of Alex Marrow. All Carlyle had to do now was enter the new name in the pool and get confirmation from Roche. He didn't fancy the last bit too much but maybe there was a way round that. 'When you get home,' he called across the road, 'tell Ali I'm very grateful for everything she's done for me today. It really was above and beyond. I owe her big-time.'

Marrow did not respond as he got into the car and drove off. Raising his gaze to the heavens, Carlyle tried to pick out some stars in the night sky. Inevitably, however, a combination of cloud cover and light pollution made it an impossible task. Stepping back onto the pavement, he trudged off in search of the nearest Underground station.

THIRTY-EIGHT

When Carlyle arrived home, the flat was shrouded in near darkness. Alice had retreated into her bedroom while Helen was sitting in front of the flickering TV, a glass of white wine in her hand. His appearance in the doorway did nothing to ease the furious scowl on her face.

'The bastards,' she snarled, 'the fucking bastards.'

Tiptoeing into the room, Carlyle glanced at the screen. A news report showed a tank trundling across a section of waste ground, to the sound of automatic weapons fire. Following on behind, a group of infantrymen, their rifles at the ready, steadied themselves for another engagement with their terrorist foes. As a rule, the inspector made a point of avoiding current affairs but even he could not fail to be aware of the latest bloody interlude in the never-ending Middle East conflict. A plague on both their houses, he thought, as the TV cut to a series of not very spectacular explosions, followed by heavily pixilated images of dead children.

The inspector winced as his usually mild-mannered spouse spat out a further stream of heavy-duty expletives. 'Tough day?' he enquired cautiously.

'I've got thirty-five people stuck in there.' Helen pointed at the screen with her wine glass. She was only the most occasional of drinkers and he doubted if it was anything other than her first glass. Even so, he could clearly detect a slight slurring of her words. 'I'm just sitting here, waiting for the call that someone's been killed.'

266

'Hm.' Carlyle didn't know what to say. Helen's job, running a medical aid charity, was far more stressful than anything the Met could offer. The news report moved on to chaotic pictures of badly injured patients being delivered to a hospital in battered pickup trucks.

'It's just so fucking . . . *shit*.'

'Can I get you anything?' he asked gently. 'Something to eat, perhaps?'

'No, I'm fine.' She took another mouthful of wine, eyes fixed on the screen. 'How was your day?' It was a question asked on automatic pilot, not requiring an answer.

'Nothing special.' He backed out of the room, dismayed by his wife's discomfort but happy at having escaped a grilling. 'Tiring, though. I think I'll call it a night.'

He had been sound asleep by the time Helen had finally switched off the TV and come to bed. The morning saw their roles reversed: the inspector left his wife snoring gently as he slipped out from under the duvet. After munching some toast, he headed for the police station with a spring in his step. Technically, he was still suspended but Carlyle knew that if he waited for police bureaucracy to catch up with the reality of his situation he would never be able to clear up the mess created by Vernon Holder and Ronnie Score.

Given the early hour, it was no surprise that the third floor was almost deserted. Trying to look nonchalant, Carlyle headed for his desk. Switching on his computer, he was delighted to discover that the IT department hadn't cancelled his log-in. Once up and running, however, he was less pleased to discover that his inbox contained 342 unread emails. Ordering them by sender, he quickly deleted all but sixteen. Amid the remainder, there was a message from Fiona Cope saying that she was still trying to track down Eric Rayner to talk to him about Richard Furlong's doped pigeons. It seemed that the chairman of the Hendon Pigeon Racing Association was no longer willing to cooperate with the police and had gone to ground. Either that or he'd buggered off on holiday.

Carlyle took the news with a sense of calm: he had more important things to worry about right now. Not least among them was fiddling the sweepstake on the father of Roche's baby. Recovering an ancient bottle of Tippex from the top drawer of his desk, he tested that it was still usable by painting over part of a story on an old copy of the Metro. Only after he had satisfied himself that it still functioned did he notice that the story concerned the identity of the body parts that Susan Phillips had been recovering from waste bins along Euston Road. In the end, apparently, almost eighty per cent of the body had been recovered. The victim had been identified by a tattoo on one of his forearms.

'Good effort,' Carlyle muttered, impressed.

The man, understood to be a Belgian national, is to be repatriated once family members have formally identified the body.

'Bloody Belgians, they're everywhere.' Getting out of his chair, he walked over to the noticeboard. Below a memo outlining proposed changes to overtime arrangements and a leaflet warning about the danger of injuries caused by ill-fitting uniforms, he found the by now rather tatty A4 list outlining the various guesses as to the identity of young David Roche's father. Carefully brushing out his previous pick – a DI from Islington with whom Roche had been romantically linked a couple of years earlier – he carefully printed ALEX MARROW in black biro.

'What are you doing?'

'Erm, nothing.' Carlyle turned to face Sergeant Adam Palin watching him suspiciously. 'Don't creep up on me like that.' He walked away from the evidence of his crime. 'You'll give me a bloody heart attack.'

Palin followed the inspector back to his desk. 'I thought you were suspended?'

'Nah.' Dropping the Tippex back into the drawer, Carlyle tried to remember if Palin had entered the sweepstake. 'It was all just a misunderstanding.'

'A misunderstanding?' The sergeant sounded sceptical.

'These things happen,' Carlyle replied offhandedly. 'It was no big deal. I've been suspended loads of times over the years.' Slumping into his chair, he began tapping at his keyboard in the hope that Palin would take the hint and bugger off. Instead, the sergeant took up a perch on the neighbouring desk.

'What can I do for you?' Carlyle asked gruffly.

'I was just wondering, have you heard from Rita recently?'

Rita? It took Carlyle several moments to recall the striking nun, the unfortunate object of Palin's misplaced affections. 'No, not since she was here. Should I have done?'

'It's just that she seems to have, well, disappeared off the face of the earth.'

Maybe she doesn't want to be stalked by a lovelorn plod, Carlyle mused. 'Have you tried her phone?'

'It seems to be switched off all the time.'

Smart woman, Carlyle thought. If I had Palin chasing me, I'd switch my phone off, too.

'I was wondering—'

The sergeant was abruptly cut off by his superior. 'We're not putting a trace on her bloody phone,' Carlyle harrumphed. 'There are limits. I mean, come on.' The deflated look on the young man's face invited a mixture of pity and scorn. 'Have you tried the, erm, nunnery?' he asked, trying to sound vaguely helpful.

'The convent hasn't seen her in over a week.' Palin choked back a sob. 'She was our only link to the girl from UCH, Isabel Corey, don't forget. We don't know where either of them is at the moment.'

Yeah, like you give a monkey's about Isabel Corey, the inspector observed. 'Isn't that case now formally closed?'

'I haven't done the paperwork yet,' Palin admitted.

'Well, you'd better get on with it. You don't want it piling up.'

'I thought we should tell Rita – and Isabel – that the investigation is being wound up.'

'I'll go back and speak to the doctor at the hospital,' Carlyle promised, if only to get rid of Palin. 'I'm sure he'll be able to track them down.'

THIRTY-NINE

Standing in the middle of the room, Victoria Dalby-Cummins pointed at the blood-splattered chair. 'Is that where Harry was shot?'

'I believe so.' Placing his hands behind his back, Vernon Holder dropped his gaze to the carpet in an attempt to hide his smirk.

The widow grimaced. 'You would have thought someone might clean it up.'

'The office is still part of the official investigation,' Holder glanced at the police tape that had been torn from the doorway, 'technically speaking.'

'I wanted to see where it happened.'

'Yes, of course.' Leaving her to her thoughts, Holder slowly counted to sixty in his head. 'This must be a very difficult time for you and your family,' he said, once the minute had elapsed. 'I am very sorry—'

'It stinks in here.' Not interested in his empty words, Dalby-Cummins stepped over to the window. Throwing open the shutters, she flooded the room with a sullen sunlight, which only served to make the place look dingier. Grunting, she tugged at the bottom of the frame. 'Does this thing work?' Answering her own question, she managed to open a gap of maybe three inches, allowing the stale air inside to mix with the traffic fumes from outside. She turned back to face Holder, a small smirk of triumph on her face. 'What a tip.'

'The police had to go through it in detail, as part of their investigation.'

'No doubt. They haven't got anything, though, have they?'

'Not as far as I know.'

'So, who shot Harry?'

'I believe that remains unclear. They may have some leads, but they'll be reluctant to tell you too much.'

'They haven't told me anything.' It was an observation rather than a complaint. 'All I know is what I've read in the paper.'

'Likewise.'

'And the police officer who was leading the investigation, he was shot too?'

'It's a messy business, but not one that need bother you, out in the country.' Holder had been surprised when Ashley Cotterill had told him the woman was coming up to London and wanted to meet him. He was even more surprised to discover that she was not the stereotypical provincial horse-riding bimbo he had imagined. Instead, he had found himself dealing with a no-nonsense hustler who wasn't going to waste her time – or his – by playing the grieving widow. She seemed even less concerned by Harry's death than Holder himself. A very good-looking woman . . . If he had been maybe ten years younger – certainly twenty – he would definitely have tried his luck.

A smile crept across Dalby-Cummins's lips as she caught him eyeing her up. 'So, I spoke to your lawyer.'

'And?'

'And you want to take advantage of the situation by buying Bob's at a bargain-basement price.'

'I think you'll find my offer is at the market rate.' Holder didn't say which market he was referring to but they both knew it wasn't London's.

Placing her hands on her hips, she stared at him defiantly. 'And what if I don't want to sell?'

'Well—'

'Will you shoot me, too?'

Holder ignored her question. 'I will respect your decision, of course,' he lied.

'It has turned into quite a mess, this little business deal of yours.'

He couldn't disagree with that. 'Look, if it's just a question of price, I'm sure there's room for some further negotiation. I don't want you to think I'm unfair. I'm a businessman, always happy to negotiate. Give me a number. What did you have in mind?'

'I don't want to sell.'

'No?' Holder scowled. This was one problem he had not anticipated.

'No. But I don't want the hassle of running this place, either. I want us to go into partnership. Combine our assets and grow the business.'

Holder took a moment to let that idea take hold in his brain. 'How much do you know about what Harry was up to?'

'Everything.'

Holder raised an eyebrow.

'Having spent the last few months on the sidelines, watching Harry make such a complete mess of things,' Dalby-Cummins continued, 'I know that I can do better. A lot better. With your help, of course.'

'I see.' Holder had to admit that the idea had some appeal. He was getting fed up with having to run everything on his own. A partner might not be such a bad idea. And if things didn't work out, well, partnerships could always be dissolved.

'Let's get out of here.' Heading for the door, she gestured for him to follow. 'We can discuss the details over dinner.'

Alison Roche looked like she wanted to punch him right on the nose. 'Did you threaten him?'

'Not really.' Carlyle took a half-step backwards.

'Not really?'

'I didn't threaten him at all. We were just chatting.'

273

'Alex was really quite upset when he got home.'

'He was?' Carlyle hadn't given it much thought.

'He schlepped all the way over to Forest Gate to bail you out and you were shitty to him. You need to apologize.'

Really horrible? What are we talking about here? Is Alex Marrow a grown man or an over-sensitive ten-year-old? 'He's a bit young, isn't he?'

His change of tack gave her pause. 'How do you mean?' she asked suspiciously.

'Well, he seemed very young,' Carlyle mused. 'He's got to be, what, eight or nine years younger than you?'

Roche frowned. 'What's that got to do with anything?'

'Well,' Carlyle smirked, 'he *is* David's dad, isn't he?'

Roche let fly with an impressive collection of expletives.

Five hundred quid, Carlyle thought happily. Money in the bank.

'Did he tell you?'

'Not really.' Carlyle thought back to their exchange outside the police station. 'It was more that he couldn't convincingly deny it. If he's going to be a lawyer, he's going to have to work on his poker face.'

'Thank you for that insightful advice,' Roche said sarcastically.

'Just trying to be helpful,' Carlyle chuckled, 'seeing as he is family, and all.'

'You are such a git.'

'Come on, why is it such a big deal?'

'It's my business, all right?'

'Sure.'

'Just make sure you don't tell anyone else.'

'Me? Never.' Carlyle placed a hand over his heart. 'You know that I'm very good at keeping a secret.'

'Hm. I still want you to apologize.'

'Of course.'

'And one other thing – don't call him Shaggy.'

'Okay,' Carlyle conceded, 'that's fair enough.'

'Thank you.'

'To be honest, given his age, I was surprised he knew who Shaggy was.'

'Are you kidding?' Her anger dissipated, Roche stifled a smirk. '*Scooby Doo* is still one of his favourite shows. He's downloaded just about every episode ever made onto his laptop.'

And you had a kid with this guy? Carlyle told himself it really was none of his business. 'That'll come in handy when the kid's a bit older,' he ventured. 'They can watch it together.'

FORTY

A second trip to South Kensington proved no more productive for the inspector than the previous one had been. Marjorie Peterson kept him hovering on the doorstep before confirming that Elke Lamoot had returned to Belgium to bury her husband, then headed to the Bahamas for a much-needed holiday. There was no certainty about when she would return to London. Having imparted this information, the housekeeper indicated that their conversation was over by shutting the door firmly in his face.

Thus his rather desultory enquiries reached a dead end. After considering his options, Carlyle took the unilateral decision to close the Furlong case. The beating in Kaplan's he would put down to experience; the Kevin Lamoot killing wasn't his problem and he was happy with that. For once, he had no particular desire to push his nose into someone else's investigation. Frankly, he had had enough of Belgians for a while.

If Superintendent Maria Lockhead needed his assistance, she would get it. However, Lockhead's investigation was said to be going nowhere. The restaurateur's killer – still unidentified – was thought to have left the country almost before Carlyle regained consciousness.

Sitting at his desk, Carlyle carefully typed out a report that was light on detail and long on bland assertion. The final verdict was suicide: Richard Furlong had destroyed his pigeons and taken his own life in a fit of depression. There was no

276

speculation as to the causes of that depression, or any mention of the failed dope tests, Madam Monica or the Belgian Mafia. 'Like the saying goes,' he muttered to himself, 'there really is no such thing as non-fiction.' After a quick spell-check, he hit send and watched the file disappear into cyberspace.

Turning to his inbox, the inspector was dismayed to find that he had somehow accrued another 1,124 unread emails. Where the hell did they all come from? Organizing them by sender, he quickly deleted all but three. Two, from the Federation, concerned the state of his rapidly shrinking pension. It was the third, however, that really made Carlyle's heart sink. Someone called Danni from Accounts had sent him a scan of Madam Monica's invoice with 'NOT RECLAIMABLE' stamped on it in large red letters. The accompanying message said: *Part of your expenses claim is not valid. If you wish to challenge this decision, you have ten working days in which to do so.*

'Bastards,' Carlyle hissed. 'That's my fucking money.' He knew better, however, than to go into battle with the bean-counters over a bill for services in a BDSM dungeon. The story would make him an instant legend among his colleagues – but not in a good way. His reputation was worth more than £225.

Still, the thought of losing such a sum caused him a spasm of acute physical pain. Waiting for it to pass, Carlyle shut down his computer and checked his watch. It was a bit early to bunk off home. On the other hand, nothing demanded his immediate attention. Considering a trip to the gym, he remembered his promise to Palin about trying to track down the nun on the run, Rita Vicedo. He didn't particularly want to schlep up to UCH. Then again, he didn't particularly want to spend half an hour huffing and puffing on a cross-trainer either.

He found the young German doctor in the hospital's staff canteen, deep in conversation with a pretty girl Carlyle remembered seeing on one of his previous visits. As he approached, it was clear that they were not discussing matters of a professional nature.

'Dr Siebeck?'

'Uh.' Startled, the doctor jerked round as if he'd just received a mild electric shock.

'Sorry to interrupt,' Carlyle lied. 'I just wondered if I could have a quick word.'

Struck mute, Siebeck blushed violently. The girl gave Carlyle a big smile and invited him to join them. 'I'm Sonia. I think we've met.'

'John Carlyle.' Pulling up a chair, he sat down.

'You're one of the cops.' The girl's eyes sparkled with mischief.

Nice to see someone happy, Carlyle thought. He nodded. 'I came over before to see, erm . . .' he tried to recall the woman's name but came up blank '. . . Miss X.'

'Anne,' Sonia giggled.

'Isabel Corey,' Markus Siebeck corrected them. Having composed himself, he asked, 'Tell me, Inspector, your father, how is he getting along at the moment?'

'Things are okay,' Carlyle said quietly. 'The old man's getting the help he needs.' He wondered what the doctor would make of a death doula but decided not to go there. 'I think he's dealing with things well.'

'That's good.' Siebeck nodded. 'I'm glad to hear it is the case. Please give him my regards.'

'I will.' Carlyle realised he should go back down to Fulham to see his dad. 'But that's not why I'm here.' He explained how he was trying to track down Isabel and also the nun who had provided her with a refuge. 'I just wanted to give them both reassurance that the man who attacked Isabel has been dealt with. He won't be a problem again.'

If Siebeck picked up on Carlyle's strange use of words, he didn't let it show. 'I'm sorry, Inspector,' he said stiffly, 'but I really wouldn't know where they might be.'

'I would,' Sonia said brightly. 'At least, I can get a message to Rita and ask her to give you a call.'

'That would be very kind.' Carlyle handed over a business card. 'But tell her to ring the general station number – it's the one at the bottom – and ask for Sergeant Palin. He's the one with all the details.'

'Sure.' Sonia tucked the card into the pocket of her jacket. 'No problem. It will be up to Rita if she wants to get in touch, though.'

'Of course. Thanks.' Having done his good deed for the day, the inspector got quickly to his feet. 'I'll let you guys get back to your chat.' Siebeck started blushing again as Sonia pulled him close. 'Have fun.'

'Where did this come from?' Helen picked up the envelope stuffed with ten- and twenty-pound notes and waved it at her husband. 'What are you doing with all this cash?'

'I won the office sweepstake,' Carlyle explained, 'on the football.' He knew better than to tell his wife that they had been betting on the identity of the father of Roche's child.

'That's nice.' Helen didn't bother to enquire any further. Instead she shoved the envelope into the back pocket of her jeans. 'A generous contribution from the forces of law and order to our emergency appeal.'

'That's not really . . .' The words died in his throat as he saw that her decision was final.

'Everyone at the charity thanks you for your contribution.' Reaching forward, she gave him a peck on the cheek. 'God knows we need all the money we can get. Things are getting worse by the day.'

Easy come, easy go. 'My pleasure,' he said weakly.

'I've got to get going.' She pulled on a coat. 'Some of our people have managed to escape the fighting. They're coming back tonight. I'm going to meet them at Heathrow.'

'Okay,' he said warily, wondering if he might be expected to traipse out to the airport as well.

Helen, however, clearly had no interest in her husband

tagging along. 'Alice is on a sleepover,' she said, 'so you've got the place to yourself.'

'Great,' he replied, discomfited at the thought of being at a loose end.

'I'll be late back, so don't wait up.' Giving him another kiss, she headed for the door.

'See you later.' The inspector padded into the living room. His backside had barely touched the sofa when Silver rang.

Dom got straight down to business. 'Good news, I've got the stuff for your dad. From a more reliable source this time. And top quality.'

'That's great.' Carlyle scratched 'Procuring illegal drugs' off his to-do list.

'When the old fella finally does check out,' Dom chortled, 'he's gonna have a hell of a smile on his face.'